DESIGN FOR HEARTBREAK

Edward walked more slowly now, studying the information on the paper. "A new gal with lots of promise," he said. "Her showroom is on the Rue Bonaparte."

"Now?" said Susan, crushed.

"I leave at five. It has to be now," he replied sharply.

He seemed to assume that she would follow along as usual. She could visualize the rest of the afternoon —Edward smiling at the designer and she waiting in some corner while he made his deals and counterdeals. "Edward, I can't go with you," she said. "I've got someone working on my orders while I'm away, and if I'm not back by tomorrow to check them, they won't be delivered on time."

His face clouded. "Orders? What orders?"

He's already forgotten what I told him during lunch, she thought. "As a designer, I have my own studio. I run a business," she said, with an edge to her voice.

"So do I, my dear, so do I," said Edward coolly.

"That doesn't mean we can't get together. You'll be coming to London one of these days. I'm still at our house . . ." she began.

"After Italy I go to New York for a buyers' meeting of all the members of the Association," he said, looking down at the list again.

He doesn't really care about me at all, she thought dismally. Meeting me is no more important to him than if I'd been a casual acquaintance—certainly nothing to delay his work for. She plunged her hands into the pockets of her jacket. When she was rich and famous, he'd *have* to care!

(Cover photograph posed by professional model)

PATTERNS

JANE VERBY

Book Margins, Inc.

A BMI Edition

Published by special arrangement with Dorchester Publishing

Copyright © 1986 by Jane Verby

Printed in the United States of America.

PATTERNS

Chapter 1

Edward had come to Schetchat Terminal with her, although she had wanted him to stay at the pension. After their quarrel last night, there was nothing more to discuss.

He looked at her now, hostility in his eyes and his chin thrust out stubbornly. "For God's sake, Susan, in all the years of our marriage this is the stupidest thing you ever thought of doing!" he said.

She was silent, remembering his derogatory remarks last night.

"So you didn't like what I did," he persisted. "Can't you just brush it aside—put it in the waste basket?"

"The way you brush *me* aside? Is that what you mean, Edward?" she almost shouted.

He glanced about him. Together with other passengers, they were standing in the boarding gate area, waiting for the London plane to be called. His photo had appeared in various European newspapers often enough so that he might be recognized. She knew that was what he feared.

Her fingers tightened around her purse. The ticket that would take her away was jutting from the outer pocket like a tiny red flag announcing her freedom. "You might have consulted me. Asked if it was okay. Those designs *did* belong to me," she said.

"If I stopped and consulted you at every twist and turn of my career we wouldn't be where we are today."

"*You* wouldn't be there." Her voice rose. "What about me? Do you think I'll float along with you no matter what you do—what you say?"

"Shhh." His gaze switched to a man about thirty—Susan's age—standing by a row of gray plastic seats, watching them. He was dark haired and did not look Austrian like the other men standing nearby, nor English either, although he was wearing a Harris tweed jacket.

The knowledge that they were being observed made her lower her voice. "It will do you good to have me gone—make you realize just how much help I give you in that crazy rag-trade world!"

"I'm not doubting it for a minute. That's why I want you to stay. The Trade Fair here in Vienna will be over in a week. Then we could go somewhere—Milan, Paris—remember the *fraises de bois* that we ate in Paris?"

"They only come in the Spring. No one carries wild strawberries now, and anyway, I know what it would be like in Paris. You running to designers' workrooms—me spending my time alone. Paris is the worst place in the world to be alone," she said softly.

Edward moved farther into the corner, turning his back to the crowd. A few feet away, windows looked out on the airfield, parched and brown from Vienna's long, hot August. Susan's breath caught as always when she saw his profile. Ever since that first night seven years ago when she'd fallen in love, his incredible good looks had always affected her this way. The light shining in picked up the star-like brillance of his azure eyes, illuminated his blond hair with the cowlick in the exact spot where he might have put it had he, himself, been in charge. He controlled so many things. . . .

"You're being damn foolish . . ." he began, then stopped.

The man at the end of the row of seats was still watching them, listening to every word. Edward crossed the marble floor to the window and gazed out. A tall man, he was slimmer than he'd ever been—from too much work, too much smoking, too many phone calls, and not enough time for love.

Take me in your arms, Edward, and I'll come back. Hold me—whisper in my ear—tell

*me what a wonderful wife I am—tell me I'm
more than (what was that dreadful word he
had used last night?) Tell me I'm more than
"a nothing"!*

"We shall be boarding flight 68 for London
in a few minutes. Anyone with small children
or needing assistance may board at this
time," a male voice announced over the loud-
speaker.

Edward strode to her side. Susan gazed up
at him, suddenly fearful over her decision to
leave. Would he kiss her goodbye? The skin
around his mouth was taut and white and a
muscle was working at the side of his jaw. He
did not look at her, but at the crowd beyond.
Out of the corner of her eye she could see
passengers picking up their books and carry-
on bags in response to the second boarding
message now blasting over the intercom. The
dark-haired man had already left.

"You won't make it, you know," Edward
said to her. "You'll last exactly two minutes
in that huge house by yourself."

Her anger flared. Important as he might
be, he had no right to predict the future.
Picking up her make-up case, she turned on
her heel and marched down the ramp, keeping her eyes facing front, determined not to
look back or waver. She hurried through the
exit door and up another ramp leading to a
smiling flight attendant who was standing at
the cockpit of the plane. Susan drew her
ticket from the pocket of her purse and

shoved it in the attendant's hand. In the moment it took to check it and give it back, tears filled Susan's eyes.

Head lowered, she hurried down the corridor of the plane until she found her seat located by the window. To her dismay, the dark-haired man who had been staring at her and Edward in the boarding gate area was sitting in the aisle seat. He stood up to let her pass. His eyes were as dark as his hair, and she wondered briefly how they could display admiration, interest and reticence at the same time.

Brushing against his knees, she sank down in her seat, the blue upholstery on the chair ahead swimming in her vision. Suddenly the risk she was taking overwhelmed her. *She would lose her husband—lose him for sure. Edward on his own. Edward among all the fashion models and female buyers who gravitated to his good looks like hungry ducks to a scrap of bread on the water.*

Ignoring the man at her side, she blotted her eyes with a tissue, then shoved her carry-on case under the seat ahead. Her hands trembled so much it was difficult inserting the metal tab into the slot on her seat belt. A fresh rush of tears came and ran down her cheeks and neck into the Hermes scarf tied loosely around her neck, washing away her make-up as a stream carries away silt. Embarrassed, she turned to the window, avoiding her seatmate's gaze. Her pride had left her no choice. How could she have done anything else but leave?

Outside, a hot breeze blew up a cloud of dust from the airfield, obliterating her view, and she shifted her gaze back to the cabin. The rumble of the plane's engines turned into a roar, the man next to her adjusted his seat to an upright position and the usual brigade of flight attendants hurried down the aisle, glancing right and left. It was a familiar scene that had been re-enacted over and over in her travels with Edward—enacted now perhaps for the last time. Was it really finished?

The plane moved out of its position at the ramp like a heavy box car, then glided more gracefully onto the runway. As it roared up into the air, an awful sense of finality came over Susan. She gazed out the window, picking out the spire of St. Stephan's Cathedral, the Prater and Ferris wheel. When she saw the roof of the auditorium where she and Edward had been only yesterday, her entire body began to tremble. "Columbus," a nickname he'd been given because of his many fashion discoveries, was minus a wife now. She still loved him, yet she had managed to make the break.

The bright light above the clouds burst into the plane with its customary abruptness and she closed her eyes. It always amazed her that ordinary people could be lifted so quickly to a spot where the sun was always shining. But despite the warmth coming in through the window, her hands were cold. Tucking them at her sides, she lay her head back, drifting into a state of semi-sleep and remaining that way until the liquor cart tinkled down the aisle.

"Would you like a cocktail, ma'am?" a female voice asked.

Susan opened her eyes and stared at the attendant, an attractive auburn-haired girl. She didn't know what she wanted. She couldn't think. The silence grew embarrassing.

"She'll have a Bloody Mary. So will I," the man beside her said in an American accent.

Turning to the cart, the attendant popped open two cans of spicy tomato juice and while Susan and her seatmate were pulling down their dinner trays, poured it together with vodka into plastic glasses. Grabbing two napkins, she set the drinks before them. The man in the aisle seat laid two pound notes on her tray but when Susan offered to pay her share, he waved her off.

"That's not necessary."

"Thanks," she breathed.

"If there's a lady who needs a drink more than you, I've yet to see her. I'm Michael Everett."

"Susan Thorwald." She took two gulps immediately, then set down the glass, waiting for the vodka to take effect.

"Feeling better?" he asked.

The square hand which held his glass was a symbol of solidity and warmth. For a moment she wondered what it would be like to have it close around her cold one. "A little. I saw you standing there before the plane was called. How much did you hear?" There was no use pretending the scene in the airport hadn't happened.

"Enough to get the picture."

"It's not a permanent separation," she explained hastily. "Once my husband tries working without me he'll beg me to come back. I do all his bookkeeping. No one but me ever opposes him, you see. It's 'Yes, Columbus; No, Columbus' until I get so frustrated I could scream!"

"*That* was Columbus Thorwald—the famous buyer—the man who's supposed to be sort of a fashion oracle?"

She nodded. "Former salesman—poor Chicago boy who worked his way up. Yes, *that* one."

"Why are you so angry at him?"

"He did something last night that I couldn't forgive. Just because we've been married seven years and he's number-one man on the letterhead, he thinks he can do whatever he wants—that nobody else has any rights."

He patted his lips with a paper napkin. "My, how the venom flies! Will you be staying in London long?"

"Not long, actually. We own a house in

South Kensington, where we used to stay when we went to London style shows. I'm going to live there until he comes to his senses. He'll see just how independent I can be." She wondered why she was prattling on so. Was it the release of being alone? Was it the Bloody Mary? For some strange reason she had an urge to confide in this fellow American.

They discussed the strange and different customs of the Europeans and the advantages and disadvantages of living overseas. He interjected philosophy into almost everything that was said. Had Edward been sitting beside her, they would have talked about fashion. Edward had a tremendous enthusiasm for his profession, and her eyes misted again when she thought of the days ahead without him.

"Edward's not *awfully* famous—how did you hear of him anyway?" she asked.

"I'm a journalist. He's gained quite a bit of print over the years not only in fashion sections, but on the front pages."

"You mean in the States. Are you vacationing in Europe?"

"No, I work in London—for the Times. I was in Vienna collecting information for a news story I'm writing."

Susan swallowed. A reporter was the last person she wanted to meet. "You're not going to write about that little scenario in the terminal?" she asked anxiously.

His laugh was frank and unself-conscious. "Only if a divorce is pending. *That* would be a juicy story."

"That's the last thing I would do—divorce Columbus. We'll work it out and he'll respect me for standing up for my rights. That's all I want—respect."

She pulled out an in-flight magazine from the seat pocket and laid it on her dinner tray beside her drink as a signal that the conversation was over. *A reporter!* This wasn't the first time her candor had trapped her, but today she had spilled out more than usual because of her anxiety. Would she ever learn?

Out of the corner of her eye she saw Michael also reach for a magazine and flip through the pages until he found the crossword.

She, in turn, opened hers and tried to read, but the tears in her eyes made the words a blur. Opposite the page of print was a perfume advertisement showing a couple fondly gazing at each other across a table. The woman was wearing a diamond tiara and the man a tuxedo. Someday, Edward and I will be like this again, she thought. She glanced at Michael, who was rapidly filling in the blanks of his crossword.

Suddenly he looked up. "What's a seven letter word for intercept, first letter 'd'?"

She paused. "Deflect?"

He studied the page as if visualizing the word in the blanks, then nodded and began copying it down.

Susan watched him inserting letters in other sections of the puzzle—the clean line of his cheek, the broad hand that held the pencil. After a few moments, she laid her head against the window and closed her eyes. The plane's engines droned on, dulling her worries about the future. When she finally looked down, she saw dark blue water.

"There's the Channel," she said.

Michael reached under the seat ahead for his briefcase and for the first time she noticed there were no rings on his fingers. "I was going to go over my notes before we got to England but I never did," he said, opening the case and dropping in a notebook that had been lying beside him. The snaps clicked shut, reminding her of Edward's many brief-cases. Being a man dedicated to success, Edward would definitely have gone over his notes.

The auburn-haired flight attendant began collecting the empty glasses. Pausing at their row, she smiled at Michael as he gave her his and Susan's.

"Did you enjoy the flight?" she asked, then paused. "Haven't you flown with us before?"

"Probably. I made this same trip last week."

"That's where I saw you, then," she said.

She dropped the glasses in the plastic bag she was carrying and with a smile, continued up the aisle.

All it takes is a good-looking man, Susan thought, and we women fall apart. But it wasn't going to happen to her, not anymore. Not a second time with Edward and certainly not with a stranger.

Chapter 2

From Gatwick Terminal, Susan took a train to Victoria Station where she climbed into one of the waiting cabs. As the driver sped towards South Kensington, she dug in her purse for her hand mirror and held it before her. She was shocked at what she saw. Her eyes were red and her face was porcelain white. Strands wafted down from her light-brown hair, drawn back from her face and secured in a chignon. She was glad the lines at immigration and customs had been short, making it possible for her to avoid a second meeting with Michael.

Unpinning her hair and giving it a quick brushing, she gathered in the stray locks and jabbed the pins back, then looked at herself again. Her hair style was severe—one that Edward had encouraged her to wear. "You're

19

pretty enough to get away with it," he had said. "Your features are so even that pulling your hair back from your face will highlight them."

Dropping the mirror in her purse, she drew out the key to her house, holding it so tightly that the bevel cut into the flesh of her palm. It reminded her of the day two years ago when Edward had dangled the key before her eyes in the dim hall of a London hotel.

"It's ours," he had told her calmly.

Looking back now, she was sure that half their talks had taken place in halls or corridors—sometimes even escalators. Edward could never sit still long enough to have a real conversation. That day she had been walking to the lift as he came out of it. At the sight of the key she turned and, naturally curious, matched her steps to his long strides back to their room.

"You have a home, now," he said, not looking at her. His blond hair shone as he passed under each of the high sconces fastened to the corridor walls, and his azure eyes held a look of priestly beneficence. As they walked, he described briefly how he'd traded a group of designer clothes that he couldn't unload for a three-story Victorian house.

She had wanted a home for years but always assumed that she'd be consulted when a final choice was made. "It's a house, not a home," she said bitterly.

The next day when Edward proudly

showed it to her and she saw its very apparent age and the ungainly arrangement of the rooms, her disappointment was even greater. She had difficulty listening while he bragged to their friends about the marvelous deal he had made. But six months later, the house tripled in value, proving that he was as shrewd in real estate as he was in merchandising.

The worth of the house did not abate her dread of living there alone, and when the driver pulled up, there was a sinking feeling in her stomach. While she stood on the pavement fishing in her handbag for the fare, he offered to bring her bags inside, but she refused, not wanting to make herself vulnerable in an empty house. She paid him, and tucking the money in his pocket, he went to the rear of the cab, lifted her bags from the boot and set them beside her.

"That's all you need then, luv?" he asked.

The words startled her. She had forgotten that the British call even strangers "luv."

"Yes, that's all, thank you," she replied and stood surrounded by luggage as he drove off.

The people on the street were gazing at her and it seemed important to get inside as soon as possible. She grabbed the handle on one bag, carried it to the door and unlocked it, then went back for the rest.

The foyer brought back poignant memories of the many times she had been here with Edward. A nylon-curtained window adjacent to the door shed diffused light across the slate floor. Curving up from where she stood was a stairway with a white wooden railing. Everything was dusty, and she remembered that Edward, who was generous about small things, always wired ahead for a cleaning woman to ready the house for them.

She began to climb the stairs. On each step there were white flakes of paint which had chipped from the peeling railing. The condition of the house didn't matter, she kept telling herself. That could be changed. What mattered was the freedom to live on her own, rather than in a world dominated by Edward.

The wooden floor in the upstairs hall also was covered with a layer of dust and she could feel grit under her shoes as she walked across it. On entering the parlor, she was struck again by its age and high ceiling. The room contained massive mahogany buffets and tables as well as a stiff Victorian sofa, all of which had come with the house. Covering the windows were velvet drapes that the sun had faded from maroon to rose.

She laid her purse on the buffet and wearily sank down on the sofa. The house smelled excessively musty, worst than most closed houses. Mingling with the mustiness was the odor of antiquity—old plaster, old drapes, ancient furniture pitted by wood worms. But the cool atmosphere pleased her, a welcome change from the sticky warmth that had blanketed Vienna for so many days. In a minute she should open the drapes and wrestle with the windows to let in the clean air blowing off the Thames. A post-crisis weariness settled upon her, making it hard to move. Shaking it off, she got up, went over to the windows and pulled open the heavy drapes. Dust balls sifted down from the rod above. She yanked at the windows until three were open, then stood gazing out. Already deep blue afternoon shadows were spreading over the quiet streets.

Last night she and Edward had spent half the night arguing and now her eyelids could hardly stay open. She would unpack, make up the bed and sleep. In the morning she'd be better able to cope.

Once she had slipped into bed, however, she became restive. The streets outside were too noisy, then too quiet; the room was too cool, then too warm. She missed burrowing against Edward's smooth back. Would she ever fall asleep?

At dawn she was sleeping soundly, only to be wakened by an insistent jangling from the hall. At first she did not recognize the sound. She wanted the noise to stop—wanted her bedroom, now blossoming with light, to be dark and peaceful again. When she was awake enough to realize it was the phone, she dropped her feet over the edge of the bed and felt about for her slippers. Then it all came back. She was in London and her slippers, which she'd forgotten, were standing beside Edward's thongs at their pension in Vienna.

She went out into the hall and picked up the receiver.

"Susan Thorwald, please," an operator said with an Austrian accent.

A tiny prickling began at the base of Susan's spine. It had to be Edward, who must have slept as little as she. He was going to beg her to come back.

"Vienna, are you still there?" the English operator asked. "Are you there, Mrs. Thorwald? Can you hold, please?"

Susan guessed that, as usual, Edward was placing calls to several parties at once. It would be worth the wait to hear his penitent, pleading voice.

"Go ahead, sir. Your party in London is on the wire."

"Dammit, Sue. Where in hell do you keep the order blanks?" Edward shouted.

Her fingers tightened around the receiver. These weren't exactly the words or tone of voice she had expected. "Where do you think I keep them?"

"How should I know? You do the accounting!"

"Try the black suitcase."

"You took it with you."

"I did not. It's in the closet where it's always been."

She could hear the phone clatter down and

sounds of rummaging. Why couldn't Edward simply say he missed her instead of focusing on little things?

"Yeah, it's here," he said when he returned to the phone. "There are all these damn details. It would solve a lot of problems if you came back."

She sighed. Step one was accomplished—now for step two. She took a deep breath. "How's Marie?"

He gave a little laugh. "Marie? Haven't seen her. I can't ask her for those sketches now," he said apologetically. "I gave them to her. She sure wouldn't like it if I took them back."

It was the same argument they'd had until 2:00 a.m. the night before last in Vienna. "Edward, you don't care how I feel. You care how *she* feels," she said now.

"That's not the point. If I can do Marie a favor, she'll do me one later. It'll help us both."

"Don't involve me. That's not the way I operate." Her voice was rising with her anger.

"Don't involve you? You're my wife. At least I thought you were until you walked out. I'm supposed to train a new gal in the middle of a fashion fair while you sit like some damn queen in London. I'd like to know what gives you the right to come and go as you please."

She swallowed. "There are a number of

things that gives me that right. One of them is
pride. Because of your popularity, you think
you can get by with anything. You were
ignoring my feelings that night and catering
to someone else's—someone you scarcely
know." In the seven years of their marriage
she had rarely taken a stand. It felt good to be
telling Edward what *she* wanted for a
change.

"Godammit, if only you'd been poor you'd
realize how well off you are. Why, there are
dozens of women who'd love to change places
with you—do all that traveling and live our
kind of life."

He spoke rapidly. She visualized him
standing by the window, the slim fingers of
his left hand angrily drumming against the
window frame. Or perhaps he was pacing up
and down, the phone cord trailing behind.

"Tell them it's not that great, Edward. That
there are a lot of disadvantages."

She wondered if she would talk to him this
bluntly if he were in the same room with her.
He had a way of putting her and other women
under his spell—all it took was that vulnerable look in his blue eyes or those perfect
teeth gleaming between sensual lips. At the
moment there was merely his voice, and
voices were easy to deal with.

"You won't make it, you know. You've
always had everything done for you. You've
never had to manage by yourself," he said.

She stiffened. "You're wrong. I used to

manage very capably when I was a teacher."

"As I recall, you lived at your parents' home then, with a houseful of servants. Manage? What's managing when you have everything? You never lived on the Chicago streets like I did . . ." He paused. There was the sound of a door opening and closing in the background. "Mark's here and I've got work to do. Are you coming back or not?"

"Not!"

"All right—but remember, don't expect any help from me. No money—no phone calls. You want to be independent, then *be* independent!" he said and slammed down the receiver.

This seemed to be a signal for her knees to go limp—which they did. She already had tried to contact her few London acquaintances, but they were all away—puttering around country cottages, vacationing on the Riviera, off on business. She was truly alone. She sank down in a chair in the now silent hall, remembering only one other time when she'd been this frightened. It was the moment she stood at the altar right before she said her marriage vows.

Chapter 3

It had always been a puzzle to Susan whether it was destiny's timing or Edward's genius that had caused her to fall in love. She had met him the year after she graduated from college and was teaching at a high school near her parents' home.

"Now don't go getting an apartment," her mother had said. "There is plenty of room here. You've been away at school so much that we scarcely know you anymore."

It was true. An only child, she had been sent to a girls' boarding school and then had attended a four-year college in the East. Many times, when she'd come home for vacations, her parents were absent, traveling. The "plenty of room" was almost laughable. The family home was a massive stone mansion in Lake Forest consisting of three floors looking out on tall cedars which lined the walkways of a five-acre estate.

Yet, despite her mother's pleas, Susan decided to get an apartment and live independently. She was searching for one she could afford on a teacher's salary when her father had his first stroke. Now tears were added to her mother's pleas. "He needs your company, dear. He gets bored with mine," she said, her blue eyes watery and her weathered cheeks wet and shiny.

Susan did not hesitate. Filled with love and admiration for her father, she welcomed the chance to be near him. He had started out with a tiny dry goods store on State Street, made it flourish into a chain of successful smaller shops, then purchased one of Chicago's largest department stores. The years of work and the demands of a lively wife had taken their toll. He sat in a wheelchair that year, able to speak and think but unable to walk.

Susan read to him during her free hours away from teaching. After six months he became strong enough to work a portion of each day, resuming his part in store management.

It was around that time when her father hired Edward, twenty-nine at the time and already making himself known in retail circles. In order to consult with his employer, Edward started coming to the

house. His first visit would always remain
etched in Susan's memory.

It had been a sleety day, the wind whipping
Lake Michigan into a gray, churning sea.
Susan had a cold but had managed to teach
all day and was exhausted when she arrived
home. On her bed the maid had laid out a
green plaid evening dress—not like the ones
carried in the family store but simpler,
featuring a bias-cut skirt. Susan had
designed and made it herself. Beside it was a
case containing a pair of her mother's
diamond earrings.

Her mother, already dressed in a black
taffeta skirt and low-cut blouse, rustled in.
"The most important man at your father's
store will be coming to dinner," she announced breathlessly. "He's a dream!" She
fingered the dress that was on the bed, then
looked up. "Your nose is red, dear."

"I have a cold, Mother. I won't be coming
down to dinner."

Her mother crossed the room, came up to
Susan and laid her palm across her forehead.
"You're not in the least warm. Just the
sniffles. Your father will be awfully disappointed," she said, glancing sideways at her.
"If he can come to the table in a wheelchair,
you can come with a cold. Just powder your
nose. It won't look red in the candlelight."

That night their massive dining room

seemed unusually dark and imposing with gloom festooning the corners like cobwebs. The only bright notes in the room were the two candles on the table and an elaborate silver coffee urn standing on a shiny tray on the buffet. Edward, who was seated across from Susan, gazed at her frequently. "Probably he's looking at my red nose," she thought. He was older than most of the young men she knew, yet there was a boyish quality to his blue eyes and an animation in his face. He talked enthusiastically about fashion, and to someone like her who had always been interested in clothes, what he said was fascinating. The thing she admired most about him was his ability to relate to her mother. He was polite, but kept her from dominating the conversation as she usually did. By the time they had reached dessert, it was easy to see that his charm had cast a spell over them all.

Impressed as Susan was, she kept telling herself she was not in love. Edward frequently came to the house that year. "Father's young genius" her mother named him. Susan usually would be upstairs correcting papers. A maid would let Edward in, and as soon as Susan heard the sound of his voice below, a thrill would pass through her. His visits were always brief, yet left in their wake vast seas on which her dreams could float.

There was little contact between them.

Sometimes on his way to her father's study, Edward would pass Susan in the hall and they would smile at each other, after which she would go upstairs and write impassioned entries in her diary. Her romantic notions stemmed from those Hollywood movies which she inevitably attended with her dates.

Throughout that year Edward's importance grew. Susan's mother was in awe of him and her father praised him, describing the innovative changes he had made in the store. It was not until the week before he left for New York that she and Edward made a commitment to each other. Now she pushed the memory into the recesses of her mind. What good would it do to remember that unbearably beautiful night when she was presently alone in London?

She wondered if she had it to do over whether she would make that commitment again. Seven years ago. Seven years of giving up her life for his until she discovered that what she was getting in return wasn't enough. Seven years to be able to tell Edward what she had over the phone just now.

She left her memories in the hall and went into the parlor. The room was more cheerful this morning. Golden light streamed through the bay window, making bright panels on the wine-colored carpet. She stood a moment admiring them, then crossed to the window and gazed below. Sunshine filled the streets, enhancing the lime green of the plane trees and bouncing off the shiny cars lined up along the curb. Since all the homes in her block had been built without garages in the days of the horse and carriage, the curb was the only place to park.

Last night, in one of her periods of wakefulness, she'd promised herself she'd clean the entire house today, but now she realized even one story would be too great a task. A parlor, kitchenette, two bedrooms and a bath were on this floor with the main kitchen, dining room and guest bedroom downstairs. All the rooms were huge. Before she could even begin she would have to get supplies.

By the time she had unpacked her clothes, taken a bath in the old-fashioned tub and dressed, it was close to 11:00 o'clock, and her stomach was rumbling from lack of food. She went out and stopped at a bakery for rolls and coffee, then went to a few neighborhood shops, buying tea, sugar, eggs, milk and vegetables. Her string bag was full by the time she started home again.

It was no longer the brilliant day in which she had started out. Dark clouds had gathered overhead and she hurried her steps, hoping to get home before the inevitable London rain. Crossing the street to her own block, she was gazing up at the peeling paint on her own house and comparing it to the shiny coat next door when she nearly collided with two scruffy-looking men standing under the street lamp.

They were wearing dirty jeans and tattered, screen-painted T shirts that might have come from a thrift shop on King's Road. The red-haired one peered at her, his eyes like clouded milky blue marbles. The other had mirror glasses and an Afro. Shifting her purse and shopping bag to her other arm, she passed them, momentarily shaken, and without looking back, hurried up her two front steps.

The parlor had the best view in the house. Quickly setting her groceries in the foyer, she bolted the door, then ran upstairs two steps at a time and hurried to the bay window, careful to stand far enough back so she couldn't be seen. Under a tree across the street stood two figures who, even at that distance, were unmistakably the same men. She watched for several minutes, then the taller one slowly raised his arm and pointed in her direction.

At dusk, Susan sat in her shadowy parlor, too nervous to read. She had been far from calm all afternoon, glancing out the windows at intervals during her cleaning to check if the strange men were still there. Supper was a disaster. The egg she poached stuck to the pan, and she burned the slice of bread she was trying to toast under the stove broiler. Cooking was new to her; the only domestic activity she really enjoyed was sewing.

The phone rang and she jumped. Was it a crank call from one of the men on the street? Was it Edward? Slowly she rose, went into the hall and answered.

"This is Michael Everett. If you recall, I sat by you on the plane yesterday. Everything going okay?"

"How did you find me?" she burst out.

"It was easy. It's a newsman's job to locate people. You're really all right?"

"Not exactly. To tell the truth I'm a little scared. London is such a miscellaneous city."

He laughed. "Miscellaneous? Don't you mean cosmopolitan?"

"Whatever. All sorts wander the streets. Odd, frightening people who stand and peer at the house."

"Want me to come by?"

She paused. She had not intended her remark as a hint. "It would be rather pointless," she said.

"I'm used to doing pointless things—following empty leads, going down wrong alleys. Besides, I'd like to see you again. You told me on the plane that you were leaving town in a few days."

"No. After talking with Edward, I decided to stay," she said rather flatly.

"You're sure you'll be all right there alone?"

Tears rose up and choked her. If only Edward had worried about her! If only he had offered to come! "Come tomorrow at 4:00. Tea," she managed to say, then quickly hung up before the sobs broke.

Chapter 4

The next morning, Susan wished she hadn't invited Michael. The house was not yet ready for visitors, but more to the point, she missed Edward so much that the thought of any other man sitting in the parlor disturbed her. If she hadn't been so unnerved last night, she would never have agreed to his coming. She had wondered, after she hung up, why she'd told him about Edward's phone call. Would she ever learn not to be so open?

She couldn't back out now, so she got out the dust cloth and vacuum and continued cleaning. The dust collected so fast on the rag that she had to go to the window and shake it over and over. Like cooking, cleaning was new to her. The pensions and hotels she and Edward had lived in during their travels had always been maintained by someone or other, and when she was growing up, her parents kept a staff of maids. She remembered how she used to meet them on the stairs, their mops projecting dangerously from their pails so that she had to duck her head to pass.

Edward couldn't seem to forget that she'd been rich. He was always throwing her affluent past up to her, and his recent remarks about her inability to cope still made her angry. Spoiled, was she? She shoved a heavy upholstered chair towards the parlor wall. She'd show him just how spoiled she was. She would get a job, live cheaply and save her money. And when the style shows were held in Paris, she would attend wearing the latest fashions. They would casually meet, and Edward would see how well she was doing and change his attitude.

She switched on the Hoover. The wheezy machine seemed to be laughing at her as she pushed it up and down the faded red carpet. Hauling out the attachments, she vacuumed the rose velvet drapes and the upholstered seats on the chairs, determined to put the house in such good shape that it wouldn't be necessary to touch it again for a month.

Next she waxed the dark mahogany tables, then dusted the books on the shelves surrounding the coal grate until the gilt on their bindings glowed. She wasn't afraid of work. Ever since she'd been small, her father had lectured her about the value of diligence and industry—how a person could accomplish anything by rising early and coming home late. His success had proved his theory, and she was sure she could do well in whatever she attempted. After all, wasn't she his daughter?

Her thoughts swung back to Michael's upcoming visit and she paused, the dust cloth motionless in her hand. Although he had seemed open and honest on the plane, he was a total stranger whom she would be entertaining alone. Her travels had taught her that not everyone was trustworthy. There was that Austrian mountain climber she and Edward had met who walked off with one of their bags and the talkative Frenchman who had taken Edward's wallet. Up until now, her husband had always been around to protect her.

It wasn't only the coming afternoon that concerned her. It was all the other afternoons —and nights. She would be living here by herself for some time and any man could take advantage of her. What did other single women do? Remembering Michael's face made her relax. His dark eyes appeared almost holy like those in Rubens' portraits. Nothing out of the ordinary would happen.

Although the cleaning was finished at 3:00, by the time she'd bathed, applied another coat of polish to her nails and slipped into the paisley skirt she'd pressed that morning, and an oversized azure cotton pullover, it was after 4:00. Michael was late. She sat in the parlor, drumming her fingers on the wooden arm of her chair until she heard the tap of the knocker on the front door.

Michael made no apologies. The front door creaked shut behind him and she ushered him upstairs, hating the awkwardness of meeting him again after her display of tears on the plane.

As she led him into the parlor, she was struck by the small size of the room. It had seemed mammoth when she was alone but now Michael's presence diminished even the huge mahogany buffet. Much taller than her own five feet eight, he was broad-shouldered and muscular with a vitality, a masculinity that made her draw in her breath. She had always considered her husband masculine, but now she realized that Edward's blond hair, slim fingers and Nordic blue eyes had a delicate quality beside the tanned skin and dark hair of this man.

He gazed about the room as if taking inventory of everything in it. Something about it made his dark eyes glow.

"Please sit down," she said, motioning to the sofa and perching tentatively on a chair opposite. He eased himself down onto the horsehair cushions and gazed at her silently. Beneath his outward calm, she sensed a nervousness matching her own.

Suddenly they both spoke at once. "I'm sorry," she said. "What were you going to say?"

He cleared his throat. "I said I was surprised when you told me over the phone that you were staying here longer than you'd planned."

"Yes . . . well, I changed my mind. I'm going to get a job here."

"Really? What kind of job?"

"Anything. I can't be choosy. As an American, I may have trouble. It might take a while to find something."

"Time passes with incredible swiftness," he said and looked away.

She had hoped for concrete suggestions, not vague philosophy. He's impractical, she decided—working crosswords when he should be studying notes. Coming late. Despite his dark good looks, she wasn't sure she liked him very much at all.

But though he lacked practicality, he was observant. During the next half hour he noticed and commented on everything—the leafy green aglaonema plant that she'd bought at the corner flower stall and set by the bay window, the polished mahogany tables, the ornate Victorian lamps. But he talked little about himself and gave her no clues as to his own living arrangements.

She served the tea sooner than she'd planned, and as they sat silently staring at each other across the table, she couldn't help comparing him with Edward. The rays of the afternoon sun shining in through the window would have produced a halo around Edward's blond head. Edward would have lifted his cup and drunk swiftly instead of in sips or would have talked incessantly about his one and only interest—fashion—eliminating those embarrassing silences they were now undergoing.

"What part of the States are you from?" she asked, trying to break a particularly long one.

Michael set down his cup. "A small town in Idaho named Wallace. You've probably never heard of it."

"No. Actually I don't know much about the West. Chicago is my home."

"I thought so. I picked up the accent as soon as you started talking on the plane." His eyes brightened. "Accents are fascinating. I'm beginning to tell which part of Britain people come from by the way they speak— even different parts of London."

He proceeded to mimic Scottish and Cockney brogues, making her laugh, and ended with "What do you think of that, love?" spoken in a Welsh sing-song. He stopped suddenly and their eyes caught and held. The "love" had sounded less casual than he'd intended, and she quickly glanced down at her plate.

"How long have you been working in

London?" she asked, purposely breaking the moment.

"Three years—off and on. I suppose I could earn more in the States but the work here is interesting. The Times sends me to cover events on the Continent, and when I'm here, I write one-column stories about fires, the Queen, parades, new plants at the Botanical Gardens—that sort of thing."

She frowned, adding lack of ambition to her assessment of him. A talented writer would have made more of himself. Why had he left America? Why wasn't he working there? Lifting the lid on the teapot, she peered inside. Only half a cup remaining. "Would you like some more tea?" she asked. "There's not much left."

"If it wouldn't be too much trouble."

They both got up at once. He offered to help, but she refused. "It's only a matter of heating up some water," she said.

From the open door of the kitchenette, she could see him wandering about the parlor. He stood before the bookshelves for a long time studying the titles, then moved from one to the other of several prints hanging from the molding.

A whistling called her attention to the electric kettle from which vapory steam was rising. She sprinkled tea in the teapot and filled it with boiling water, savoring the fragrant aroma. When she looked again,

Michael was still studying the print of the Battle of Ucello. Edward and his friends had ignored any decorative attempts on her part, and Michael was the first one to pay any attention to the prints she'd hung two years ago.

Picking up the teapot, she started to carry it in, then paused in the doorway. A man who liked art couldn't be *all* bad. From a side view his features were almost perfect—a clean unfettered chin, a shapely nose and wavy dark hair that sprung from his forehead at a point neither too high nor too low. She went in and called out to him.

Once they were seated and the tea was poured, he said, "Tell me more about yourself. Did you live in Chicago proper? And what did your father do?"

"He owned a department store on State Street, but our home was in Lake Forest."

His eyes widened. "A department store?"

"It's sold now," she said. "Dad died of a stroke two years ago, and since I was traveling and had no brothers or sisters and Edward was committed to his own career, there was no one left to manage it."

"I'm sorry. I mean about your father."

"Is *your* father living? What's his line of work?"

"He owns a silver mine in Idaho." Suddenly he smiled, his entire face lighting up. "No, that's not true. We were poor. I was the youngest in a family of five kids and although there were mines where we lived, my older brothers, not my dad, worked in them. I worked there too until my uncle staked me to an education."

She thought of Edward, who had been poor as well.

As if he'd been reading her mind, Michael said, "I went through the microfilm of past copies of the Times and found some articles on Edward Thorwald. He's even more important than I thought. Does he really manage twenty-five stores?"

"Even more. He's a buyer for the women's departments of Thadius, a chain of department stores with twenty-eight branches in the States and seventeen overseas. You've probably heard of them. Edward has very innovative ideas—that's how he got the name Columbus. Everyone is amazed at how successful the stores are."

"It seems an unusual kind of existence."

She bristled. "Not really. Edward is someone to be proud of."

"Then why did you leave him?"

She stared at him. "I didn't *really* leave him. He begged me to come back when he phoned."

"So are you going back—and giving up the job idea?"

"No, I'm staying."

He looked puzzled, as if waiting for an explanation. There was a long pause, during which she studied two tiny tea leaves floating in the bottom of her cup. The silence was so awkward that she felt compelled to fill it.

"During his call," she began, "Edward made some remarks about my background and we started to argue. He said he didn't think I had the courage to stay here by myself." She paused. "I asked him how Marie was."

"Marie?"

"Marie La Joy—a famous designer he works with. It was over her that we had the argument."

"I've heard of Marie La Joy. She runs a modeling school, doesn't she?"

"When she isn't running after Edward. But there were other reasons I left besides her. For one thing, Edward thinks I'm spoiled—incapable of handling my own affairs. That—and some of his other views—came out in the argument we had the night before I left."

"You don't appear spoiled to me. In fact you seem extremely capable."

His praise acted on her raw wounds like a soothing lotion. "I wish Edward thought so," she said, then went on, happy to have a sympathetic ear. "It was just that until we quarreled I had no idea he felt that way—as if I were some weight dragging him down. I can't go back until I show him I can manage alone—until I prove I can do something on my own."

She gazed at him, and the tension that she'd felt ever since his arrival eased. Here

was an ally, a man she could talk to, a friend
in this alien city. Who he was didn't matter,
only that he was someone who might come
occasionally and allay her fear and loneliness.

Chapter 5

The interest Michael had shown in Marie made Susan wish that she'd told him her entire story during his visit. In the bright glittery world of fashion where Susan had lived, Marie was the queen. Edward knew it—the other buyers knew it. Her style shows, in which she presented her collections, were gaudy affairs, extravagant and lavish. After one glance at the kangeroo trademark on her designs, customers were willing to pay top prices. Despite Marie's success and popularity, it had always puzzled Susan how she could afford to squander so much on her shows. Such large outlays of money didn't seem natural for Marie, who, like Edward, had worked herself up from a background of poverty. And how Edward admired Marie! Susan hated her for bringing out the very things in Edward that she herself wanted—a regard bordering on worship and an over-abundance of attention.

Only last week in Vienna, Susan had been in the auditorium with Edward when Marie minced up on her spiked heels, gushing and beaming—as if meeting the famous Columbus were her only reason for existence. She was a handsome woman—jet black hair pulled back in a bun at her neck without an errant wisp, eyelids covered with blue, cheeks rosy with blusher, her long swan-like neck set off by a single gold chain.

Kissing was as necessary to Marie as sticking stamps on letters, and when she reached them, she slipped an arm around Susan's waist, pecked her on the cheek, then turned and kissed Edward full on the lips. It was all Susan could do to keep from slapping her, wanting to see that bright come-on look turn into one of shock. But wives don't slap designers who are vital to their husband's careers, so Susan joined in their chatter about which new creations were collecting attention at the Trade Fair.

The rest of the day was ruined for Susan. Bedazzled, Edward followed Marie to all the style shows, sitting by her side whenever possible. When the threesome grew to be too much, Susan returned to the pension, leaving Edward at the Fair. The meetings finished after 11:00 o'clock, and since the bar closed early, Edward brought Marie up to their suite for a drink.

Susan was already in bed. The designer's low melodious laugh drifted from the living room, glasses thudded on the coffee table; ice clinked.

"I thought Sue would be up," Edward said.

"It wouldn't be right to wake her," Marie replied sweetly.

Listening from the bedroom, Susan found nothing amiss. The conversation centered on business—what had taken place in the showrooms, what colors were popular this year. Edward began talking about his work in the States, a monologue that soon expanded into his life story. At the point "From Chicago it was only natural that I'd go to New York," Susan turned over and began drifting off to sleep.

The sound of papers rattling woke her. "I found them in a box under the sofa when one of my cufflinks rolled under there," Edward was saying. "I suspect she's forgotten about them."

Susan sat bolt upright. During their travels she'd sketched designs as a hobby, storing them in a suit box. The last time she'd seen it was on the floor by a chair. Had a maid shoved it under the sofa?

"Columbus, you're sweet but I really couldn't take them," Marie replied.

"She never does anything with them," said

Edward. "Not that you could use many. Some of them are wild!" The papers rattled again and the two laughed.

"Do you really want me to have them? What about Sue?"

"She won't care. Here."

And so Edward had given her designs to Marie. Each was drawn carefully on a separate page and labeled with the colors Susan felt were appropriate—mango, saffron, sunset pink. Like most buyers hoping to gain favors from designers, Edward had wanted to obligate Marie.

Susan wondered now why she hadn't rushed out and stopped him. She visualized the scene: she in her nightgown, hair loose and wild, tugging at one end of the box with Edward, his cheeks flushed with embarrassment, holding onto the other. The sketches probably were worthless, but that didn't give Edward the right to surreptitiously hand them to Marie without her own say-so.

Thoughts of Marie had put Susan in a somber mood. Marie was self-sufficient; supposedly she was not. The money she had brought with her from the Continent was slipping away each day. Out of £500, £400 was left. If she were to carry out her plan of living independently, she must find work—and find it fast!

After listing the phone numbers of London public schools, she began calling them, hoping some headmaster would take her on as a teacher. She received a variety of answers: "No, madam, one must have a work permit in order to teach here." "Actually, as an American . . ." "The system in Britain is quite different, you see. I believe you would have to take some type of training . . ." After the tenth call, she realized the field of education was firmly closed to her.

She considered getting a job as a waitress or secretary, but those positions required alien work permits that took months to obtain. At a loss over her next step, she simply went back to her cleaning.

The parlor was the only room completely finished. Today she hauled her equipment into the guest bedroom and started there. After dusting the top of the bureau, she opened all the drawers to check for moths. The contents quite surprised her. Inside were remnants from designers' cutting tables which she'd forgotten, as well as new fabrics she'd purchased on their last trip across the Channel by ferry. She had taken up sewing as a teenager to avoid buying the mass-produced clothes displayed in her father's store. There had been little time to sew after her marriage, but collecting fabrics remained a hobby. Once while she was in London waiting for Edward, she even had purchased a sewing machine and had it delivered here.

She went through the drawers one by one. There was a green watered taffeta, several skirt lengths of plaid wool, yards of wheat-colored raw silk and a number of pieces of linen in various pastel shades. Enough for a year's sewing. Enough, she decided, to try making a dress to sell!

When her cleaning was finished, she took a bus to Knightsbridge and got off near Harrod's Department Store. She visited the pattern sections of all the fabric stores in the surrounding area, and at the last one she discovered a design by Roccoco, an Italian couturier who was a favorite of Edward's. Buying a size 10 pattern, she returned home and excitedly began. She cut out the pieces from raw silk, then sewed diligently for the next three days, hoping that this one dress might be the start of a new career. When it came time to try it on, she was doubtful about the fit. She usually wore an American size 10 and British sizes usually were smaller.

The dress surprised her by being too large. She'd grown slim enough for her shoulder blades to show, either from tension or lack of long dinners and cocktail parties at style shows.

Pirouetting in front of the mirror, she decided that the dress looked even better than expected. It had a jewel neckline, deep armholes and three-quarter length sleeves. The flaxen color was neutral enough for anyone to wear. There was an elegance about the total effect, and with the right accessories, it could look sensational. Suppose she brought it to the boutique and it sold? Would it really be so hard to get started as a dressmaker?

She stood still and gazed at herself. Now that she no longer could afford biweekly visits to the beauty parlor, her severe hair style looked untidy. Even the color seemed drab. Why not change the shade and have it cut?

The next day she packed the dress in a box, and taking it with her, went to an inexpensive stylist to have her long locks cut off. The new style, ash blond and "windswept," as the stylist said, made her feel five years younger. Filled with confidence, she then took her dress to several boutiques in the area, hoping to get one of the shopowners to take it on consignment. Refusals at three made her approach the fourth more hesitantly.

The shop, nestled between an antique store and a florist's, had a striped green awning over the front window, making it dark inside. A bell clanged when she opened the door. Once inside, she strode to the counter and waited, wondering if anyone were there. The scent of perfumed candles from a nearby display enveloped her with its waxy sweetness.

After several minutes a blond woman wearing a black dress and large turquoise earrings came out from a fitting room, holding several dresses on hangers in the crook of her finger. "May I help you?" she asked.

Susan explained her visit, laid the box with the dress on the counter and opened it. The blond woman clicked her burden onto one of the garment racks, then came back and examined Susan's handiwork.

"I doubt if it will sell very soon," she said. "Sales this summer are a bit slow, actually."

"But you will take it on consignment?" Susan asked eagerly.

"I'll give it a go." The woman scribbled something on a sales pad, then looked up. "My name is Veronica Jones—Mrs. Jones— and here's a receipt for the dress."

Dropping the slip in her purse, Susan left her own name, then hurried out before Mrs. Jones could change her mind.

When she arrived home, the phone was ringing.

It was Michael. "This is the third time I've called," he said. "I was afraid you might have gone back to Vienna. How's it going?"

"I think I've visited every boutique in South Kensington. I've decided to take a chance in the fashion world," she said, and told him about making the raw silk dress and taking it to Veronica's Boutique.

"Do you have business cards?"

"I'll attend to that tomorrow." It was such a good idea that she wished she'd thought of it herself. She remembered a shop in the neighborhood that promised them within a day.

"I'm glad things are going so well. The Times is sending me to Italy for a while but I'll check with you when I come back."

They said goodbye, and she put down the receiver with an uneasy feeling. Subconsciously, she had relied on Michael's reassurance and help. She had meant to ask him about the lock on the front door which jammed somewhat everytime she used it. She had also meant to ask him what neighborhoods were unsafe in London. And what would happen now if she ran out of money?

She went to the desk drawer where she kept her cash and counted it again. Buying a pattern, thread and food had taken the amount down to £350. If the boutique sold her dress, there would be no cause for worry, but if the dress wasn't sold. . . .

Sinking down on the bed, she gazed at the wall opposite. Brown water stains streaked down the blue floral wallpaper, and up near the ceiling where the paper was peeling, a patch of plaster showed. Would the house hold together long enough for her to start a career? She sighed. She had to show Edward that she could make it on her own!

Chapter 6

The next morning Susan's sewing was interrupted by the ring of the phone. Throughout the night, she had listened to odd sounds in the house, missing the warmth of Edward's body beside her and worrying about her finances. Hoping the call probably was good news about the sale of her dress, she hurried to answer the phone.

"I hope you're enjoying yourself in that big house all alone," Edward began.

She sensed by the tone of his voice that he was in a better mood than when she'd last talked to him. She decided to put up a brave front. "Things are going quite well, actually. My only problem is that the lock on the front door sticks."

"You must have done something to it. It worked perfectly when we were there last."

He paused. "I called to get Lou Goldstein's address. I need to contact him about some orders."

"Just a minute," she said and put down the receiver. After Edward's threat about never phoning her, his call was a pleasant surprise. She quickly found Lou's number in an old address book that was in her desk and gave it to him.

"By the way, your mother called," he said.

"Mother?"

"I told her where to get in touch with you. She seemed excited about something."

"Edward . . ." There were a dozen questions she wanted to ask him—who he had found to help him, where he was planning to go after Vienna.

"I gotta go, Sue. Talk to you later," he said hurriedly.

She said goodbye and slowly put the receiver back in its cradle. She was turning away when the phone rang again.

The excited bubbly voice on the other end was unmistakable. "Darling, it's Mother!" There was a note of triumph as if a call across the Atlantic were an accomplishment. "What in heaven's name are you doing in London? I phoned Edward's office in New York and the girl there said you were both in Vienna. When I talked with Edward, he said you were living in that dreadful house at Sumner Place."

Susan's heart sank. It had been months

since she'd heard from her mother, and this was exactly the wrong time.

"I'm only here temporarily," Susan began.

"Never mind explaining, dear. I want to see you. I have something to tell you that can't be said over the phone. Are you really living alone?"

"For the time being. How's Chicago?"

"There's a lull now. I thought I could jet over and spend a few days with you. Wait until you hear my news!"

Her mother had a habit of dramatising events of minor importance, and this news was undoubtedly trivial. Besides, she was reluctant to have anyone who lived as luxuriously as her Mother see the peeling paint and wallpaper. "When would you be coming?" she asked hesitantly, hoping to come up with an excuse to delay the visit.

"Tomorrow. I'll arrive tomorrow. My travel agent was lucky to get me a seat at such short notice. Never mind about meeting the plane. I'll take a cab."

Susan sighed. It would be a major battle to get her mother to change her mind. Inopportune as the visit was, she might as well get it over with. She said goodbye and hung up, dreading the coming day. Her mother would want to know everything, then scarcely listen to her answers.

She abandoned sewing to give the downstairs a hasty cleaning, then checked the pantry. Other than tea and breakfast supplies, she would need little food since dining out was one of her mother's favorite pastimes. They would go to the fanciest restaurants in London, drink the finest wines and eat the choicest food, half of which would be left on her Mother's plate.

The next afternoon at 4:00 o'clock a taxi horn beeped on the street below. Hurrying to the window, Susan looked down and saw her mother coming up the walk with the cab driver who was carrying one bag. That was a good sign—for it meant her visit would be short.

Once inside, the older woman planted a lip-sticky kiss on Susan's cheek. "Like your hair! Turn around. Yes, that's nice—quite becoming, in fact. Tell me," she said, patting her own locks, "do you think a trifle less bleach? Annette says to keep it the same, but sometimes I think a little more brown might make me look younger."

Susan studied her. Her mother looked like what she was—a slim, sixty-year old woman trying to look forty. Rouge covered the sagging muscles of her cheeks, and the painted arch of her plucked brows over her blue-lidded eyes gave her a constant expression of surprise. The fingers on her purple-veined hands were loaded with diamond rings, which sparkled under the foyer light even more brightly than the crimson polish on her nails.

"You look good to me, Mother, whatever the color of your hair," Susan said, planting a kiss on her wrinkled cheek.

"How long has it been since we've seen each other? A year—year and a half? I was *so* sorry not to be able to meet you and Edward that time in New York," the older woman said.

"It's been *three* years, Mother."

Her mother laughed. She picked up her bag and glanced up the long stairwell. "You told me when Edward first bought this horror that the guest bedroom and parlor were on the second floor."

"My bedroom is there, too. Silly, isn't it?"

Her mother started up the stairs. "Tell me about Edward," she said. "Is he still as attractive as ever? I love that boy—so good to your father after he had his stroke. Remember how he used to . . ." She paused, teetering on her high heels.

Susan, who was close behind, reached for the bag. "I can take that, Mother."

The older woman shook her head but began climbing more slowly. "I don't want to be any trouble. I can make it to the landing, at least," she panted.

When they reached it, Susan took the bag and carried it the rest of the way into the guest bedroom. While her mother was changing into a robe, she made tea. She carried the pot and cups into the parlor on a tray, placing it on a coffee table between two chairs that were facing each other. She suspected that her mother would withhold the reason for her visit until they were lost in some trivial conversation, then lead up to it dramatically.

After the tea was poured, the older woman picked up her napkin and slowly wiped the rim of her cup. "Now, tell me, for heaven's sakes, what you're doing in London. I couldn't get a word out of Edward," she said, without looking up.

Susan drew her sweater closer about her neck, then reached for her steaming cup. It was a gray, cool day with intermittent squawls of rain, and it felt good to be inside. Despite its aged furniture, there was something cozy about the parlor. "I guess the best way to answer you is to say that I'm embarking on a career," Susan said, taking a large gulp of tea.

"You're not falling for all that bunk about two breadwinners in the family? What about children?"

Susan set down her cup with a loud click. "You know that Edward doesn't want any."

Her mother gave a little laugh. "He'll change his mind once he has one. That's where you should be, Susan. At his side, helping him. Why, I never left your father. I was always there. Any minute he needed me, I was there."

But not for me, Susan wanted to add, remembering her lonely days at boarding school—all those postcards her mother used to send her with pictures of beautiful castles and gothic buildings reflected in European ponds. Her mother had been partial to ponds.

"You didn't ask what my career was," Susan said.

"What is it?"

"I'm going to make clothes and eventually design them. I've already made one dress," she answered proudly.

Her mother moved her index finger over her tea cup in a stroking motion. "I remember all the outfits you used to make during vacations. But in spite of all that sewing, you couldn't mend a broken slip strap. I had to get Nancy to do that for you."

Susan smiled. "That was because sewing dresses was more interesting."

Her mother glanced about the room. "This house reminds me of the one on Jenks Street where I lived as a child. How can you bear it here alone? You should be with Edward— such a fabulous young man. I simply can't see how you can stay away from him." She took a sip of tea and wrinkled her already wrinkled brow. "What kind of tea is this, anyway?"

"The green kind that Harrod's sells," Susan replied.

Setting down her cup, her mother got up and crossed the room to the bay window, then stood gazing out without speaking. The light from the lamp made her silk dressing gown shimmer and her pale hair glow. She was as slim as she was when Susan had last seen her, but her back was slightly rounded. "Alan saw me off at O'Hare," she finally said.

"Alan Hennessy?"

"Yes. Remember him? At country club parties, he always used to dance the next to the last dance with me. The last one was reserved for your father. My, how Alan could make his feet go—still can, in fact." She did a slight twirl to emphasize her point, then fingered the velvet drapes nervously. "Alan's law practice is faltering—too many young lawyers in Chicago now. Of course, he's nearing retirement anyway." She turned and her gaze was direct and innocent—almost like a child's. "He wants to marry me!"

Conflicting emotions filled Susan. From rumors she'd once heard about Alan's questionable reputation, he didn't seem the right man to marry, yet her mother was too vibrant to enjoy being single for long. "Are you asking me or telling me?"

"Of course, I said yes. Alan and I . . . well, everyone's doing it these days . . . and it's darn hard, you know, after you've had sex for so many years . . . you can't just cut if off. Don't you agree?"

Susan looked away. It was a question she'd have difficulty answering. Fortunately her mother continued, too involved in her own concerns to wait for a reply.

"We're going to the Bahamas and we thought before then, it would be fun to have a little ceremony and party—nothing fancy—a case or two of champagne—some caviar. Now you and Edward don't have to come. Alan has no family whatsoever, and we were thinking of getting married on Christopher's yacht. It can sleep six. Wouldn't it be fun being married on a yacht?"

"Very."

"I didn't want to tell you all this over the phone, you see." Her mother's eyes misted. "I miss your father terribly."

A wave of love swept through Susan. In the past she had resented so much about her mother—her fanciful attitudes, her yearning to have a good time at all costs, her lack of compassionate attention—but now she felt sorry for her. She seemed so lost, almost frail. She watched as that customary bright smile crept back on her mother's face.

"The girls at the tennis club think it's fabulous. Of course they know that Alan and I have been living together—what is it?—six months now, but I was surprised when he asked me to marry him. We were there in the living room, the mailman had just come. As I recall I was opening the envelope containing my quarterly dividend from the mutual fund, when suddenly he proposed! Alan might have chosen a more romantic time but I guess the old adage is true—'beggars can't be choosers.' " Crossing the room, she sat down opposite Susan and gazed at her. "You're like me—you're susceptible to men—highly susceptible. A sensuous type. Anyone your age who bleaches her hair has to be sensuous."

"Oh, Mother!" But Susan couldn't deny it. Sometimes merely being near an attractive man could give her a rush of wetness.

"Edward is a woman's dream. If I were you, I'd hurry back to him. You can't leave a man that attractive alone for too long."

"If seven years working by his side hasn't made him love me, I don't know what else will." She, too, had worried about his attractiveness, but wasn't going to admit it to her mother.

"Hah! Little you know about men. They can't stand empty beds. I wouldn't say that the thought of your inheritance hasn't kept him in line, but all in all, there's a lot of temptation in that world of fashion."

Susan's teacup was almost to her lips. She set it down so suddenly it clattered on her saucer. "What inheritance? The money from the sale of father's store is yours, Mother."

"Half is in trust for you, dear. Edward knows that. Your father talked to him before he died."

It was strange that Edward had never told her. But it really didn't matter. "Edward doesn't need money. He's got a six figure yearly income as it is," she said.

"That's all the more reason you should go

back to him," said her mother. "Alan, on the other hand, isn't doing as well as he might, and wants a change. He has passed the Florida bar so he might pick up some clients down there."

"You're going to live in Florida?"

"That's the other thing I was going to tell you. Yes, we're moving to Florida!"

That evening, Susan and her mother ate at the Savoy Grill and the next night at Mirabelle's. The following morning Susan went with her to Heathrow Airport to see her safely on the plane. Still bubbling with energy, the older woman stopped at the Duty Free Shop and bought perfume for herself and liquor for Alan, arranging with a porter to put them on the plane for her. They reached the boarding gate moments before the scheduled departure.

Susan's mother kissed her quickly. "Life's great if you don't weaken," she said then, with a little wave, started down the ramp to the exit door, her eyes moist and glowing. When she was almost there she glanced back at Susan, smiled, and like an actress in a play, swept through the door with chin held high.

As Susan walked through the terminal to the area for London buses, the brittle bravado she had exhibited before her mother went limp. The older woman had pushed doubts into her head—doubts about Edward

—doubts over her own career, Why couldn't her mother have praised her for her courage and independence? Why couldn't she have agreed that Edward needed to be taught a lesson? Why did she always have to take *his* side?

As she walked Susan's spirits sank lower and lower. Was she really doing the right thing? How long would Edward wait before he became interested in someone else?

Chapter 7

The next day Michael called and arranged to come by that evening, and Susan couldn't have been more delighted. She was glad he was back. There was something about his calm eyes and his reassuring silences that she needed right now. Despite her new-found tolerance for her mother, the visit had been an ordeal, bringing with it concerns over a forthcoming marriage Susan felt would be far from ideal.

That evening Susan was careful to select a sweater that would complement her new hair color, which Micheal had not yet seen. She finally chose a black turtleneck which she pulled down over her mauve striped slacks until it reached her hips, then fastened a black leather belt around her waist.

Michael arrived in a cab, which he left

waiting at the curb. As soon as she answered
the door and he saw her new haircut, he
smiled his approval. Once they both were in
the cab, Michael told the driver to take them
to the Thames. Noticing the footpath along
the bank, they made plans to walk as far as
Tower Bridge, arranging with the driver to
pick them up there in an hour.

A cool fog was descending over the river
and its shores, making the air chilly. Mis-
placed seagulls soared above the darkening
water, crying to each other. Even in the
fading light Susan could see that Michael's
face was tanned. "How was your stay in
Italy? You look like you've been lying in the
sun," she said.

"Scurrying around, mostly—had a half-
dozen interviews. I have more writing to do
tonight, but I wanted to see how things were
going with you. As soon as I arrived at my
flat, I dumped all my notes on the desk and
called you."

"Wait a minute," she broke in. "You called
me this morning. You had all day to write."

"Not exactly. I went back to the Times and
worked on an assignment there. What I was
writing in Italy is an investigative story that
will take months to finish."

"Being a journalist sounds grueling."

"But exciting!"

She strolled slowly by his side, glancing
at him periodically. It was different than

walking with Edward who, no matter how fast she walked, always managed to be a step or two ahead. She was content to listen to the gulls and the distant traffic without much small talk.

"So your mother visited you?" he asked, picking up on what she'd said in the cab.

"Mother and I have never been very close, but this time I felt a little something for her. She's getting older and wants to get married again, but I'm not too crazy about the groom she's chosen." She gave him a sideways glance. "She also kept urging me to go back to Edward."

"I hope you weren't influenced."

"Not in the least . . . Well, maybe a little. At the moment, the dress I made isn't selling and things look rather bleak."

Michael watched a gull strutting across the grass towards a discarded popcorn container. "You'll make it. You've got courage and determination. Not many woman would have the guts to live alone—or come here in the first place."

"It was staying in Vienna that was the hardest. Sometimes, when all the beautiful models and buyers crowded around Edward and I was left in the corner, I thought I would die."

"I suspect there's miles between being married to a man like Columbus and loving him."

She'd never considered it that way. *I do love him,* she thought, *and I miss him and there's no getting around it.*

Stopping, Michael pulled a pack of cigarettes from his pocket and shook one out in his palm. Compared to a stereotyped chain-smoking reporter, he smoked very little. The orange glow of his lighter made her realize how dark it was getting. Tower Bridge was far ahead.

"We should hurry—the cab is probably waiting," she said.

"Let's jog. I have to finish my cigarette first, though."

He stamped it out when it was half smoked, and they started to run single file over the footpath. They arrived breathless and laughing. A lock of Michael's hair had fallen over his forehead. She couldn't bear to think of what hers looked like, but Michael was so different from Edward, she doubted if he would care.

The cab appeared out of the gloom as miraculously as those in detective novels. After they had climbed into it, Michael said, "If it's okay with you, I'll take you to a fish n' chips place near your house and we'll eat our dinner off newspaper."

"I'm starved enough to eat it off the floor!"

They laughed a lot as they stood waiting in a queue at the restaurant. When they finally received their orders, they carried them toward the back of the room and sat at a tiny table.

"Plaice used to be inexpensive," Michael said as he bit into his batter-fried piece. "Now poor people can't afford it. It's lucky the British are stocking the Thames with fish."

"You know a lot, Michael—a lot of little interesting things."

He looked away, a somber expression clouding his face. "Yeah, I know a lot."

They had both finished. He got up, and when she rose, he took her arm, steering her past the crowd.

They walked through the mist, passing through large circles of diffused foggy light shining down from the street lamps. The air was damp and filled with the faint scent of roses. Having Michael at her side made Susan feel calm—not as frazzled as she had felt with her mother.

When they finally arrived home, Michael waited while she jiggled the lock in order to open her front door, then remained standing on the steps.

His eyes studied hers. "You're pretty," he said. He lifted his hand to her chin, placing it underneath and stroking it gently with his thumb. "Very pretty."

She leaned towards him. She was sure he was going to kiss her.

Suddenly he dropped his hand and turned.

She swung open the front door. A panel of light shone out from the lamp she always left on when she went out. "Come in," she whispered.

"Can't. Have to work. G'night," he said.

She watched him hurry down the steps and over the pavement, with a strange yearning inside. It made her wonder if her mother's comment about her sensuousness might not be true.

By Friday, the dress at the boutique still had not been sold. She sewed all weekend on a green silk one, but when she brought it to the shop on Monday, Veronica discouraged her from hanging it on the rack. "Your first one isn't selling. It's a bit premature for me to accept a second," she said.

Susan canvassed the streets in Knightsbridge checking out other boutiques that might take the dress, and after a number of refusals, returned to Veronica's in hopes she could persuade her to change her mind.

Veronica was adamant and barely glanced at the green silk dress, insisting that Susan put it back in its box. As she was tucking the tissue around it, a tall woman strode into the tiny, dim shop. Susan paused and gazed at her. Her hair was a bright, blazing shade of auburn, but her skin was olive and her huge brown eyes were fringed with black lashes. She looked Indian or Arabian—Susan couldn't tell which. She was wearing an

attractive beige knit suit and carried a tan
leather purse which matched her sandals.
Her hair was in an upsweep that only a professional beautician could have arranged.

"I buy a blouse in here the other day. You
haf something new?" the woman asked in a
foreign accent.

Veronica quickly stepped out from behind
the counter, led her to a rack of clothes, and
helped her sort through the size 10 dresses.

The customer studied the first dress Susan
had made but passed it by. "I think it is not
what I like here," she said.

Would Veronica remember the dress on
the counter, Susan wondered? It was also a
size 10 and that particular shade of green
would look gorgeous with the customer's
hair.

"An afternoon dress came in a few minutes
ago. Would you care to have a look?"
Veronica asked.

The woman followed her to the counter.

"Tamar Mahbouba; Susan Thorwald. Mrs.
Thorwald is a designer from America who
uses fabrics with exquisite taste." The tissue
paper rustled and before Susan knew it,
Veronica had lifted the green dress from its
box and was spreading it over the counter.
"Lovely, isn't it? Pure silk!"

Tamar smiled for the first time. "I try it,"
she said and marched off to the fitting room,
followed by Veronica with the dress over her
arm. A few minutes later she returned. "Mrs.

Mahbouba is an Arabian who used to live in Iraq and is partial to western styles. She's very selective. I hope it will fit," she whispered.

After several minutes she went to check, then came back. "The style is fine, but it's too low waisted for her figure. After seeing it on, I've decided to hang it on the rack with the other dresses. It's more attractive than I thought. What price do you want me to put on it?"

"Seventy-five pounds including commission," said Susan, hesitant to name such a high figure.

The blond woman paused, then nodded. Just then, Tamar stepped from the dressing room and came toward the counter, her eyes on Susan. "Your card, pulice," she demanded.

Grateful to Michael for his advice, Susan drew one out from her purse.

"Do you—how do you say it—custommake?" the Iraqi asked, opening her handbag and dropping the card inside.

"The price is higher—but yes, I do."

"No matter, I phone you." There was a snap as her purse clicked shut followed by the staccato tap of heels as she went out.

"A bit of money, that one has," Veronica said after the door closed behind her. "The Arabians come and stay in London for weeks, paying fabulous prices at our best hotels. I suspect she could buy the entire street if she were in the mood."

Laughing, Susan hurried over to the rack where her first dress was hanging. "No doubt you want me to collect the dress I left here before."

Veronica paused, then smiled. "I'll lower the price and give it a few more days. We've had quite a few calls for summer suits. I know the season is short, but if you could bring in something right away—say next week—tailored, simple, in a washable fabric . . ."

"Lined jacket?"

Veronica nodded.

"I'll begin on it today," Susan said, pleased at the sudden change of attitude.

Hurrying out, she walked home at a fast pace, her arms swinging freely now that she no longer was encumbered by the dress box. She had almost reached her block when she saw the same two men who had been standing under the street lamp near her house the week before. Today they were wearing open jackets and looked a trifle less scruffy. They turned the corner before she passed and disappeared into the side street.

The sight of the men made her so uneasy, it took two cups of tea before she was able to settle down to her work. She went upstairs and began going through the fabrics in the spare bedroom, searching for one she could use for the summer suit. A violet linen seemed the most appropriate. Carrying the material out to the bay window in the parlor, she studied it under the light, visualizing a stand-up collar and a row of lavender buttons.

The street was empty now, the sun was warming her shoulders, and the sweet remembrance of Michael and their walk along the Thames enveloped her like a heady perfume. She smiled. The future seemed brighter than it had since her arrival in London.

Chapter 8

As she had promised, Tamar Mahbouba phoned the next week and asked Susan to come and show her fabric samples at her suite of rooms at the De Vere Hotel. During their half-hour telephone conversation, Susan learned that Tamar was a recent widow whose husband had died while having open heart surgery in London. She had lived in Iraq up until that time. Periodically she spoke of "when the oil come" as if it were the dividing point between segments of her life. She explained that she was anxious to dress well for her friends and her mother, who had come to London from Iraq at the outset of war.

"My mother and aunt, they say my dresses are too bright," she whined. But the more she talked, the more Tamar's strong interest in fashion became apparent. "Will skirts be slim and have pleats at the hems? Will the waist be high or low?" she asked.

Susan carefully and knowledgeably answered her questions, aware that Tamar possessed what Edward usually considered the two prerequisites of a good customer: a love of clothes and the means to pay for them. If anyone could, this rich and pampered Iraqi could bring her success.

It had rained for a week, but the morning of her appointment with Tamar was sunny. On getting up, Susan opened every window in the house. She'd caught the European habit of airing the rooms whenever possible, and she wanted to take advantage of the breeze blowing in from the Thames. She stood for a moment by the window in her bedroom, breathing in the fresh, invigorating scent. A gull screeched overhead, its cry punctuating the distant roar of early morning traffic.

Once dressed and ready, she decided to walk to Tamar's hotel, wanting to check out everyday fashions on the London streets. According to Edward, the real trends in fashion appeared among the street crowd—for those alert enough to pick them up. It was a "look" a designer searched for—baggy slacks, low-cut transparent blouses, high heels—a look that could be reshaped into innovative designs.

Sunlight streamed down. The pavement was crowded, so Susan edged over and walked next to the shop fronts to avoid being jostled. Periodically she glanced in the wide windows, surprised that the reflection of the slim blond woman striding along was hers. On her last shampoo, she'd darkened her hair slightly, making the shade more natural.

The nearer she came to the hotel the more nervous she grew. She gazed up at the ornate red brick building. Carrying a satchel containing her measuring tape and samples, she seemed like a professional seamstress, but she scarcely knew what else to measure besides hips, waist and bust. She would have to bluff her way through.

Tamar's rooms were on the fourth floor of the hotel. Afraid of being late, Susan took the lift, then hurried down the corridor and tapped lightly on Tamar's door. She was relieved to see that her client was smiling when the door opened. The shop had been dim the day Susan had first met Tamar, and now as she entered the sunny room, she noticed a small but not unpleasant gap between Tamar's front teeth. She was wearing a slim green skirt and a taupe tunic blouse that had a mandarin collar. Today her hair was the color of strawberries.

Susan followed her into the room, past a parrot in a cage standing by an open window. The sunny room was spacious and had been modernized but still contained some vestiges from the Victorian era when the hotel had been built. The muffled sounds of a vacuum came from far down the hall.

Tamar insisted that Susan sit on the sofa. Before her was a glass-covered table on which she spread out her fabric samples. Sitting down beside her, Tamar picked up one sample after another and, holding them in the light from the window, examined the swatches of material with her long red-tipped fingers, while talking incessantly.

"The operator—she burn the ear when she blow-dry the hair," Tamar said, describing her session at the beauty parlor that morning.

She rejected the voiles and light materials, protesting that they grew limp in the London climate. After looking at all the samples, she ordered an off-white crepe to be made into a flowing dress with a cowl neckline.

"I pay 5 pounds more than you charge for the green silk dress," Tamar said abruptly.

Susan was silent. She'd expected to earn more for a custom-made dress but it seemed foolish to argue when she'd had so little experience—so she agreed. She asked Tamar to stand up and then began taking her measurements with swift, efficient motions, copying those faceless women she'd watched in countless fitting rooms with her mother.

Tamar stood still for a few seconds than began to complain. "My legs ache. How much longer it take?"

There was only one word to describe her, Susan decided—*petulant.* Her high hopes were dwindling. Whatever she made for this woman would be received without praise—and possibly, rejected. She finished the measurements and gathered up her patterns, fabric samples and measuring tapes, dropping them into her satchel.

The parrot squawked and fluttered in its cage and Tamar ran over to attend to it. "Mortecai, my sweet Mortecai," she said, making little kissing sounds with her lips. "Is my baby frightened?" So absorbed was she with the bird that when Susan said goodbye, she scarcely looked up.

Riding home on the bus, Susan gazed out at the shiny rhododendron bushes lining the pavement. It was a beautiful day, warm and radiant, and she wasn't going to let her visit with Tamar spoil it. She had closed every window in her house when she'd left, but would open those in the parlor again and then cut out the dress for Tamar while the breeze blew in on her.

The red two-decker bus pulled up to the curb. She got off and walked the block from the bus stop to her house. As she mounted the steps and looked up, a shakiness came over her. The front door was ajar. She remembered locking it when she left. She pushed it open further and was met by the same musty odor that all the airing in the world would never eradicate. And the quiet was there, too, the customary stillness. She set down her satchel in the hall.

Sunshine slanted in from the nylon-curtained window by the door, dust particles floating in the golden rays. Why dust particles? And why was there dust hovering in the stairwell?

She mounted the stairs, her fear crystallizing. Someone had been in the house! She could sense it, almost smell it. On every other step she stood still and listened, but only silence enveloped her. The closeness in the stairwell bore down on her as she climbed, steadily now, beads of sweat breaking out on her forehead. Clump, clump, up, up. At the top of the stairs she stopped. In one long trail from the bedroom clothes were scattered— slips, bras, panties, blouses—trampled and crushed!

She rushed into her room. The drawers of the dresser and desk had been pulled out and dropped on the floor. Her address book lay on the carpet, and the box that had once contained her money lay beside it—open and empty!

How could this have happened? That lock on the front door had to be the cause!

She ran downstairs to check further. All the cupboard doors in the kitchen were open and the shelves bare. Whoever it was cleaned her out of food as well. Hurrying across the room, she pulled open the door to the fridge. The shelves were empty accept for the lower one where an egg lay splattered.

She sank down on a chair, burying her face

in her tembling hands. It seemed so unfair! Her career was barely started and her chances of success had looked so bright. Now all her money was gone—even her food!

Chapter 9

The kitchen wall kept changing from dark tan to light ivory as the afternoon sun intermittently slanted through the windows. Susan sat by the table in a state of numbness. The weather was not making up its mind what to do and neither was she.

Edward would have known. But then, being meticulous in everything, he never would have left the lock unfixed in the first place.

Just the thought of Edward made her more alert. Not repairing the lock had been a mistake, but she wasn't going to let the consequences get the best of her. She must stop being so indecisive and deal with the burglary in a mature way. The first and logical thing certainly was to call the police.

She climbed the stairs, her knees trembling

at the thought of the clothes strewn over the hall above. She wondered how she could endure tonight—and all the following nights here by herself. A few weeks ago she would have been even more frightened. But her days and nights alone had seasoned her so that she no longer jumped at the slightest sound. She had learned to recognize the thump of the paper as it hit the front steps, and the footsteps of the postman, could identify the whistling the wind made through the cracks around the windows or down the fireplace flue. There were few times when she had to stop her work, trying to identify a strange sound.

When she reached the hall where the phone was she averted her eyes from the clothes. Finding the number under "Police" in the white pages, she dialed and waited patiently for someone to answer.

"Kensington Station," a deep voice boomed.

"I want to report a burglary on Sumner Place."

"Name and address, please."

Steadying her voice, Susan gave her name as Mrs. Edward Thorwald and told him the house number.

"Would you mind popping into the station to fill out some forms?"

She hesitated. Images of the men she'd seen lurking on her block, who might very well be the burglars, made her reluctant to go out on the streets.

"Can't someone come here?"

"I'm afraid that would be a bit awkward, madam. Is your husband there? Perhaps he could pop in."

"No, I'm alone. I'll come," she said and hung up.

Glancing at the phone book lying open before her, she saw the address of the station was 72 Earl's Court Road, a distance from her house. There was not even enough sterling in her purse to pay for either a bus or a tube. She would have to walk to the station and back. And after that—what would she do without money then?

Once outside, she walked fast to get away from her neighborhood where the men might still be hiding. By the time she reached Earl's Court Road, she was breathless. Projecting from a brick building was a neon sign glowing with the word "Police." A number of steps led up to the entrance and she climbed them with her remaining strength, wondering if she were ready for an onslaught of questions.

She swung open the door and entered. Before her, a counter about five feet tall threatened her with its height. Behind it a bobby in a dark blue uniform was holding a black telephone receiver to his ear and speaking gruffly into the mouthpiece. Under his jacket he wore a white shirt and spotless black tie, making him look overly neat in contrast with the clutter around him.

She crossed the dark wooden floor scuffed by dozens of heavy shoes. Lining the wall was a row of chairs with dark stains on the yellow wall where greasy heads had rested. She sat in one and waited for the sergeant to finish his conversation. Tacked on the wall behind him were photographs of "wanted" men. She studied them to see if any matched the two she had seen on her block.

Just as the constable put down the phone, another man wearing tan pants and a jersey came through a rear door and stood at the end of the counter, a pad and pencil in his hands.

She went up to the counter. "I'm Susan Thorwald, the woman who called from Sumner Place."

The constable began asking her questions and jotting down her answers on a form. "The exact address, madam? The crime took place when you were away, right? When did you leave the house? When did you return? How did the burglars gain entry? How soon did you discover the crime?"

She noted that the man in the jersey was also writing.

The constable reached behind him for another mimeographed sheet and slid it over the counter. "On this form we want you to list everything that was stolen with complete descriptions and serial numbers."

The man in the jersey closed the pad on which he'd been writing and went out. She had a vague fear that he might be a newspaper reporter. She puzzled over the sheet the sergeant had given her for a long time, trying to recall every item that was missing.

When she returned the form to the sergeant, she told him about the two men she'd seen twice on her street, and jotting down their descriptions, he promised to call her if anything came up. Satisfied that she'd done her best, she left the station and trudged the long way home, wondering how long before the sergeant would contact her.

It took courage to enter the house again, and more courage to go upstairs to the phone. She called a locksmith who came within the hour and fixed the latch on the front door, promising to bill her for the work. The lesson she'd learned had been costly, but it was one she would never forget.

She was certain this first night after the burglary would be the worst, and as she went about her tasks, she forced herself to stay calm. Her ears were attuned to the customary sounds of the house—the clicking of the waterpipes when the water drained, the intermittent purr of the fridge, the hum of the overhead lights—and she knew if there were some strange noise, she would know it.

Suddenly the other noises in the house were interrupted by the rattle of the brass knocker on the front door. At first she was so startled she couldn't move. Robbers never knocked, she reasoned, and it might be the police coming to check for fingerprints. Steeling herself for the worst, she opened it.

Michael was standing under the entrance light, his thick brows drawn into a frown. She was so happy to see him she almost threw herself into his arms.

He hurried inside and quickly closed the door behind him. "Are you all right?" he asked. "I got here as fast as I could."

"You know about the burgarly?"

"Yes. I was talking to someone at the city desk when one of our reporters phoned it in. I caught the words 'Sumner Place,' then checked the house number."

He studied her as if to make sure she *was* all right. His mouth was compressed in a severe line and there was a dark shadow over his cheeks and chin from a day's growth of beard. She couldn't help contrasting his face with the memory of Edward's, whose whiskers were so blond they never showed.

"It's the first time I've ever been robbed," she said. "Drawers were pulled out, clothes strewn all over. The thieves got in through the front door somehow, although it was locked. The two rooms they really hit were the bedroom and kitchen. They broke into my money box and took all the cash I had—200 pounds! They even took my food. It's got to be those two men who've been lurking on our street ever since I got here," she said.

"What two men?"

"They usually stand under the street lamp. One has red hair, the other an Afro and mirror glasses. I described them to the police sergeant. Will the news story be on the front page?"

He smiled. "It may not get in the paper at all. At best it will be used as a filler. In London, burglaries are as common as the rain."

"Good. I wouldn't want Edward to see it."

He raised his brows. " 'All going well in London.' Is that what you're writing him?"

She glanced down at her feet. "I don't write at all," she said. "How soon will they catch the men? I know I won't sleep until they do. My hands haven't stopped shaking."

"I hate to disillusion you, but I doubt if the police will do much. Food and a missing 200 pounds isn't a very weighty crime. London bobbies have too much else to deal with to spill their guts over something so minor."

"You mean I'm going to have to live in fear?"

"I'm often in this neighborhood. If you'll give me more details, I could watch for the men."

"Besides what I told you, they're about my height. They look scruffy and the one with red hair has pale, milky skin." Suddenly she was very tired. She had thought that filling out the forms at the station would alleviate her worries. Obviously it wasn't that simple. "Let's go upstairs and sit down," she said.

Shaking his head, Michael reached in his back pocket and drew out his wallet. "I've got a deadline to meet and can't stay. I probably shouldn't have taken the time to come, but I wanted to make sure you were okay. If they cleaned you out, you'll need this." Opening the wallet, he pulled out two £20 notes and held them out to her.

"No, I couldn't . . . I couldn't take money from you," she protested.

"You'll have to take money from someone."

"Isn't there some charity—some emergency loan I could get?"

"As a poverty-striken American? Don't be foolish. You can pay me back—it's only a loan." There was a flash of white as he smiled, then a devilish gleam came into his dark eyes. Drawing back the bills, he opened his wallet as if to insert them. "Of course, if you'd rather ask Edward . . ."

In a flash, she had whipped them from his hand. "I'll pay you back within two weeks," she promised.

"I suspect you will," he said and went out laughing.

Chapter 10

Somehow, Susan got through the night, sleeping with Michael's two bills under her pillow for safekeeping. The next morning she bought tea, milk, eggs and bread, and after breakfast, started on her sewing. She was grateful for Michael's kindness in lending her the money. No one else in London would have helped her. Her friends were away, Veronica was much too busy, and Tamar's wealth seemed to form an invisible enclosure around her.

Following her burglary, Michael came frequently, often appearing without notice and rapping so loudly on the front door that he made her jump. But she never complained. The moments he spent with her were gratefully welcomed since only then was her anxiety alleviated.

During his visits he either roamed about the parlor or sat gazing at her, rolling up tiny scraps of paper into neat little tubes as they talked. Sometimes they were labels from her fashion magazines (he seemed to like sticky things that would hold their shapes), sometimes tiny pieces of notepaper which she'd find in various corners of the parlor after he left. These little quirks displayed what she felt was nervousness—over what she couldn't say. He was difficult to know and often looked away when she tried to meet his eyes.

She welcomed the opportunity to have a friend, however. Up until now there had been few chances for lasting relationships. She and Edward had traveled extensively through Europe—away from her childhood friends in Chicago, away from his associates in New York, away from relatives like her mother. Edward's job had usurped any spare time, and because she believed so utterly in his future, she had acceded to this way of life.

On each visit, she found ways in which Michael differed from her husband. Michael enjoyed conversation, but he often appeared with a history book under his arm, revealing an interest in reading as well. He possessed a broad-based knowledge that surprised her, but also a lack of practicality that infuriated her. No matter what time they arranged to meet, he was always late. He certainly was more spontaneous than Edward, who planned every move, never making one until he had thought out all the angles. The two differed in their openness as well. Like her, Edward was quick to reveal his thoughts while Michael was indirect if not oblique. Susan was at a loss to know what he was thinking when his eyes grew serious or he suddenly turned away.

Perhaps she might have read him better if she'd had more experience with men. Most of her childhood had been spent in girls' boarding schools, and as an only child there had been little give and take with her peers. Michael could be deluding her or he could be sincere. It was difficult to tell.

Since neither of them had money to burn, their dates were simple. They spent an increasing amount of time together strolling through Hyde Park or Shepherd's Market, visiting interesting landmarks or going to the Tate Gallery—anything and everything free.

One night at dusk as they were walking home from the Victoria and Albert Museum, Susan stopped still and grabbed Michael's arm. Ahead, on the grounds of St. Mark's Church, was an array of card tables loaded with crockery, linens, and pots and pans. A sign with the words "Jumble Sale" in black lettering stood on a wooden easel nearby. Leaning against the sign were the same two men she had seen twice on her street. She studied them. The skin of the man with the

Afro seemed a shade darker in the fading light. A shoelace was dangling from the Nikes of the red-headed man.

"It's them!" she whispered to Michael.

He locked her hand in his and they kept walking, his eyes focused ahead. She was aware he was picking up as much as possible through his peripheral vision.

When they arrived home, he was hesitant to leave, knowing that the sight of the men had frightened her. "If I could only stay," he said, "but I promised Alan Morgan, my editor, that we would go over a story I wrote this morning. I'm to meet him at 6:00 o'clock."

She insisted that he must leave—his job was more important than her fears.

Around 11:00 o'clock that night he called to check on her. "Mr. Morgan approved my story," he said. "I've arranged with him for a job as a police reporter."

"Is that a promotion?"

He laughed. "Obviously you know little about the newspaper business. I'll be doing the same thing as that guy you saw at Kensington Station. A police reporter hangs around waiting for action and calls in any newsworthy crimes. It's night work and a starting job for most journalists. The city desk says I can have a temporary beat on the south side of London, so maybe I can find the men who ransacked your house."

She didn't know how to answer. Her peace

of mind certainly wasn't worth disrupting his career. "Maybe you shouldn't, Michael. Why not keep on with the work you've been doing?"

"It's only temporary," he said. "The change of pace will do me good."

Two weeks went by, and due to his new hours, Michael was no longer free in the evenings. Susan used the time for sewing. The summer suit she'd made had pleased Veronica, who ordered another as soon as the first was sold. Tamar's off-white crepe dress needed some alterations, but Susan was confident that the Iraqi would accept it after the next fitting, giving her enough money to pay back Michael's loan.

Knowing that he was on the lookout for those men made her feel more secure. A bobby had come the afternoon following the burglary to take fingerprints but she had heard nothing since. She still suspected that the man with the Afro and his red-haired friend were involved.

One night Michael phoned and announced breathlessly, "I saw your suspects in a line-up!"

"Where?"

"At a station in the dock district. They were released after some mug shots. I'm going to work through the Paddington Green Police Station and see if we can learn more about them."

Several days later, he appeared with a white paper package tucked under his arm. "Your burglars are safely in jail," he said. "After a long chain of thefts, they tried to steal some art treasures at a gallery. The alarms went off, and off they went in the paddy wagon. According to the officer I talked with, they confessed to robbing your house as well as nine others. Have this with your dinner and sleep well," he said, handing her the package.

Opening it, she found a bottle of Macon Blanc Village Jadot. She smiled, glancing from the bottle to his smiling face. "You'll have to help me drink this."

"I thought I might when I bought it. Now I learn that the city desk has me booked on a flight to France at 7:00 o'clock tonight. They were good about letting me have the police station beat, so I can't refuse to go."

She set the bottle on the buffet. "Then I'll save it until you're back."

He nodded and reached for the doorknob.

"Michael, thanks," she said. Going over to him, she brushed his cheek with her lips. His day's growth felt scratchy. She had meant it as a simple gesture of gratitude but immediately she was sorry. His nearness made her long for something more.

He too hesitated a moment, then pulled open the door. She caught a glimpse of his shining eyes as he went out.

She went to the window beside the door

and watched him trudging down the steps in his tan raincoat, a lump forming in her throat. He had done her two favors—loaned her money and now saved her from worry. She wondered if the situation had been reversed, would she have taken the time to be of that much help?

Chapter 11

The week after Michael left, Tamar Mahbouba accepted the crepe dress Susan had made for her and gave her a check large enough to pay back Michael's loan as well as a few outstanding bills. As if this weren't good luck enough, the second summer suit at the Boutique sold, and Veronica ordered one exactly like it in a heavier fabric for fall.

The fact that she was surviving on her own made Susan proud. As the wife of the famous Columbus, she had received some passing recognition, but such secondhand glory didn't compare with the satisfaction she felt now, delivering one garment after another. She had made something out of nothing, had created her own little business—and best of all, she was no longer dependent.

Not long after Susan delivered the crepe

dress, Tamar called and asked her to come to her hotel so that she could order another outfit. Susan had been working on the suit for Veronica and was anxious to finish it, but stopped sewing immediately, knowing she was not well enough established to ignore any business that might come her way.

It was a rainy blustery afternoon—another reason to delay the visit—but she took the bus, got off a block away and splashed through the puddles on to Tamar's hotel. When she arrived her shoes were soaked and she could feel a cold coming on.

On reaching Tamar's door, she knocked and waited but there was no answer. She could hear voices inside, and once or twice she heard a laugh that sounded like Tamar's. Finally the doorknob rattled and a vaguely familiar male voice said, "I really must go. You have another visitor. I'll come again with more photos."

"No, stay," she heard Tamar say. "It's only my dressmaker. She can wait."

Blood rushed to Susan's face. *Only my dressmaker!* That's how Tamar viewed her—as a mere servant. The tower of pride that she'd built up over the past weeks suddenly collapsed in a cloud of dust. Tamar's tone of voice had revealed her disregard—a disregard bordering on contempt.

Nothing could induce Susan to visit her now. She'd starve first! Turning, she squished down the hall in her wet shoes.

When she was almost to the end of the corridor, Tamar's door opened then closed with a click. The man must be leaving. Footsteps padded on the soft carpet behind her. She hurried until she came to the elevators, then pressed the button and waited.

The man neared her, and with one glance, she recognized him immediately. "Joel Adams!" she cried.

A puzzled look crept over his face. "Susan Thorwald?"

She nodded as he came closer. Joel was an American who worked under Edward as manager of the London branch of the Thadius chain. He was about Edward's height, and extremely thin—one of the thinnest men she'd ever known. The slender fingers of his right hand clasped the handle of a maroon leather briefcase.

"I didn't recognize you at first with your hair that way. You look great!" he said, gazing at her admiringly.

The surprise meeting wiped away her former feelings of inadequacy. She had always liked Joel whom she'd run into more than once at various style shows.

How is Edward? was on the tip of her tongue. Instead, she asked, "What brings you to the De Vere Hotel?" She was sure that since he worked in London he couldn't be staying here.

"I was visiting one of our important customers who lives on this floor. I brought some photos of the gowns we're currently showing. She's a woman who likes personal attention."

It took only a moment for Susan to realize that Joel had been the man in Tamar's room. "Is her name Tamar Mahbouba?" she asked.

"You know her?"

"Yes, I met her a month ago." A thrill passed through her. Her handmade clothes were hanging on the same rack in Tamar's wardrobe as extravagant gowns sold by Thadius!

The elevator came, and as they stepped in, Joel asked her to have a cup of coffee with him. "We have a lot of catching up to do," he said.

She agreed, and they went to the hotel restaurant where they sat at a small table near the window. The rain was coming down now in sheets, sweeping against the glass, almost obliterating the outer world. There was no way she could get to the bus stop right now without getting drenched.

The waitress came and quickly took their orders, bringing their coffees immediately. Susan gazed at Joel who was seated across from her. Seeing him again brought back fresh memories of Edward. The two men were somewhat alike—both in the merchandising field, both tall with slender hands and blond hair. Yet the intense energy and charisma that Edward possessed were missing in Joel.

A frown crept across his face. "I can't quite put it together," he said. "You're living here in London while Edward's in Vienna. Are you tired of the fashion circuit?"

"What you really want to know is, are Edward and I splitting up?"

He looked down at his cup. "Rumor has it that you might be. That—and certain activities of Edward."

She almost choked on her coffee. Setting the cup down on its saucer with a loud click, she leaned forward. "What do you mean?"

"It's probably all gossip . . ."

"Joel, tell me. Is Edward seeing someone?"

"You know how people talk—that's all."

Susan's thumping heart moderated somewhat. The fashion crowd was constantly gossiping and Edward was too popular not to have his every move noticed. The women he had been seen with were probably associates. Deep down he would be loyal. He often had talked in a scathing manner about husbands who were unfaithful.

"Marie La Joy still in Vienna?" she asked, trying to erase a tiny doubt that remained.

"She's in Paris working on her collection. Her show is coming up soon."

"And Edward's still in Vienna?"

Joel nodded.

She sighed. That settled it then, since she felt Marie was her principal threat. She could safely change the subject. "So you've been selling clothes to Tamar Mahbouba. I've made her a dress myself."

"You sew professionally?"

"Yes, it's something I've always wanted to do."

His eyes swept over her. "Did you make that suit you're wearing? I noticed it at the elevator."

She nodded.

"Your sense of proportion and balance is outstanding—very refined."

She knew the suit looked good on her. It had a knife-pleat skirt of delicate houndstooth check and a fitted jacket of the same fabric that fell only an inch below the waist.

He continued to study her until she felt a flush creeping over her cheeks. As Edward's employee he dared not ask her out, but the bold blue eyes caressing her over the rim of his cup conveyed the message that he wanted to. When she and Joel finished their coffee and decided to leave, he leaned close as he pulled out her chair, then escorted her out of the restaurant. Her confidence soared. To him, she was more than a servant or a seamstress. She was someone special.

They said goodbye, and although his words were a simple "See you around," his eyes seemed to be asking a question.

She watched him go through the revolving door, then rushed to the house phone and asked for Tamar Mahbouba's suite. "Tamar, I'm late," she almost shouted. "I'm terribly sorry. I'm in the lobby. Could I come up now?"

Joel must have put Tamar in a good mood as well, for she readily agreed. The visit went swimmingly, and after she placed her order, she invited Susan to stay for tea.

The next time Susan came to the De Vere, Tamar showed her all the clothes she'd bought at Thadius' London store. "The manager—he is nice," she said. "He pick out for me what I like, but the dresses do not fit so well—not as good as yours."

Susan smiled. The slight of being called a dressmaker was forgotten.

"The clothes Mr. Adams is showing you have been there all summer. If I were you, I'd wait until next month when the new shipment arrives."

"He tells me nothing of this. How do you know about this shipment?"

"It's the way things work in the retail business. Edward Thorwald, the regional manager, is my husband."

"You—*he*?" Tamar cried with a little laugh. "But, of course. Thorwald is your name." She sank down in a chair and leaned forward. "All the time I read about this wonderful man, Columbus, who knows so much of fashion. I go to Paris. I see his name and hear the whispers. I cannot believe it. You and he husband and wife and you sew for me—Tamar Mahbouba! Tell me what he says is new."

Susan quickly related Edward's predictions for the coming year: accented shoulders, plunging necklines, tightened belts.

"The . . . uh . . . bottom?" Tamar asked, motioning to her hemline.

"Whatever looks best on you," Susan assured her.

During the days that followed, Tamar's attitude towards Susan changed considerably. She began inviting her to cafes where they sat for entire afternoons, talking over their drinks. Sometimes she asked her to come to her suite and had room service bring the specialties of her country—sausage rolls, peppers and unusual sweets. As they became better acquainted, Susan realized that they had much in common. We are both foreigners, she thought, both trying to live alone, both without husbands we loved. There was one big difference, however. She could still look forward to joining Edward someday; for Tamar, whose husband was dead, that part of her life was finished.

Although she ordered many outfits, Tamar was not always pleased with the clothes Susan made for her. "This color is no good for me," or "I cannot wear it with the skirt so full," Tamar would pout. Susan would try again. The outfits Tamar accepted were shown to full advantage by her tall, perfectly proportioned body. When the two of them walked down the street, heads would turn; when they sat in restaurants, there seemed to be a constant queue of people who made it a point to pass by their table.

Tamar often talked nostalgically about her own country. "In Iraq a man can have more than one wife," she said. "The groom's parents choose the first one. They put her through tests to see how well she can work. They pull her hair to see if it is real. The first wife, she chooses the other wives, usually her friends. Having more than one wife is good because extra help is needed on the farm."

Susan grew to enjoy her company. Her mother's visit and her encounter with Joel had planted tiny fears about Edward's fidelity, but Tamar's lively chatter made her forget them.

One day she phoned Tamar and said, "Remember the sketch of the dress I showed you —the one with the spaghetti straps? I'm going to take it to Teena's Boutique and see if they'll take it on consignment."

Popular with girls ages twenty to twenty-five, Teena's was a large boutique on Oxford Street where Susan was anxious to have her work displayed.

"I know Teena's," said Tamar, "but I like the little shops better."

"Will you come with me?" Susan asked. "I need your support."

It took a great deal of persuasion before

Tamar agreed to join her. That afternoon
Susan came to her hotel and they took a cab
to Teena's. The sky was heavy with clouds,
but the Iraqi refused to wear a raincoat over
the mauve slacks and tangerine blouse Susan
had made for her. Huge pendants, studded
with sapphires, dangled from her ears. Susan
wore a crisp gray cotton suit, cut from a new
pattern she'd designed herself.

As they stepped from the cab onto the pavement in front of Teena's, rock music blared
from the open door. Mannequins with their
hands on their hips looked down from inside
the shop windows, strobes flashing on and
off from the lamps at their feet. As she and
Tamar went in, an odor of musk oil combined
with the distinctive scent of new fabrics
filled their nostrils.

Marching up to the counter, Susan asked to
see the buyer. The girl paged her on the intercom, and as Susan and Tamar stood waiting
for her to appear, the music grew louder and
drummed in their ears. Two pink-haired,
"punk" girls came in and began sorting
through dresses on a rack nearby. Finally a
black-haired woman wearing heavy, dark-
rimmed glasses hurried from the back of the
store to the area where they were standing.

"I'm the manager. You wished to see me?"
she said.

Explaining her errand, Susan laid her box
on the counter and unwrapped the dress. The
manager took a long time inspecting the

seams and examining the binding near the zipper while Tamar gazed out the open door, her lips looking like they had been pulled in with a drawstring.

Finally the manager held up the dress, looked at it a few seconds, then turned to Susan. "It's too ordinary. It isn't original enough for us," she said flatly.

Scowling, Tamar turned away so suddenly that her earrings bobbed. She was at the door in seconds. Quickly stuffing the dress in its box and jamming down the cover, Susan tucked it under her arm and followed.

Outside, the Iraqi's eyes flashed. "They cannot tell what is good. They are—how you say?—cheap. A cheap shop!"

"Oxford Street does more business than most, and Teena's has a good reputation," Susan protested.

Rather than answering, Tamar stepped to the curb and flagged a cab. "Come, we go to hotel!"

As they were drinking rich aromatic coffee in the hotel restaurant, as if to make up for the manager's cruel words, Tamar repeated over and over to Susan how much she liked the clothes she'd made for her. Susan listened politely, but she was certain the buyer at Teena's had been right. So far she'd produced nothing truly distinctive. Her creations were "nice," well-made but lacking in originality.

"Why do you call them your designs?"

Tamar asked. "You use patterns made by others."

"Not always. The suit I'm wearing is my own design."

"Is nice. Why not for me?" Tamar asked.

"I wouldn't dare."

Tamar tipped up her cup and drank the remaining coffee, then set it down on her saucer decisively. "You must. You, who have seen so much of fashion, you must not be afraid."

That evening Susan did not sew as usual, but sat at her desk sketching. She longed to make the gowns that she was designing. Tamar's praise had encouraged her, but she knew that by daring to cut her own patterns, she could lose the small business she had—as well as ruin yards of expensive fabrics.

The phone rang, and hoping Michael was back, she laid down her charcoal pencil and hurried to answer. When she picked up the receiver and said hello, the clicks and buzzes of a long distance connection came over the phone. Could Michael be calling from France?

"Sue, do you have any old account books in the house there? We seem to have lost track of some orders," Edward said.

His familiar voice so surprised her that it was a moment before she could get her thoughts together. "There's a file here with copies of orders we made two years ago after the show at Hermes. That's all I know of."

"I want the orders of last November. Any idea where they might be?"

"Last November's . . . let me think. They should be in that brown suitcase—the one with the stripe around the middle."

Edward began talking to someone in the room with him who she guessed was Mark, his assistant. There were sounds of footsteps, punctuated by thuds. The phone clattered down, more footsteps, then the sound of heavy breathing as it was picked up again. "It's O.K. We found them."

"Where are you calling from?" she asked.

"It's my last night in Vienna. I go to Paris next. How's life in London?" he said in a more relaxed tone. Obviously, he was relieved about finding the records.

"I'm doing quite a bit of dressmaking. Eventually I hope to go into designing."

He was silent for a moment. "I'm surprised. You know how fierce the competition is."

"How's the bookkeeping?" she asked, hoping he would tell her he missed her.

"Oh, I found someone to do the books. No problem. We'll get by."

What did he mean "we?" Something was wrong. He was not complaining.

She was about to tell him about her friend Tamar when a female voice, sounding very close, called "Eddy-e-e."

"I've got to go," he said. "Talk to you

later." There was a click as he hung up.

Then it hit her. It wasn't Mark who had been with him—it was a woman. Was she living with Edward? Her heart began thumping wildly, and her hand was shaking so that it took two tries to get the receiver back on its hook.

A damp coldness came upon her, easing itself over her entire body. The naked overhead bulb shed its cold blue light down as she stood there, overcome by an acute feeling of loss.

Sketching was impossible now. All she wanted to do was crawl under some warm blankets. She went into the bedroom, and as she shed her clothes, shivering all the while, her mind wearily tried to accept the harsh truth. The rumors had been true. She had not only left Edward. He had left her—just as her mother said he would.

Chapter 12

Although Susan crawled into bed, drawing the blankets tightly around her, there was no sleep for her that night. Back and forth, back and forth, her thoughts went. Sometimes she was sure Edward was living with the woman who had called out to him; other times she decided she was wrong. The woman might have been there innocently working on his accounts. Innocently? They had been in his room, all right, or the suitcases wouldn't have been close by. Perhaps she had just stepped into the room. Could that be?

Up until now she had been quite certain that, like her, Edward had been faithful to their marriage vows. She'd caught designers, models and other buyers giving him fond looks, but there never had been any talk of affairs. She had worked with him so closely she would have known. She also knew that infidelity was the one thing Edward abhorred.

One look at his background explained it. Edward's mother, Sara, was a Catholic while his father, John, had attended the Protestant Church. The couple, together with Edward and an older son, had lived in Chicago near the stockyards where John worked sporadically. Staunch in her religious beliefs, Sara refused to use birth control after Edward was born, trying to limit their family through abstinence. A handsome red-haired man, John waited until Edward was four then, deciding he'd had enough, found a more compliant woman to live with, shifting his meager support to her. When Edward grew old enough to understand, he resented his father greatly for his betrayal.

Without funds and near poverty, Sara got a job in a neighborhood bakery, working even after Edward's older brother became a car mechanic and Edward, at age sixteen, started a greeting card business. The years of impoverished diets of oatmeal and homemade soup caused Edward to hate his father and revere his mother. It was that hate—and a fear of being like his father—which Susan believed had kept him faithful.

Up until now, that is. Now Edward was in a situation like his father's, deprived of connubial rights and wanting the sex and love denied him. What else was there for him to do but find a mistress?

And if it were so? Her bonds of loyalty were broken as well, and the small guilt feelings she'd felt over her friendship with Michael were dissolved. If Edward were living freely, that meant she could, too.

But that was not the way she'd envisioned her life! She couldn't give up Edward! A sinking feeling crept over her when she thought of losing him.

She simply couldn't stand by while Edward . . . Exactly what was he doing? She had to find out.

The next morning, she phoned Joel Adams at the London Thadius Store and arranged to meet him there at 10:00 o'clock. He seemed surprised to hear from her again.

She dressed in the same gray suit she'd worn at Teena's, applying some blusher on her cheeks to cover their paleness. Dawdling over her make-up, she missed one bus and had to take a later one.

By the time she arrived, it was 10:30. The store looked empty when she entered. It was the first time she'd been in the London branch but it was similar to all the others Edward so carefully tended—one of those exclusive shops where nothing is visible except a broad expanse of lush carpeting and a few well-placed triple mirrors.

A woman in a simple black dress came

from the back of the shop, but before she could reach Susan, Joel appeared. He had difficulty disguising the triumph in his smile as he circled past the sales lady and rushed up to greet her. "I thought you would come, but I didn't know it would be so soon!"

He had sent out romantic signals at their last visit, and now he was acting as if she were responding to them. The man was as egotistical as Edward was at times! "I think you have me pegged wrong, Joel. I came only to ask you some questions," she said icily.

He glanced at the woman in the black dress who, having gone to the front desk, was sorting through sales slips. "You're sure you want to ask them here? There's a nice Chinese place not far away and it's almost lunch time."

Susan glanced at her watch. "It's 10:30, Joel."

He shrugged. "Coffee then?" He turned to the woman at the desk. "Mrs. Banks, I'm going on a break for a while. If you need me, I'll be next door."

Edward's phone call had taken away Susan's appetite. The thought of coffee nauseated her but she went with Joel anyway, deciding it would be easier to talk in the privacy of a booth.

She ordered nothing for herself and had a difficult time biting her tongue until Joel's coffee had arrived.

"You mentioned rumors about Edward the

other day," she said as soon as his cup was before him. "What rumors?"

Joel looked down and gave a little laugh. "There are always rumors when two people are apart. Far be it for me to give away my boss's secrets."

"Even to his wife?"

"I tell you, I don't know anything but gossip."

"And what is everyone saying?"

"Well, it isn't Marie La Joy—and it isn't anyone else important. If I were you, I wouldn't worry. Nothing solid—perhaps all false rumors." He took a sip of his coffee.

"I do worry, Joel. I worry very much. I knew I was taking a chance when I left him, but staying with him wouldn't have solved much either."

He sat with his left arm stretching across the table and abruptly his warm hand closed over hers and the light in his eyes softened. "Edward's a difficult man to work with . . ."

She pulled her hand out from under his grasp as delicately as she could. Working closely with Edward had caused her problems, and it was gratifying to hear someone else confirm that the fault might be his. But it had been a mistake to come. Joel was noted for his amorous affairs, and she might have known he would give her that special sympathy reserved for single women. What she really wanted, rather than sympathy, was information.

"Can't you tell me the truth, Joel?" she asked, her voice rising and tears springing to her eyes in exasperation.

"I can tell you what I think. I think you should calm down. Give Edward a little freedom. You're doing your thing—let him do his."

She sighed. "I should have guessed you'd be on his side. If only you'd tell me what that thing he's doing *is*!"

"If I knew, I'd tell you—honest." There was no coyness in his gaze and she believed him. He simply did not know.

"Sorry," she said. "I'm afraid I've wasted your time." She got up and moved out of the booth.

He quickly joined her, leaving money for his coffee and a tip on the table.

They walked out together and went next door where they stood under the awning above the curtained windows of Thadius.

He took her hand and patted it. "You could never waste my time, Susan," he said. "Never."

"I appreciate your friendship. Let me know if you hear anything—and thanks," she said, then headed toward the crowd on the corner waiting for the bus.

At the bus stop, she turned and was surprised to see Joel still where she'd left him. He had been watching her all the way, and she didn't know whether she liked it or not.

* * *

She spent the next three days worrying about Edward. On the fourth morning, trying to break out of her blue mood, she put a lively record on the stereo, then went to the front window and gazed out. It was almost autumn. The leaves on the plane trees were turning color, the rose petals dropping from their stems. Early that morning it had rained and some yellow leaves lay pressed against the dark pavement. For several minutes she stood watching the postman in his peaked black cap and gray jacket as he stepped over the puddles on his way from house to house. Finally she turned away and began tidying the room. Above the music came the sharp rattle of the metal cover on the mail slot. Swaying her hips to the beat of the electric guitars, she went downstairs to collect the letters.

Four were spread out like a fan below the mail slot. Picking them up and examining them, she found a letter addressed to Edward from Marie La Joy. All the will power in the world couldn't keep her from ripping it open. Inside was an engraved invitation to a style show of Marie's new collection, which was to be held in Paris.

The high spirits she had been trying to build up disappeared, swiftly replaced by hatred for Marie. Crumpling the announcement in her hand, she began slowly trudging up the stairs, distasteful memories meeting her on every step. When she reached the top, the paper had become a tight ball. Why did trouble come in batches? What evil force was trying to break her down? Going into the parlor, she switched off the stereo and tossed the announcement into the waste basket.

From the parlor she went into her work room. Panels of new sunlight spread themselves across the green carpet and pieces of white eyelet stood on the table in a neat pile. Picking out the front and back yokes of a blouse, she sat down at her machine and began sewing them together. The crisp eyelet felt good under her fingers. If only she could stop thinking about Marie!

She recalled the designer's work shop, bare except for a diploma on one of its walls. Suddenly she raised her foot from the pedal, letting the machine whir to a stop. Why hadn't she thought of it before? Marie was successful because of her training!

Seconds later, she was standing before a chest near the phone with the heavy London phone book spread on top and a pencil in her hand. She began calling each of the design schools listed in the yellow pages, making large checks by the names as she gathered information about costs and schedules. Deciding that St. Martins School of Design was the best one for her, she dialed the office back and registered for the fall semester.

"We'll ring you up if there's other information we need," the secretary said. Susan was on her way back to the sewing room when the phone did ring, but it was Michael, not St. Martins.

"My plane from France just came in," he said. "If you're free, why don't I come to your house from the airport and take you to dinner?"

The call was the best thing that had happened all week.

She laughed. "Remember the 40 pounds I owe you? I think I should take you?"

"No, let me pay this time. I'll charge it to my expense account. I should be there in about half an hour."

She hung up, puzzled. Michael was honest above all else. How could he include her dinner on his expense account?

A glance in the mirror brought her back to more immediate concerns. Her hair needed washing, and she must heat up the iron and press whatever she was going to wear. There was not much time to do any of these things. Rushing to her wardrobe, she began sorting through her clothes, her thoughts tumbling over one another as she pushed the hangers over the wooden rod. Joel and Edward were of the same mold—like all the other retailers and buyers and sellers on the Fashion scene. Michael was from a far different world. There was something about his dark eyes that could pull her away from the tinsel brightness she was used to. She could hardly wait to see him.

Chapter 13

When Michael came to get her in a cab, she was waiting by the front door. She had managed to wash and blow dry her hair, but instead of pressing her violet shantung suit with its collarless waist-length jacket, she'd saved time by steaming it when she took her bath. Sitting by Michael in the back seat, she had an urge to tell him all that had happened since their last meeting—all about Edward. The feeling was similar to that which makes one talk about the recently deceased—a need for release.

But she did not mention her husband. Instead, she told Michael about enrolling at St. Martins School of Design and receiving the announcement from Marie La Joy. The latter seemed to interest him most, and he quizzed her about when and where the style show was

131

to be held, listening intently to her answers.

At a loss over what to say next, she leaned back in her seat. They had come through the worst of the traffic and were now driving through the twilight, past the twinkling lights along the Thames. The streets were quiet except for a few pedestrians strolling along. Far ahead the jagged outline of Parliament was silhouetted against the pale layered sky.

"We're going to Taylors. Have you ever been there? It's over a pub and I'm told the food is fabulous," Michael said.

"No, I never have," she said, remembering the luxurious restaurants where her mother had taken her.

"I think you'll like the atmosphere," he said.

They rode the rest of the way in silence. When they pulled up in front of a gray Victorian building, Michael got out, and stuffing some bills in the cabby's hand, opened the rear door and helped her out. His hand lightly touching her elbow, they walked through the crisp air to the entrance. He was so close to her she could feel some of his vitality, like a current passing between them. He smelled of tobacco and after-shave—masculine scents that seemed foreign to her now. Once they were inside, the man behind the bar pointed them to a door leading upstairs.

The restaurant was larger than Susan expected and was filled with the fragrance of good cooking, the hum of voices and the clatter of silverware. Black-coated waiters with white towels over their arms were moving swiftly between tables crowded next to one another. She was relieved when the maitre d' led them to the back of the room where there was a table somewhat apart from the others. As she and Michael sat down, the maitre d' lit a candle in a red glass container, then handed them two menus.

While Michael was perusing the menu, Susan studied his face in the candlelight. He was thinner than when he'd left and there were black smudges beneath his eyes from lack of sleep. He seemed more tense than when she'd last seen him.

"Shall I order a cocktail for you?" he asked.

"Wine will be enough unless you want something." She was beginning to feel nervous and uncertain about how the evening would go. Except for snacks at museums and fast food restaurants, it was the first time they'd been out to dinner together. She wondered if another woman somewhere was looking across a table at Edward. She glanced about the room, then at Michael who was watching her over his menu as if measuring the restaurant by her reaction.

"I know this isn't as elegant as the places Edward takes you, but the food is as good as anywhere. I'd recommend the plaice—or perhaps you'd like to try the Dover sole.

Roast beef or pork?"

She laughed. "I'll be fine, Michael." He seemed as nervous as she. A lock of hair kept falling on his forehead, giving him a boyish quality.

When the wine steward came, he ordered a bottle of the same wine he'd given her— Macon Blanc Villages Jâdot.

"Would you like an appetizer?" he asked.

She smiled. "No appetizer, thanks, just the small steak."

Besides their entres, Michael ordered side dishes of oven-browned potatoes and cauliflower in cheese sauce. When the waiter had gone, he launched into a description of the flight he'd had, mentioning how the pilot almost grazed one of the trees near Heathrow when he landed. He was still talking about it when the wine steward appeared, uncorked a green bottle and poured a little wine in his glass. He took a sip, and when he nodded his approval, the steward filled both glasses, then placed the bottle in an ice bucket by the table.

Susan watched the receding figure, grateful that the preliminaries were over. "Thanks again for making it possible for me to sleep nights," she said.

"No more burglaries?"

"None. Let's not even talk about it. What's going on in France and Italy, Michael, that you have to go there so often?"

He pursed his lips. "Shhh. It's a secret.

Unfortunately I can't tell you until the story breaks."

"When will that be?" She wondered if all reporters were this reticent to talk about their work.

"Three to six weeks. I'm having trouble getting information."

He lapsed into silence. These stagnant periods when he did nothing but gaze at her made her self-conscious.

"I'm excited about enrolling at St. Martins," she said. "Classes begin next week. Michael, I've got a feeling that this is the best place for me now. It will give me a chance to meet other design people just starting out. I'll learn how to cut my own patterns, and presto!—I'll be discovered."

"Discovered?" He smiled and took a sip of wine.

"Yes, discovered," she repeated.

"No one is going to simply appear and discover you."

"I'm not so sure. I'll work hard, do a good job on every assignment and someone will pick me out of the crowd."

He set down his glass and gazed at her. "You're the most naive woman I know. It's my guess that you've been living in a cloistered world with Edward. Things aren't that simple. Do you realize how many people are sitting around waiting to be discovered? It amazes me that you think some fairy godmother is going to tap *you* on the shoulder."

The waiter came at that moment, staggering under the weight of a tray held on his upturned palm. Swinging it down onto a holder, he began placing dishes on their table. When each had been placed in the exact spot he wanted, he tucked the empty tray under his arm and left.

Her steak was tender and rare, a treat after the meatless dinners she was used to. As Michael began on his prime rib, he returned to the former topic. "It would be nice to be picked out of the crowd. Rarely does that happen, however."

"You're like Edward. He's always regarded me as an impractical dreamer," she said, then felt like biting her tongue. Why did she always bring her husband into the conversation?

They ate slowly. Michael ordered another bottle of wine, and the more she drank the more able she was to fill the gaps in the conversation. Prompted by his questions, she told him all she knew about Marie La Joy, relating a number of anecdotes about the designer.

When his plate was empty, Michael laid his knife and fork across it and looked up. "I've always wondered. How did you and Edward meet anyway?"

"It was my dad. He wanted us to meet. He could see that Edward was special when he hired him. And when Dad invited him to dinner—well, from then on I think I had a crush on him."

"Edward worked for your father?"

"It was the year Dad had his first stroke. Edward always was doing kind things for him," she said.

"I'll bet." Michael offered Susan more wine, then slowly filled his own glass. "So Edward married the boss's daughter?"

"It isn't the way it sounds. I knew Edward would make it beyond Dad's store. Why, the very next winter after I'd met him, he had a job with a fashion house in New York. But let's talk about you," she said. "You've never married. Why?"

He frowned. "Do you think anyone back home would marry me knowing that . . ." He stopped, crimson spreading over his cheeks.

"Knowing what, Michael?"

He turned, raised his hand and motioned for the waiter. "Do you want dessert?"

"No, I want you to go on," she said quickly.

"It's a long story. I can't tell you here."

She studied him. His head was lowered and candlelight flickered across his dark face. His forlorn expression wrenched at her heart. Who had hurt him? What was he hiding?

When the waiter finished clearing the table, Michael asked for the bill which he settled with his credit card. On their way out, they passed a number of people on the stairs who were waiting for tables. Michael had been right when he'd told her that the restaurant was popular.

By the time they reached her house it was past midnight, and when she suggested they have an after dinner drink, Michael refused. He brought her inside and stood facing her in the foyer, waiting to say good night.

"You're right about its being late," she said. "Edward thinks twelve is early, but he sleeps half the morning."

Michael's face darkened. He lifted up his hands, put them behind her ears and began threading his fingers through her hair. "If only I could make you forget him . . . If I could take that lovely head of yours and squeeze those memories away." But his fingers were gentle, pressing against the bones behind her ears, then stroking the underside of her hair. She did not feel frightened, only curious over the intense look in the brown eyes that gazed at her.

Suddenly he drew her face closer, leaned down and kissed her with a completeness that took her breath away. His hands slipped down over her cheeks and neck to her shoulders, then his arms tightened, pressing her close. His lips were evoking sensations she'd never felt before. She tried to speak but his mouth still covered hers, and she found herself yielding—sinking downward into a dream.

Abruptly releasing his hold, he turned

toward the door. He did not say a word—
merely pressed the latch with his thumb,
pulled open the door and stepped out into the
night as suddenly as he had kissed her.

Chapter 14

The next morning Susan had difficulty keeping her mind on her work. She had liked the kiss. Being kissed—especially by someone as interesting as Michael—made her feel special. But the dinner conversation had disappointed her, and she felt she knew little more about him than after their first meeting. Why was he reticent to open up? What dark secret was he hiding?

Over the next few days she found herself waiting for her phone to ring, and when it did, hoping it would be Michael. Saturday passed without a call, but on Sunday her mother phoned from Christopher's yacht. The connection was poor but Susan made out that she and Alan had been married the night before. When her mother had Alan get on the phone, Susan congratulated him but could think of little else to say. Alan's voice was cold and disinterested. He certainly was no substitute for a father and she doubted whether her mother would like him as a husband in the long run.

Rather than giving way to such concerns, she tried to concentrate on her own affairs. The fall semester at St. Martins was to start the next day and she was looking forward to it. Getting out would keep her from worrying about her mother and curb her imagination about Edward.

She was up early on Monday. Uncertain who would be in her classes and what the dress code was, she selected a softly draped gray wool suit and yellow-striped blouse from her closet and slipped them on. After breakfasting on a roll and a cup of coffee, she rinsed the dishes and, gathering up her purse and schedule, hurried out.

It was a bright cool morning and as she waited for the bus, a wave of excitement passed through her. Who knew what her days at St. Martins might bring? Then came a wave of doubt. Could she do the work required?

As soon as she stepped inside the school, her tension eased. The corridor, glowing with golden wax as well as the odor of fresh paint, reminded her of the year she'd taught. When she checked in at the registrar's office, the secretary beamed at her.

"Welcome to St. Martins, Mrs. Thorwald."

Susan slid into her seat at her first class and looked around her. Most of the students were younger than she and were wearing jeans and T-shirts. During roll call when she gave her name, several class mates, surprised by the American accent, turned around and gazed at her.

During her morning classes, each teacher went over the content of his or her course, listing requirements during the term. The prospects of her design class thrilled her. At the end of the term an adjudicator was to come to the school and select one of the student's designs which would be modeled in a group style show. "Perhaps this is the way I'll be discovered," Susan thought as she doodled in her notebook.

The class after lunch was Textiles, taught by Professor Barnes, an Englishman about fifty, who made Susan feel conspicuous by frequently glancing in her direction. His hair was a silver-gray, parted on one side and combed over the top of his balding head. He had the ruddy complexion common to his countrymen and was wearing a gray suit designed for a man half his age. The coat stretched across his protruding middle, held together by a single button. Susan liked the rapid and efficient way he presented his material, however, and when the final bell rang at the end of the class day, she was happy she'd enrolled.

Over the next three weeks her opinion of

St. Martins did not change. She learned much more than she could have learned by herself, and was able to do her homework and still have time for sewing. The days went by so fast she had little time to think about Michael. When she did, she grew increasingly angry over the fact he had not called. What right had he to kiss her then desert her?

One afternoon Professor Barnes stopped her as they were passing in the hall. "Mrs. Thorwald, may I have a word with you?" he asked.

She nodded. Today he was wearing a conservative navy suit, and cascading down from his pocket was a blue polka dot handkerchief, matching a loose bow tie.

"You're older than many of my students," he said. "May I ask if you've been to school elsewhere?"

"If you mean design school—no," she replied.

"Actually, you seem far ahead of the others. Some of these elementary courses that you're doing aren't necessary at all. I should like to be your adviser. Have you been assigned one?"

"Mrs. Cartwright."

"Yes, well, she gets many of the first year students. I'm going to arrange for you to be transferred to me," he said. He gazed at her for several minutes, then cleared his throat. "I've been in this field long enough to recognize talent when I see it. I should say you have a great deal."

She was astounded. "But, sir, I've taken only one test from you. You've seen nothing of my work!"

"It's the way you dress—simply, elegantly —with a style all your own. Another Coco Chanel, shall we say?" He smiled broadly, turned and strode back toward his office.

When classes were over that day, Susan rushed home, dialed Tamar's number and told her all that Professor Barnes had said. "Let me make you a dress with one of my own patterns. If he likes the clothes I make for myself, I know it will work. You've given me so many orders that now I'll make you a bonus dress—not like the others, but something wild."

"I pay."

"I wouldn't hear of it."

"Mr. Adams was here today—I buy a few of his as well," Tamar said apologetically.

Susan knew that Tamar was buying from Joel only because she liked his visits, and aware that loneliness was a powerful force, she readily forgave her.

"If you don't like the dress I design for you, you needn't wear it. I'd enjoy making it, however."

"I always wear what you make for me."

"Good, I'll bring it over as soon as it's finished and we'll see how it fits."

Susan began cutting out the dress that evening. She had designed it some time ago with Tamar in mind and was using some gold jersey from her storeroom which she felt would complement Tamar's coloring.

Susan had often wondered if she had enough talent to be a designer. The professor's praise destroyed her doubts and buoyed her spirits, giving her the confidence to cut into expensive fabrics using her own patterns. She finished Tamar's gown, and in the days that followed, she sewed with new zeal, a creative energy that she'd never believed possible. Her next creation was a startling black cocktail dress which she planned to sell at Veronica's Boutique.

There was a new brillance to Susan's world now. The late roses that grew beneath her kitchen window delighted her with their deep reds, the tile rooftops and forest of chimneys visible from her sewing room windows seemed delightfully quaint, and the pigeons that picked at debris on the streets had changed from nuisances into interesting little creatures.

With each new creation her self-confidence rose. She was no longer trailing in the shadow of Edward but had some worth of her own. Her enthusiasm caused her to plan a party. Setting the date for a Tuesday, she invited Tamar, Professor Barnes, Veronica Jones and a number of girls whom she'd met in class. Two days before it was scheduled, Michael called.

"I thought I was never going to hear from you," she said.

"I've been in Paris checking on a few things for my story. How's everything going for you?"

"Fabulous!" Satisfied that he had a good excuse for not calling, she invited him to her party, and not even waiting for his answer, went on to tell him her good news. "Michael, I've been discovered, exactly as I predicted. Frederick Barnes, a professor at St. Martins, admires my work."

He laughed. "The school needs you well-paying students."

"Not exactly. Yesterday he arranged a scholarship to pay for my next quarter's tuition. He thinks I have talent."

"And you're naive enough to believe him? How many times, I wonder, has that old game been played? He's attracted to you."

She was silent. She had believed the professor's praise; now Michael was telling her it was only flattery. How unfair he was! All her life people had considered her looks as her main attraction. She was disappointed that Michael should be like everyone else and see only that side of her. "I don't see why you don't believe me," she finally said. "I think you're being petty. Professor Barnes is at least fifty—and married, for all I know. The party begins at 8:00 o'clock. See you then,'' she said sharply, then slammed down the receiver.

Ever since his kiss, Michael had created a tension within her. Why couldn't he accept the fact that she might have some talent? Were all men alike? Taking down the receiver, she began untwisting the knotted, tangled phone cord. There was so much that bothered her about him. Unpredictable—that's what he was! Constantly asking her questions but never sharing about his own life. A typical journalist—someone willing to observe but never get involved. She put the receiver back in its cradle and turned away, almost sorry she'd invited him to her party.

Chapter 15

Susan dressed early on the night of the party. She had designed and made her party clothes weeks ago—a thin white viole blouse with a wide collar worn with a narrow calf-length velvet skirt. She applied her make-up, then studied her reflection in the mirror to make sure no threads were dangling from the hem.

Fifteen minutes before the guests were to arrive, she stood at one end of the parlor inspecting it with the concern of an artist after the last brushstroke has been applied to a painting. Neglecting her sewing and studying, she'd spent two days preparing for the event, that morning buying refreshments and the previous day getting the house in order. She was determined to make sure no details had escaped her.

Glowing candles stood on shiny dark tables at various points in the room, and the lamps, turned low, shed exactly the right amount of light. The pillows on the sofa had grown fat with yesterday's shaking and plumping and lay against the back of the sofa, their deep pinks, blues and purples blending like flowers in a garden. On the table, pyramids of apples and oranges rose from ornate glass plates. Beside them were decanters of red and white wines, a dish of pineapple cubes on toothpicks, a platter of Brie, Swiss and Cheddar cheese cut in bite-sized portions and a long basket of crackers. Stacks of plates stood beside the wine glasses. Where were the napkins? Susan hurried into the kitchen-ette to get the floral ones she'd bought that morning, and as she was stacking them on the table, the brass knocker rattled down-stairs.

Yesterday she'd asked Katie, one of her classmates, to help her during the evening by opening the door and ushering the guests upstairs. It was too early for anyone else so it must be her, she decided as she hurried down the stairs. The guests were to put their coats on the bed in the sewing room, as vacant and pristine as a nun's room since she'd stored her leftover fabric in dresser drawers and shoved the sewing machine into a closet.

When she was halfway down the stairs, the knocker rattled again amid sounds of shuffling feet and laughter. She ran down the remaining steps and flung open the door. The group of girls, shy and giggling, were standing on the porch with Katie in the center. All had the translucent skin and flushed cheeks so famous in English girls.

"Come in, come in," Susan said, smiling as they all trooped inside. "You can put your coats upstairs in the bedroom to the left of the parlor. Katie, I'll take yours up for you if you'd like."

Slipping out of her tan jacket, Katie handed it to her.

"You're sure you don't mind waiting here in the foyer and sending people up?" Susan asked.

Katie's brown eyes glowed. "I like to see people come. I like to see what they're wearing."

"Spoken like a true designer," said Susan, mounting the stairs behind the other girls. "See you in a little while."

The guests arrived in a steady stream, one or two at a time. Those who had come with Katie attacked the wine and cheese so ferociously that Susan began worrying about having enough. She was just returning from the kitchen with more when Tamar entered, wearing the mauve slacks and tangerine blouse that had become her favorite outfit. Susan brought her over and introduced her to the girls, stumbling over a few names but proud she had remembered so many.

Next the professor who taught "Clothing

Design III" arrived with his wife. Susan chatted a moment with the couple, then introduced them to Tamar.

Like all parties where there is a mixture of people of different backgrounds, the first half-hour was plodding. Michael's arrival made it more lively. He was wearing a new navy suit and a burgandy tie over a white shirt. Formerly, he'd worn sweaters or open collars, and Susan was amazed at how handsome he looked. His brown eyes were clear and rested, his cheeks were shaved closely up to his sideburns, and his hair had the perfect shape that comes at the hands of an expensive barber.

After her sharp words, she wouldn't have been surprised if he had stayed away. As she came up to greet him, their eyes met and the same sensation she'd had when he kissed her passed through her again. Tossing back her head, she tried to ignore it.

She led him up to the girls. "This is Michael Everett." She repeated all their names perfectly this time.

As they responded to Michael's good looks, their cheeks grew rosier and eyes brighter. Susan turned away, certain that they would be entertained and he would be kept busy.

She passed Tamar who was gesturing in an excited manner as she still talked to the professor and his wife. She caught the words "shift" and "shirtwaist" and guessed they were talking about fashion—Tamar's favorite topic.

Susan welcomed another professor and his wife and stood chatting with them beside the refreshment table, periodically glancing over at the laughing group on the other side of the room. Michael was standing in the center, flocked by smiling girls on both sides who were pouring out charm the way she was now pouring out wine. "Help yourselves to cheese and fruit," she said to the newly arrived couple as she handed them their full goblets.

A knot of tension grew within her whenever she looked at Michael. He was now bending over the record cabinet, pulling out albums and stacking them on the turntable with the help of several girls. Just as she was about to join them, the parlor door opened and Professor Barnes and a white-haired woman about his age strode in. The woman was tall, with bright azure eyes and a skin as smooth and unwrinkled as a young girl's. Barnes came up and introduced her. "Susan Thorwald, Mary Seaton."

Mary's handshake was strong and firm, and when she smiled, a dimple in her cheek transformed her face and gave it an aura of radiance.

"Mary is one of the best seamstresses in the city," Barnes said.

Rather than blush as other women might have done, Mary accepted his compliment with mature composure. She chatted a moment, then left Susan and the professor together and headed toward the group of students, waving at one she obviously knew.

For Susan, the party was now complete. Here was the man to whom she owed so much. She felt a warmth towards him, and couldn't help but sense the same response in him. They talked about today's popular designers and fashion events in Paris and New York. She could feel the blood rising to her cheeks either from the wine or from the excitement—she wasn't sure which. During a pause in the conversation she glanced at Michael who stood watching them, his hands shoved deep in his pockets.

Immediately Susan led the professor over to him, introduced them, then left to go downstairs to fetch Katie.

"Whoever comes at this hour will have to let themselves in," she called out.

Together they climbed the stairs to the parlor, and when Katie joined her classmates, Susan collected the empty platters and took them into the kitchenette where she filled them with more edibles. As she was bringing them out, Mary approached her.

"Would it be too much trouble if I asked for a cup of tea?" she asked. "I rarely drink wine."

"Not at all. I'll make you one," said Susan, setting the platters down and hurrying back to the kitchenette.

"Lemon only," Mary called after her.

In the fridge was half a lemon that had been there for some time. When the tea was ready, Susan squeezed the lemon juice into the cup, then placed a doily between it and the saucer to make everything look more attractive. As she was bringing it out to Mary, she couldn't help but overhear what Professor Barnes was saying to Michael.

"There's not many like her," he said. "She has an innate sense when it comes to clothes —a flair for color, a sense of shape, a genius for accessories, an imaginative freshness in her designs . . ."

She wondered whom the older man was talking about.

She handed the tea to Mary, who looked pleased when she caught sight of the doily. "Thank you. Frederick tells me you're one of his students. Have you been in London long?"

"About three months. I began classes at St. Martins a month ago. And you're a seamstress? Where do you work?" Susan asked.

"At Dior, London."

"Dior! That must be fascinating."

"It is, but I feel a bit . . . well, rather insignificant. Professor Barnes calls on me to teach once in a while—that's why I know so many of the girls. The break from the sample room takes away some of the tedium." She smiled. "He told me of your talent."

"*My* talent?"

"The clothes you wear. He says they're quite unuşual." Her eyes swept over Susan's almost transparent voile blouse and she smiled. "I see what he means."

"The professor has been very encouraging," Susan replied.

"He's coming this way," whispered Mary. "He never stays at a party long. I hope I can finish this before he wants to leave," she said, motioning to her teacup.

The professor came up and grabbed Susan's elbow in a firm grip. "So pleased you two could meet," he said. "I've had a lovely chat with that gentleman over there and I should like to get acquainted with some of the others, but my schedule is a bit hectic tomorrow. A first-class party, I might add. Are you ready to go, Mary?"

Mary set her empty cup on the buffet, placing her napkin under it. "It's been lovely meeting you, Susan," she said, giving her hand a little squeeze, and hurried out with the professor.

After they left, Michael made his way over to her. "I guess you were right," he said. "You actually have been discovered."

"Why do you say that?"

"Barnes spent all his time talking about your talent. He seemed sincere."

She gasped. "You two were talking about me?"

"*He* was. I was listening." He smiled and the tiny laugh lines at the corners of his eyes deepened. "Congratulations. You may surprise Edward after all."

Her eyes met his—now filled with admiration—and a tingling sensation passed over her. Would he kiss her again tonight? she wondered. Would he stay after the party?

But when the other guests began their "goodnights," he joined them, quickly following them downstairs and outside.

When the door closed after the last departure, Susan remained in the hall for several minutes, the yearning inside her greater than it had ever been.

Chapter 16

That night, as she sudsed, rinsed and dried the wine glasses after the party, Susan tried to look at her future realistically. Having someone like Professor Barnes as her mentor was flattering, but it was she, herself, who must come through in the end. How many talented people made nothing of themselves? Sewing dresses for Veronica's Boutique plus a few unusual creations for herself and Tamar was only the first step. She'd never get anywhere without a style show.

She carried a trayful of crystal into the parlor and carefully placed each goblet onto a shelf in the buffet. There was one piece of pineapple left on the platter and, as she carried a dish to the sink, she slowly ate the pineapple, letting the juice trickle down her throat, its tangy taste reminding her of spring. Dipping the platter in the sudsy water, she swirled the dishcloth over it, her mind on the party. All the people whom she'd invited had come except Veronica who had not even called with an excuse. Her absence meant that she didn't want to be obligated and could continue being choosy about Susan's designs. But where did that leave her? Buying fabrics for a collection would require a steadier income than her present one. To make money, she had to sell in greater volume; there was no way around it.

She held the platter under the hot water, watching the tiny soap bubbles pop and disappear, then wiped it dry. She had been standing or walking on high heels most of the evening and now her feet ached. She kicked off her shoes. Standing there on the cold floor in her stocking feet, she washed and wiped the remaining platters, put them away in the cupboard and hung her dishtowel on the rack.

After the evening's gaiety, the house seemed unusually quiet. Going to the parlor window and pulling back one of the drapes, she peered out. The streets were dark except for the ghostly circles of light shining down from the street lamps. How foolish she was not to go to bed. Unless she got some sleep, she'd be exhausted tomorrow. She let the drape fall shut. Noticing a thin strip of light across the carpet where the curtain had not quite closed, she tugged at it again until it neatly overlapped, shutting out the light.

On sudden impulse, she unzipped the skirt she was wearing and slid it down over her hips. Bringing it under a lamp, she examined it—the tucks at the top, the closing. She held it up to her waist. It shouldn't be cut this way —it should be wider so there would be fullness at the bottom like a bell. Hurrying into the kitchenette, she grabbed two damp dishtowels from the rack and worked with them—an overlap in the back like so, a tuck here and here. Then, in a blinding vision, she saw the design for an entire skirt. She ran to get her sketch pad and for the next half hour drew front, back and side views until the design was fixed in her mind.

Tomorrow she would work with fabrics to see which would lend itself best to the design. Leaving a trail of shoes, dishtowels, skirt and sketch pad, she made her way to the bedroom, and quickly changing into her nightgown, slipped into bed. She lay for a long time between the cool sheets, staring up at the dim ceiling with a curious sense of anticipation—a sense of nearing a goal of some sort.

The skirt Susan had designed late that night was an instant success. After experimenting with various fabrics, she finally chose fine cotton and made the skirt of a double thickness in sizes small, medium and large. Veronica bought one for herself as soon as she saw them, and the three that Susan left at her shop sold immediately. Orders came in so fast that she had to take time off from school to fill them.

One day she was putting the final touches on the thirtieth when the phone rang. Hoping it might be Michael, she quickly picked up the receiver.

"You haven't been in class for two weeks. You're not ill?" Professor Barnes asked.

Susan explained how the new skirt had taken up all her time.

"It sounds as though you need help. Could you afford to pay a part-time seamstress?" he asked.

She paused, remembering her last check from the boutique. "I think I could afford someone full time. I'm sure I could keep her busy."

"Capital," said Barnes. "I'll see what I can do. One of our graduates might be interested."

The girl whom he sent had spent her childhood on a farm in Wales and was an excellent seamstress. In no time, Susan taught her how to cut out the skirt, what mistakes to watch for and how to sew the double layers of fabric together so that there would be no wrinkles. Susan inspected every skirt the young girl made. "Quality control," she joked, but the girl's work was so perfect that there were few garments that needed to be altered.

By the end of November, the skirts were selling even better than when they first came out. Susan hired a second dressmaker and bought two new sewing machines.

She had not seen Michael since the party, then one afternoon without warning he came to her house. One of the seamstresses answered his knock, and when Susan was told who it was, she rushed downstairs to greet him. She was wearing a pink smock she always wore at work and there was a pin cushion tied to her wrist. Instead of bringing him upstairs, she ushered him into the downstairs dining room where there was more privacy.

He was wearing a new looking leather jacket and looked as neat as he had at the party, except for lines of fatigue around his eyes. Busy as she was, it was a treat to see him.

"I have something to show you," he said, pulling a folded newspaper clipping from his pocket.

"Is it an article you've written?" she asked.

"No, something that concerns you," he said, handing it to her.

She took the clipping and opened it carefully. A large photo of Edward sitting at Marie La Joy's style show appeared before her. For a moment her breath caught. He had not changed. He was as glowingly handsome as ever, his profile as glorious. His legs were outstretched, his eyes were focused on the model, and seated on either side of him, to her relief, were men. The rumors must have been false! A nostalgic yearning filled her and she could not speak. She had seen him that way so often—had sat by his side as he viewed dozens of runways in dozens of countries. Her cheeks burned as she gazed at the clipping and her fingers tightened around the edges as if it were her only remaining link with Edward.

Suddenly she became conscious that Michael was scrutinizing her. She quickly switched her gaze to the headline, translating it aloud. "Cutaway Steals Show." The model in the photo was wearing a long black dress with a white insert down the front. She brought it to the window so that she could see it in more detail.

"It's mine," she gasped.

"What's yours?"

"The dress," she cried, shaking the clipping in fury. "Marie took one of *my* designs, had it executed and featured it in *her* show."

Michael gazed at her as if she'd gone crazy. "Wait a minute. Where could she possibly get one of your designs?"

She flung the clipping on the table. "Edward—that's where! He gave Marie sketches of dresses and sports clothes that I made as a hobby during our travels. It was one of the reasons I left." She could scarcely get the words out she was so angry. Copying was common in the fashion world, but it was unfair of Marie to exhibit the dress as her own creation.

Michael questioned her until she had told him the entire story. His eyes were glowing when she'd finished. "Do you know what this means, Susan?" he said, grabbing her hands.

"Marie has no right to use my design—not without my permission, not for a show!" she sputtered.

He continued to hold her hands. There was something hot and vital and exciting about his grip. "But she did," he said, "and the press and buyers liked it. Don't you see? It means that you're *good*, Susan. Professor Barnes isn't the only one who thinks so." He emphasized his final words by squeezing her hands, then releasing them.

Suddenly she realized how silly she was to be angry. Michael was right. She should be celebrating, not grumbling. She read the rest of the article, translating the French as best she could. The show had been a hit, largely because of the cutaway dress—*her* dress.

Michael folded the clipping and slipped it back in his pocket. "Can you tell me more about Marie La Joy's modeling school?" he asked.

"I don't know too much about it. Everyone says she never hires models from her own school for her shows. She always gets top name girls—where the money comes from to pay for them I'll never know. One of the girls in the school whom I've always admired is Debbie Novak. Despite her perfect figure, she's never given a chance. Instead, Marie pays high prices for well-known runway models."

Michael's brown eyes flashed. "Could the school be a cover?"

"For what?"

"I'm not certain, but . . ."

The phone began ringing in the upstairs hall, and the seamstress who answered called down to Susan from over the banister. "A Mrs. Veronica Jones wants to speak with you."

A call from Veronica meant more orders for skirts, and excusing herself, Susan went to answer. Veronica told her how well the ones she'd brought in last week were selling, then tried to make up her mind about what colors to order next. Before the call was over, Michael came halfway up the stairs and waved goodbye. She hung up as quickly as possible, but it was too late. She reached the landing just in time to see the front door close behind him.

Chapter 17

As if the photo hadn't been enough, the letter in the next morning's post sent Susan's thoughts again tumbling back to Edward. "Please, Susan," her mother had written, "appreciate your marriage. Go back to your wonderful Edward before it's too late." She went on to describe the fun she was having with Alan under the Florida sun —the friends they had made, the parties they had flitted through, the dinners of excellent seafood which Susan, aware of her mother's habits, was sure went unfinished. The letter was as bubbly and chatty as her mother's conversation, yet did not seem quite real. Life was too good, too sweet, too sunny.

"Go back to Edward. Go back to Edward." Like a marching song the words rang in Susan's ears all day. At 6:00 o'clock after all the seamstresses had left, the phone rang.

It was Joel Adams. "Pulling a fast one on me, aren't you?" he began in a teasing voice. "I visited Tamar Mahbouba today, and she was wearing the maize dress you designed. Amazing! How can Thadius compete with originality like that?"

No matter how much he pretended irritation at the competition she was giving him, he couldn't disguise the admiration in his voice.

"You liked my design?" she asked.

"Let's put it this way. Tamar is good looking, but not exceptional. In *your* gown, she was stunning!"

"So you fell in love with her?"

"Almost. Of course there are other pretty women in London—violet-eyed beauties like yourself—but seriously, I didn't call to chat. I called for another reason."

A wave of fear shot through her. He was going to report further rumors about Edward. "Does it concern Edward?" she asked almost too quickly.

"Yes, he's left Vienna. If there *was* someone, she didn't go with him."

"So you think the rumors might have been false?"

"Could be."

She was so relieved she felt like jumping up and down. "Thanks, Joel. I can't tell you how much this means to me."

"You do me a favor, too. Forget that

remark I made the other day about Edward being difficult to work with. It's been bothering me ever since."

"Joel, I wouldn't betray you. You know that."

"He's a successful bastard—so successful it sometimes hurts."

"I know."

Joel seemed placated by the time he ended the conversation. He was like all merchandisers—jolly and well-met but with concerns like everyone else's hidden behind their smiles. Staying a step ahead of the fashion whims of the public was never easy.

From the phone she went into the parlor and stood gazing out. Up until now she had prided herself on her ability to block out the past. But today . . . Joel's phone call, her mother's letter, yesterday's newspaper photo produced an acute nostalgia. Her thoughts drifted back to that night over seven years ago when she'd fallen in love. It was then that she'd discovered the secret behind Edward's charm—that quality of daring that made whatever he touched glitter and glow.

Since they did little more than pass each other in the hall during Edward's business visits to her Father, there was nothing to assure her of his interest. She could only sense that, like her, he was attracted.

One evening, when they met outside her father's study, Edward said rather hesitantly, "I have to go back to the store tonight to check the displays. I wonder if you'd care to come with me."

Beaming inside, she agreed almost too quickly. It seemed impossible that her dreams were coming true at last.

It was a Friday, two weeks before Christmas, and a light sparkling snow was falling as they came out of the house. Away from the massive stone mansion and the leathery odor of her father's study, Edward seemed more relaxed.

They drove in his Ford to State Street where he parked. It was past 10:00 and the last of the Christmas shoppers had hobbled home. Quickly, he unlocked the store and they climbed the stairs to the third floor department containing Women's Apparel. Edward strode ahead of her as proudly as if the store were some enchanted realm of which he were king.

"The door here was taken out and this counter put in. The racks were removed here and replaced by easy chairs. What woman doesn't like to sit down a minute to rest her feet while she's shopping?"

He strutted before her over the thick carpeting pointing out other changes and smiling. He was wearing a fashionably cut suit which accentuated his slimness. He seemed so positive, so pleased with results, that a matching enthusiasm grew within her.

"I haven't been here for months. I like what you've done," she said. But more than that she liked him. There was a vitality about him that was captivating. He was so pleased, so eager. Unlike many of her friends, Edward never regarded anything as dull, even the most mundane things.

He paused at a display of green, lilac, and navy shoes, piled in a triangle and capped with a red pump on top.

"What do you see?" he asked.

"Shoes," she replied.

"I see a rainbow." After adjusting a shoe so that its tip pointed toward the center, he went over to a spangled silver evening dress, like those of the thirties, which was draped on a mannequin.

"What do you see?" he asked.

"A gown."

"I see Ginger Rogers." He gave a little bow. "May I have this dance?" he said and laughed. "The man who does these displays is a real artist. Your father should reward him —give him a huge Christmas bonus. Sales have picked up amazingly since he came."

"And since you came, I hear."

He laughed again. His eyes glowed with pleasure at everything around him.

He flicked a switch and a miniature Santa Claus began bending over and stuffing jewelry in a sack. Everything before them was festive—aglow with red and green and tinsel brightness.

When they had toured the entire floor, he took her hands and gazed down at her silently. At his touch she could feel her love blossom. His eyes studied her face for a long moment, but he said nothing.

"What do you see?" she whispered, a current coursing through her, making her even more alive.

"I see violet eyes set off by dark, glistening lashes—a flawless complexion. I see lips . . ." But they were covered now by his, and although silence surrounded them, Christmas bells were ringing in her ears.

She smiled between his kisses, so happy was she in knowing of his love. It wasn't the store that had pleased him, he told her the next day. It was the fact that he could measure everything by her eyes.

She prided herself that even then she had not been naive. Beneath Edward's gaiety, beneath his strong desire for approval, and beneath the attention he lavished upon her, were contradictory feelings—sincerity coupled with self-interest.

But by then she was lost. Two objectives had formed in her mind. She wanted to marry Edward and she wanted to make him truly love her, so that his momentary enthusiasm could solidify into something deeper.

The next year she accomplished the first goal and married him. And so Edward started out as a man who was never quite hers—and remained so.

Maybe this challenge of never having him

completely kept her in love with him. She only knew that the photo had brought out the same old feelings, tempered with the knowledge that real love on his part would never come until she could gain his esteem.

In the following days, filled with Michael's frequent visits and her work, she had little time to think about Edward. She was surprised at how many questions Michael still asked about Marie La Joy especially after all the information she had given him during their dinner together.

One afternoon as he was leaving, he complained that the Times was sending him to cover the auto races in Italy. "It will delay the other story that I'm working on," he said. "It also means that I won't get to see you for some time. How about having dinner with me when I get back on December 20th?"

She laughed. "December 20th is a long way off."

"You're getting so busy that unless I ask ahead, you might be booked and refuse." His eyes suddenly turned sober. "Refusals are hard for me to take."

"I promise to work it into my schedule," she teased.

Life was going well for her—she couldn't deny it. The skirts she'd designed were selling so fast she could scarcely keep up with the orders, producing an income that both surprised and pleased her.

If the sewing machines weren't humming overhead and two delivery men weren't carrying bolts of fabric up the stairs, she suspected, from the look in his eyes, that Michael might have kissed her goodbye. But he didn't—and was gone.

A week after Michael's departure, St. Martins closed for the Christmas holidays. On the final day when her design class was almost over, the instructor announced the winner of the style show competition. All eyes turned to the green velvet dress Susan had designed which he held up for display.

It was a lavish gown with a low-necked fitted bodice closed with a row of tiny velvet-covered buttons. Its deep-yoked gathered skirt descended to the floor in graceful folds.

The instructor gave a short lecture on the reasons for its selection, praising the way the velvet skirt had been shaped and swirled without bulkiness and the bodice lined with stiffer fabric to give it body.

Susan scarcely heard him. The announcement that she had won had put her in a sort of trance and when the lecture was over everything seemed to happen in a dream— the passing out of tickets and the instructor's repitition of the time and date, 8:00 P.M., January 8th. "Remember, Mrs. Thorwald," he said, making her jump, "you are responsible for finding your own model."

That afternoon when the final bell rang,

Susan had mixed emotions. The other girls went home to relax, but for her, the holiday meant a heavier work schedule. The next day she joined the new seamstress she had hired, and side by side, they worked on orders for skirts. As Susan sewed she kept thinking of who might model the green velvet dress. Having something of hers modeled before an audience would bring publicity, and she couldn't afford to have a girl less than perfect. After a great deal of thought she decided to write Debbie Novak at the LaJoy School of Modeling.

Debbie's reply came by return mail. She was thrilled at the offer, would love to see London again, but needed expense money. Susan sent her a check immediately with a letter telling her to arrive January 5th, three days before the show.

Susan worked ten hours a day until December 20th. That evening she stopped sewing as soon as her staff left, then bathed and dressed and at 7:00, the arranged hour, sat down to wait for Michael. She had not heard from him since he left, but since it was not his habit to phone before he came, she thought little of it. When the hands of the mantel clock pointed to 8:00 and he still had not appeared, she grew concerned. At 8:30 she took off the zebra-striped blouse and flared black skirt she'd designed for the occasion, and changed to a robe. Giving up on dinner out, she heated up some soup in the kitchen. She listened all evening for the phone, then finally dialed Michael's home number. The phone rang a number of times but there was no answer.

The next morning she phoned the Times and talked to one of the editors who knew Michael. "He was due back from Italy yesterday," the editor said. "Sometimes he calls in a bit late but he usually keeps us informed. He's needed round here. There's not a chap on the staff who can cover a story as thoroughly."

"Do you think there might have been an accident?"

"It's possible. We lose one or two reporters every year, particularly if they discover information a bloke would rather not have reported."

"But he was covering the auto races. There's nothing dangerous about that," she said.

"He did cover the races, but he's researching something else at the moment."

Susan thanked him and hung up, now suspecting that the new assignment might have delayed Michael. But if such were the case, he would have called her long distance. It was not like him to stand her up without a word. There were two seamstresses in her house at all times to cover the phone when she was out, so no calls had been missed. She couldn't understand it.

Chapter 18

The 21st, 22nd, and 23rd passed, and each day she checked with the staff at the Times for news of Michael. At five o'clock on Christmas eve she was sitting before several half-finished sketches at her desk in the parlor. Unable to think of any more details, she laid down her charcoal and leaning back, turned her head toward the glowing fire.

The room was deserted. She had dismissed the seamstresses at noon so that they could get ready for the Christmas holiday. Besides the coal fire and tiny bulbs on the Christmas tree by the window, the only light in the room was the lamp at her desk. She switched it off and gazed at the dim objects around her. Over the mantle was a large wreath of holly, its red berries scarcely visible. Silver tinsel bordered the windows. The two young

seamstresses had been excited when she suggested decorating the workroom. One of
them, Peggy, had gone to the corner stall to
get the tree and had strung the lights with
such exactness that the new girl had smiled
behind her back. While looping fir branches
over the stair railing, both girls had laughed
and squealed with excitement.

Susan got up, added more briquettes to the
fire and sank into an easy chair nearby. The
little tree reminded her of the Christmases of
her childhood. But once she was married, the
charm of Christmas faded. Edward usually
had kept on with his work until Christmas
eve, which he usually used for catching up on
sleep. One rare holiday season he surprised
her by taking her skiing in Switzerland, but
more often she bought her own present with
his obligatory cash gift. "I do enough buying
during the year," he used to say. "I'm sick of
looking at merchandise." She always had
bought a present for him and this year had
sent him a maroon silk dressing gown that
she'd designed and made. She was wondering
if it had arrived when the knocker rattled on
the front door.

She rushed downstairs, her heart
thumping loudly. *I mustn't get excited. It's
probably the newsboy or the milkman coming
to collect.*

When she opened the door and saw
Michael, she gasped. Purple bruises covered

his handsome face and black stitches, resembling cat's whiskers, closed a cut above his left eye.

He stepped inside and grinned. "The warrior returns."

She stood staring at him. "Come upstairs to the parlor where it's warm," was all she could think to say.

He disliked being fussed over, but once he was seated on the sofa, she fussed over him anyway, bringing him a crystal snifter half filled with brandy, then adjusting the cushions behind him. "Who did this to you?" she asked.

He laughed. "I was in a drunken brawl with some cowboys in Italy."

"Don't joke. Tell me what happened."

"Actually, I was abducted and held."

It took a moment for the news to sink in. "Why? Who would do such a thing? And why you?" she cried.

"That's what I have to find out. Three guys came to my hotel, lowered a sack over my head, then stuffed me in the trunk of their jalopy and drove to an old villa in the country. I was there three days. On the third night,I knocked the guard's gun from his hand and after a nasty struggle managed to make it into the woods. I walked all night and in the morning came to a highway where I flagged down a car."

"I still don't see why they chose you."

He shrugged. "Maybe my research has been too extensive."

"I've been calling the Times every day. You have no idea how worried I've been."

His brows shot up in surprise. "You mean I share some of your affection with the famous Edward?"

She was silent.

"Why is it that whenever I mention Edward you get a certain look on your face?" he asked.

"Why do we have to mention Edward at all?" Edward was probably with another woman at this very moment, and chances were he wasn't just catching up on sleep.

Michael slowly sipped his brandy. The flames from the fire shed their light on his face, illuminating the dark shadows beneath his eyes. Suddenly he set down the glass with a loud click.

"How has your work been going?" he asked, the expression in his eyes changing from weariness to interest.

"Very well," she replied. "I'm able to pay my staff and make money besides. My next goal is a fashion show."

His eyes narrowed. "You're talking about a tremendous layout of cash."

"Of course, but I think I know how to get the money." She would earn enough from skirt sales to pay for fabrics and eventually finance the show by borrowing from her trust.

"You're going to ask Edward for it."

"Not on your life."

She rose, went to the fire and stood gazing into the coals. "Borrowing from Edward would defeat my purpose. I want to show him I can survive on my own—show him I'm just as good as any of those other designers."

"Why does it mean so much to you?"

She was startled by the question, and unsure how to answer it. It did mean a lot. Was it because Edward meant so much? Yet, after she'd recovered from seeing his photo in the newspaper, her work had consumed her to such a degree that there had been days when she'd never given him a thought.

Without answering, she came back and sat down beside Michael. There was a long silence, broken only by the sounds of the sputtering fire and the clock ticking on the mantel. It was quite dark now with the Christmas tree and glowing coals the only bright patches in the room. The sewing machines in the center looked like dark alien intruders. By one wall a stack of fabric bolts loomed up in the dimness.

"Maybe it means so much because it's my first try at independence. Maybe it's a matter of proving myself. I don't know, enough talk about me. Let's play some Christmas music."

Going to the stereo, she began stacking it with records, glancing at Michael as she did so. He had taken out a cigarette and a match flamed from the corner of the couch where he sat, illuminating his sober eyes. He rarely smoked, and she wondered if, like her, the approach of Christmas made him homesick.

His face gave no clue. She had often tried to imagine his other life—imagine him hammering out a news story on his typewriter, or, notebook in hand, hurrying to the scene of a fire or accident. If only he would talk more about himself! Determined to draw him out, she flicked the button on the stereo, then came back and sat by his side as the strains of "White Christmas" flooded the room.

"What did you used to give your girl at Christmas?" she asked.

He mashed out his cigarette in the ashtray, keeping his face turned away. "I told you before. No girls would have me."

"Don't be silly. You're an attractive man."

"The girls here keep telling me that. I suppose I could marry one of them, but despite all their charms, I don't fancy eating brussel sprouts or custard the rest of my life."

She laughed. "You don't really mean that."

He turned his head and gazed at her, his brown eyes reflecting the orange glow of the fire. "No, I don't. I never fell in love, I guess. Perhaps that's it."

His eyes lingered on hers until she grew uncomfortable. She wondered what he would be like were he in love—what light his eyes would reflect then.

For the next half-hour, above the soft music flooding the room, he described his childhood—how in winter he and his brother hitched sleighs to horses and with bells jingling drove up the steep logging roads of the mountains, how most of his Christmas gifts came from his uncle and aunt. The firelight played on his face as he talked, and for a moment, he seemed to be that young boy again.

"My mom used to bake for weeks," he said. "Flour and sugar. If we had them, we felt like kings."

"You never mention your dad."

The light in his eyes dulled. "He wasn't part of the fun." He paused, then told her how he and his sister would go into the mountains to find and cut a Christmas tree and spend hours sledding before they returned.

Susan sat there, dreaming of the crisp American air, hearing the jingling bells and almost smelling the scent of pines. She remembered how a slight touch would make a branch dump its snow in a silvery shower, remembered the sounds of feet stomping off snow on their welcome mat, remembered houses where entire rooms were warm, not just a portion like here.

"Do you think we'll ever get back to the States?" she asked.

"When we're ready . . . I can't face home just yet," he said.

She gazed at his bruised blackened cheek and the stitches above his eye, then turned away. Had he been in some trouble back in America? Had he run away? For all she knew he might have killed a man. But gazing at him again, she knew it wasn't so. Not Michael with the laugh lines at the corners of his sensitive eyes and the sudden smile.

"Why can't you go back?" she asked.

He turned away. "I have to make a name for myself here, first."

She sensed that was not the true reason, yet she sympathized. He was like her—willing to spend some time sorting out his life and maturing in a small country so he could face future challenges in a large one. To them, England was the new land—the land of opportunity. It seemed amusing.

"What are you smiling about?" he asked.

She took his hand in hers and gave it a little squeeze. "That you're safe . . . that you're here."

He moved closer, lifted his arm and let it rest on the sofa behind her. *In a minute I shall put my head on his shoulder*, she thought, *and all my frustrations shall diffuse in the warmth of his closeness.*

The phone jangled in the hall. She turned to him. "Shall I answer?"

He raised his brows and shrugged, as if to indicate it was her decision. The phone rang again and slowly she rose. The mood had been broken, and as long as the ringing continued they would have no peace. Going into the hall, she lifted the receiver.

"Hello. Yes, this is she. Yes, I'll wait."

There was a buzzing on the wire then an unmistakable voice.

"Merry Christmas to you, too, Edward. Look for a package? Yes, I will. I *will!*"

Chapter 19

On the next day, Christmas, Susan had many opportunities to reflect on Edward's call. It was the first time he'd phoned for any reason other than business, and a pleasurable tingling went through her when she considered the possibility of his having a change of heart. What had prompted his call? Was it memories or the dressing gown she had sent him as a Christmas gift? Perhaps it was the loneliness of a hotel room.

Around noon a florist delivered a vase containing a large bouquet of cut flowers. Placing it on a table, she reached down among the fragrant roses and carnations and found a tiny envelope. "Merry Christmas—Michael" was scrawled on the card inside. He must have ordered the bouquet before he visited last night, for after Edward's phone call he had left abruptly, his eyes averted and his face flushed.

The flowers were lovely and fresh, and she arranged them on a table downstairs where Michael would see them the next time he came.

At 5:00 p.m. the knocker on the front door rattled and she hurried to open it, suspecting it was him. Instead, Veronica was standing on the porch, holding a poinsettia plant with three scarlet blossoms. She was wearing a tweed coat, and under her fox fur hat her blue eyes were bright from the cold. "I thought you might be a bit lonely," she said, stepping inside and handing her the plant. "Merry Christmas!"

This simple gesture of friendship smoothed over Susan's former irritation of Veronica ignoring her party. "It was lovely of you to bring this, Veronica," she said, gazing at the colorful blossoms.

"I decided that rather than mailing your check this month I'd deliver that as well." Opening her purse, Veronica drew out an envelope and handed it to her. "It's been a good year for me, largely because of that fantastic skirt you designed."

It was the first real appreciation that Veronica had shown. "Could you stay for a cup of tea?" Susan asked, setting the plant down beside Michael's flowers and tucking the envelope in her pocket.

"Thank you very much indeed, but actually

I'm on my way to my Aunt Ruth's. My husband is waiting in the car." At the door, she turned. "I don't expect you to work on Boxing Day or New Year's, but I could use three more skirts. The navy ones sell best."

Working intensely on the skirts, Susan got through the next two days. Edward's present, an expensive bottle of French perfume, arrived the day after Boxing Day. She put it on the dresser along with the card, "Love, Edward," in handwriting other than his. She couldn't help but wonder how many bottles he had ordered. But a gift was a gift and she was pleased that, for once, she had not had to select it herself.

Once New Year's Day was past and the three sewing machines in the workroom were humming again, she relaxed. She had made it without family or friends through the holidays. She could make it from here on.

"Did you have a nice Christmas?" Michael asked when he phoned the following week.

"A lonely one," she replied. "The flowers you sent helped cheer me up."

"I thought Edward might have come," he said.

She couldn't tell whether he was joking or meant it. Was that why he had left her alone? "Edward usually works on Christmas," she said. "He starts planning for the haute couture fashion shows held in January.

Speaking of fashion shows, you must come to ours on January 8th. My dress won the competition at St. Martins, and Debbie Novak, the girl I mentioned before, is coming from Paris to model it.''

Michael was silent for a moment. ''Debbie Novak? Coming here especially for the show?''

''Yes. I'll introduce you.''

Debbie arrived three days before the show. She was an extremely tall, slim girl who slunk across a room in the typical posture of models—pelvis forward, shoulders back. Her pale blond hair was cut in a Cleopatra style, and she had the habit of nervously smoothing her bangs while deep in thought.

In her letters, Susan had invited the model to stay with her, but Debbie insisted on a hotel near Charing Cross Road. ''I want to be where the action is,'' she explained when she came to try on the dress. ''I want to see the chestnuts roasting, hear the street vendors and go to the theater. I want to do London— as they say here, pub crawl—that sort of thing.''

Except for some fullness at the bust line, the green dress fit Debbie well. Susan pinned up the hem and took in the sides of the bodice a half inch. Determined that the dress be as perfect as she could make it, she asked Debbie to return for another fitting the day before the show.

After the model left, Susan got out her check book and studied her balance. Debbie had made it clear in their correspondence that she expected Susan to pay her expenses. Now, besides her meals, the cost of three days at a London hotel would be added to the bill. It would take most of her money, yet wasn't it worth it to have the green dress shown to an audience?

Having promised Michael that she would introduce him to Debbie, Susan arranged the second fitting for Saturday at an hour when he was there.

"I'm so glad to meet an American," purred Debbie when she came into the parlor and saw Michael. "Frenchmen are nice, but eccentric. Look at those shoulders—straight out of a cowboy film." They exchanged the usual pleasantries, then she glided past the sewing machines and across the room to the windows, her knit suit clinging in just the right places.

Gazing at the street below, she said, "Such a quiet neighborhood, so dull. I like to be where the action is, don't you?" She turned and gazed at Michael, her mascara resembling soot in the bright light shining in from outside.

He enthusiastically began listing the famous landmarks she should see in London. Assuming that Debbie was too shallow-minded for anyone of Michael's intelligence, Susan was surprised at his interest in her.

Going over to the dress rack in the corner, she lifted off the green velvet dress and brought it over to Debbie.

"I've altered the waist, and I'd like to see how it fits. We can use my bedroom as a fitting room."

Debbie turned to Michael and smiled. "Promise to stay until I come back," she said.

Michael nodded—almost too vigorously, Susan thought.

As soon as they reached the bedroom, Debbie put on the dress. The waist was tighter now and the folds of velvet fell from her hips in dramatic swirls. Susan circled her, trying to get the total effect. The gown couldn't fail to be a sensation. Susan went to the wardrobe and brought out the shoes she'd bought to go with the gown. While Debbie was trying them on, Susan gave her a card with the address and explained the location of the auditorium where the show would be held. Debbie listened in an abstracted manner. Slipping out of the shoes and gown, she hurriedly dressed, then went to join Michael.

There was no mistaking his attraction to her, and shortly after Debbie returned to the parlor, the two arranged to share a taxi to Charing Cross Road.

Ten minutes later they were gone. Susan watched from the upstairs window as they stood laughing and talking until a cab pulled up to the curb. Michael opened the rear door, waited until Debbie had climbed in, then jumped in beside her.

Susan turned away, surprised at the feelings churning inside her. She had always liked Debbie—had been on her side because she'd felt that the model had been treated unfairly by Marie. Now she was irritated with her. Anyone who used flattery on a man the way she had on Michael—who could look at him and bat her eyelids as coyly as she had —couldn't be sincere. And Michael—how could someone of his intelligence be taken by a woman so blatantly false?

In her own dealings with men, she prided herself on being honest. She told a man what she thought and didn't try to entice him as Debbie was doing. Why, Michael knew exactly where she stood!

She clenched her hands into fists and strode to her desk, plunking herself down hard in the chair, then sitting there staring into space. There was no reason why she couldn't have gone with Michael and Debbie to "do" London as the model had planned. Obviously Michael wanted to be alone with her—that was the surprising thing. So surprising and unexpected that the thought came back to haunt her time and time again as she prepared for the style show.

Chapter 20

Although Susan had been to the auditorium on Great Russell Street in the past, the lights on the marquee had never seemed to burn as brightly as they did on the night of the show. She watched them blinking at her from inside her cab window as the driver edged up to the pavement in front. The green velvet dress she'd designed was in a plastic bag beside her—almost like another passenger. She was sure it would draw applause.

One of the first to arrive backstage, she immediately set about pressing the gown before other designers needed the irons. When finished, she hung it on one of the wardrobe racks, then crossed the stage and pulled the plush curtain back an inch. She watched as early spectators came in and paused, search-

ing for seats with the best view of the stage.
Members of the orchestra appeared with
bulky instruments in their arms, lugging
them down the center aisle to an area below
the stage. As music stands began to scratch
and rattle on the cement floor, she let the curtain fall shut, turning around to watch the
backstage activity.

The designers and models had congretated
in a little group. There were bursts of
nervous laughter and "oohs" and "ahhs" as
they drew garments from plastic bags and
shook them out. All the irons were now in use
and the table near Susan was almost
completely filled with hair dryers, curling
irons and cosmetics.

Susan was sorry she'd pressed her dress so
early, for now she would have liked something to keep her occupied. As she watched
the activity around her, a cold layer of sweat
spread over her palms, and her knees felt so
mushy that she sank down onto a trunk in the
corner. To her left was a long string of
mirrors where a few models, dressed in the
outfits they were to wear first, were applying
their make-up. The styles of their gowns
varied greatly, of course. These days it was a
challenge to predict the public taste.

Susan slipped the shoes that Debbie would
be wearing from their plastic bag. Such
pretty shoes—of green leather and low-
heeled like ballet slippers. How ravishing
Debbie had looked in the dress, her blond

hair glowing and her fine figure molding the green velvet into a perfect shape. As Susan watched, more models crowded up to the mirrors and the air grew heavy with the scent of powder and perfume. Unless Debbie arrived soon, there would be no space for her.

The hands on the wall clock moved to 7:45 and Susan shifted her gaze to the backstage entrance, calming herself with the thought that at an event this important any delay would make anybody jittery. Chances were that Debbie would come rushing in with tales of being caught in traffic. She wondered if Michael had come yet. Her annoyance over his date with Debbie had vanished, and she wished she could talk to him. Even if they said little, his presence at her side would be calming.

When the musicians began tuning their instruments, a numbness came over her. Suppose Debbie wasn't coming? Oh, but she would come! She had to! She'd rush in panting her excuses in that sensuous low voice of hers. The fact that no one had answered when Susan had called her hotel room a few minutes ago meant that she had to be on her way.

The backstage director called out, "two minutes," and the models began queuing up. Susan's heart fluttered momentarily, then she relaxed. Her dress was number 65 and would be shown during the second half of the style show. There was still time.

The other designers began congregating stage left of the front curtain where they planned to stand on tiptoe and watch. Susan had wanted to do the same, but when the first model raised her hand to her hip and tossed back her head in preparation for her entrance, she decided to stay where she had a better view of the backstage door. More designers crowded together to watch the stage, completely blocking what little view she had. She was conscious of movement, heard the bursts of muffled applause out front, and watched the other designers hugging each other or lapsing into silence according to the reaction of the audience.

By now Susan's thoughts were centered on alternative plans. What should she do? If another model wore the green dress, it would drag, losing its flowing lines. Even she was too short to wear it.

The models hurried back from their appearances on stage, throwing off wraps or dropping jewelry into dressers' hands. There were only six outfits ahead of Susan's green dress now. Going up to the director standing at the head of the queue of models, she explained her problem. The woman turned to the girls in line and said firmly, "Forget number 65. 66 in line after 64." It was all so simple. For her.

Friends and relatives came backstage after

the show to congratulate the designers, and
when Susan glimpsed Michael in the
doorway, she rushed up to him. His dark eyebrows were raised in a quizzical expression.

"Debbie didn't show," Susan said.

A flush of crimson spread over his cheeks.
"Damn her!"

Silently they walked to the rack where the
green velvet dress was hanging. Michael
unzipped the plastic bag and helped Susan
slip the hanger through the hole on top and
insert the bulky velvet folds, then stood
holding it while she gathered up the green
shoes, the make-up case and her purse. When
all was ready, he swung the bag over his
shoulder, letting it fall against his back.

Outside a line of cabs were waiting. They
climbed into one and rode to her house
without speaking. Not wanting to discuss
anything about the show, she huddled in her
corner of the cab with the dress between
them—a cruel reminder of lost hope.

When they arrived at her house, she tiredly
climbed the stairs to the parlor, wishing that
Michael would leave her alone to an evening
of tears. But the sound of his footsteps
padding on the carpet behind announced his
continued presence. They came into the
parlor where she had left a small coal fire
burning in the grate. While she was closing
the door to keep out the chill of the hall, he
switched on the light. The sight of the sewing
machines, bolts of fabric and mannequins

draped with half-finished garments brought a rush of tears to her eyes. How excited she'd been when she'd left. How could Debbie do this to her?

Michael hung the dress on the clothing rack by the door, then reached into the coal bin for more briquettes and added them to the fire. She sank into a chair and watched him. When he was finished, he wiped his hands on his handkerchief, then sat down opposite. He leaned forward, clasping his hands in front of his knees. "I suspect it's my fault that Debbie didn't come," he said.

"*Your* fault?"

He looked down at his hands. "I spent a lot of time quizzing her when we left on that day she was here for her fitting. Maybe I scared her."

She stared at him. "Michael, what you're saying doesn't make sense. Quizzing her? Why?"

"To get information for a feature story that I'm writing," he said.

She leaned forward, suddenly alert. "Feature story . . . about what?"

Haltingly, he explained that the story was an exposé of the white slave traffic in Europe. From what Susan had told him, plus investigations of his own, he'd discovered that the La Joy School of Modeling was not a school at all but a place where girls were brought under the guise of being trained as models and forced into prostitution. "Debbie confirmed some of the facts that I'd dug up during my trips to France and Italy. She was looking for girls herself," he said.

Susan jumped up. She could scarcely believe what Michael was saying. Debbie a procurer? And Marie La Joy the head of it all? But somehow it made sense. No wonder the designer could put on such lavish style shows!

In all the time she'd known Michael, she had never seen him as disturbed. He was pressing his hands together so tightly that the knuckles were white. His face was blanched and his eyes fearful and apologetic. "It wasn't my intention to spoil your big chance. I was aware that my questions frightened Debbie, but I never dreamed she'd be too scared to show up."

Thoughts tumbled through Susan's head. It was easy to see why instinctively she'd always hated Marie. Now she was learning that Debbie was no better. But why should Michael feel so guilty? She wanted to go to him, take his hands in hers and tell him she forgave him—but something held her back. It was a tiny question which was forming in the back of her brain—one that she was afraid to ask. "How long have you been working on this story?" she finally whispered.

"Off and on for months—even before I met you."

She sank down on a chair. That explained his visits. He had come for information—

hadn't really cared for her at all! He had taken her to dinner—paid for by the Times— loaned her money, and acted as though he were concerned only because of the story. Why, he had even kissed her!

She glared at him. "Did I give you enough facts? Anyone who has been as solicitous as you ought to get their just due . . ." Her voice was icy.

"Susan, please . . ."

"How about a few anecdotes? Did you know that Marie goes without a bra and drinks only champagne? Put that in your story! She only smiles when she wants a favor from you. She's a double agent in every-thing she does." It was awful. She had con-fided in Michael without knowing he was using her. She had thought he was her friend! "But in a way you're the same, aren't you?"

He looked up, his eyes meeting hers. "You actually think I've been coming here only for information? I came because I admired you. I like people who are dissatisfied with things as they are and have the courage to change them."

She was not going to be taken in by his flattery. Not any more. He was a con man— that's what he was! "You like people who are dissatisfied with things? What were you dis-satisfied with, Michael? A promising journa-list—young and attractive. Why didn't you stay in America?"

He shifted in his chair. "The Times is a good newspaper. Maybe I wanted to work there."

"Maybe, but I suspect there were other reasons you left."

He was silent. He had never shared his true self with her—not once!

"You're not willing to tell them to me?" she asked.

"They're very personal. Something I don't want to talk about."

Tears blurred her eyes. No, despite what he said he wasn't her friend—only a stranger who had used her for a story. She rose from her chair.

"Look, I wouldn't have written the story if I'd known I was going to hurt you." He got up, and coming over to her, extended his hands in a pleading gesture.

"Don't touch me!" she almost screamed.

Dropping his hands to his sides, he began moving to the door. The room was very still. The once glowing fire had turned to embers, the sewing machines had forsaken their usual hum and the windows were closed against all street sounds. All seemed dead.

Michael turned from the room. Footsteps clumped down the stairs, then the front door creaked open and closed with a loud click. She stood there motionless, filled with an excrutiating sense of loss. It was all over. She would never make it as a designer. She would have to go back to Edward and eat humble pie the rest of her life. With Michael gone, she would be frightened and vulnerable, without the spirit to go on.

Chapter 21

The next morning when Susan awoke, guilt had replaced her anger towards Michael. Had she been too harsh? Had the hostility she'd felt towards Debbie been misdirected to him? How much fault really had been his? Reviewing the past five months since their first meeting, she decided that she had used him as much as he had used her— used him for friendship, to confide in, even used his money when she needed a loan. Priding herself on being fair, she decided to apologize.

She called his number at the Times and being told he was away from his desk, left her name. There was no word from him all day, and in the late afternoon she called again.

"Mr. Everett is out of town on assignment.

He will be gone several weeks," a girl told her.

It was obvious to Susan that he wanted nothing more to do with her or he would have called to say goodbye as he'd done in the past. What a muddle she'd gotten herself into and how unfair she'd been!

But that sense of loss she felt when Michael had walked out no longer disturbed her. She had thought her career was somewhat dependent on his support, but now a new determination filled her. She would succeed despite past mistakes—completely on her own.

Both Veronica and she had agreed several weeks before that, if she were to keep designing, she must have her own label. Up until now she had used typical dressmaker's labels marked "Handmade by Susan" which, as her business grew, were becoming meaningless. But if she used her last name of Thorwald, people would connect her with Edward, and she was too proud to capitalize on his success. After much thought, she decided on the name "Susan Whitaker" and had it printed in square letters on five hundred silky labels.

"Over there are our Whitaker skirts," she overheard Veronica say one subsequent afternoon when she was in the Boutique. The sound of the name pleased her. She wondered what Michael would think of it.

Occasionally she thought of Edward. She had written him a thank you note for his gift of perfume, but he had not responded—certainly not unusual for Edward, who rarely wrote letters. He *could* write—beautifully, in fact—essay type letters filled with predictions for fashion trends. There was nothing he couldn't do well. When he was in grade school all his teachers were amazed that such an intelligent little boy could come from one of those tottering shacks near the stockyards—the type of home that social workers always were visiting. But the teachers didn't see the emotional scars that Susan found later—his fierce hatred of a father who had deserted the family and his near worship of his mother, both of which were responsible for many of his future neuroses. The problem was complex. He was a poor boy who had married a rich girl whom he disliked for being rich.

But perhaps his attitude was changing. Joel's news that gossip about Edward had stopped, as well as the unexpected Christmas gift, made her feel that the tide might be turning in her favor.

It was the time of the January fashion shows in Paris—a time when she had once dreamed of displaying her success to the world. She knew a meeting with Edward was premature, but suppose she went anyway? Getting away would do her good, and one glimpse of Edward might be all she would need to make her forget about Michael and set her world straight again.

The following Wednesday, as she was coming out of her second class at St. Martins, she saw Mary Seaton walking down the hall. Mary's face looked drawn, and she was thinner and less composed than when they had met at Susan's party.

"I'm taking a leave of absense from Dior," Mary said after Susan's warm greeting. "I'm doing a bit of teaching here at St. Martins."

Puzzled, Susan asked Professor Barnes about Mary after class that afternoon.

"As I understand it," he said, "there was a personality clash at Dior, and Mary left. She's a bit of a perfectionist, you see. We're giving her all the work we can here at St. Martins."

That evening, as Susan sewed, she kept thinking about Mary. An experienced seamstress like Mary could handle the workroom while she went to France. The orders could be cut out beforehand, and under the older woman's supervision, the garments could be made.

The next day she got Mary's number from Professor Barnes and phoned her. In five minutes everything was settled. Mary agreed to meet the seamstresses on Thursday and look over the work orders. On Friday Susan would take the boat-train to Dover and the English Channel.

While busy packing, making reservations and exchanging British pounds for French francs, Susan did not question her decision. Seeing Edward again would give her incentive to carry on, and the style shows would keep her aware of current fashion trends.

Mary approached her new job with confidence, and on Friday Susan departed, pleased to leave her workroom in such good hands. Her years with Edward had taught her to travel lightly, and she took only one bag, containing all she needed for a three-day stay in Paris.

As the train left the station, a wave of excitement passed through Susan. She watched out the window as they skimmed past vine-covered buildings, green playing fields and tacky walled-in gardens situated behind endless row houses.

It had been months since she'd been outside London, and the novelty of what she was seeing held her rapt at the window. She watched women in smocks standing in doorway conversation, watched signs for Walls Ice Cream and Whitbread fly by, watched villages appear and disappear until the lush green countryside, dotted by clumps of sheep, took over.

Once she had reached Dover and had

boarded the Sealink boat, her enthusiasm began to wane. A cold wind off the Channel was blowing back her hair and flattening her eyelashes, and the swell of the waves was unsettling her stomach. For the first time she had doubts about her journey. Edward might not be in Paris, or if he were there, she might not be able to find him.

She went below deck. At one corner of the bar were a group of Americans, one of whom resembled Michael. They saw her looking at them, nudged each other and nodded. Ignoring them, she went to a soup bar towards the stern and sat on a high stool opposite the mirror that covered the wall behind the counter. The tea she ordered was hot and refreshing, and she drank it all. The boat was creaking and shuddering less now, and after she slid down from the stool, she found she was able to walk without swaying from side to side. She climbed the stairs to the deck.

She stood at the rail, watching the churning blue water for a few moments, wishing the man at the bar had been Michael, wondering if the yearning inside her would be satisfied by a meeting with Edward. Then the penetrating chill of the wind drove her below again.

The boat docked and there still was another rail journey. By the time she'd checked in at Hotel Wagram near the Arc de Triomphe and unpacked her clothes, it was after 10:00 p.m. All her former excitement was extinguished now. It had been foolish to come. She had run away—run away from something she couldn't understand.

She took a hot bath, then dressed and walked to La Pergola, a cafe on the Champs Elysées. Between courses of a dinner of chicken and pommes frites, she studied the phone book in the hall, copying down the addresses of a number of fashion houses. Tomorrow she would visit them and request tickets to the style shows scheduled for the next three days.

In the short span of ten days, there were to be at least forty-five shows, many held in a large circus tent near the Louvre. Had she been the average visitor, obtaining tickets to them at this late date would be impossible, but because she was Edward's wife, the fashion houses would immediately honor her request. Edward, of course, would have his usual seat in the front row.

The next day she called at the firms of Christian Dior, Pierre Balmain, Nina Ricci, Jean-Louis Scherrer and Pierre Cardin and picked up tickets. On learning that she was the wife of the famous Columbus, the attendants at these houses received her graciously, and the invitations were easy to obtain. She blessed the Metro over and over for making her trips about Paris so easy. Being viewed once again as Edward's wife made her tense, and she was nervous over the prospect of running into him when she least expected. In the late afternoon she took a walk to calm herself.

Paris differed from London in that few buildings, with the exception of an attraction such as the Eiffel Tower, were taller than seven stories. Most were built of stone smudged by centuries of urban fallout. There were broad avenues and narrow streets, and on a number of corners and squares, monuments lent historical significance. On the streets along the Seine artists had placed their colorful paintings over the sidewalk, and more than one black-haired man stared at her as she passed. The water in the river was muddy, and a musty odor rising from it irritated her. As soon as the sun dipped below the horizon, she started back to her hotel.

Back in her room, she grew excited again. Tomorrow—she could scarcely believe it— might be the day she would see Edward. She stretched out on the bed, day-dreaming until it was quite dark, then rolled over on her stomach and reached for the phone. "Room service, please," she said into the mouthpiece. When the attendant answered, she ordered soup, tea and croissants.

Pulling herself up, she sat with her legs over the edge of the high bed, waiting for the knock that would signal the arrival of her tray. Across from her was a dark mahogany wardrobe and beside it a nineteenth century chiffonier with a cloudy mirror. The gas heater on the wall had to be fed with coins. The room might not be lavish, but it was refreshing to get away from her drafty house on Sumner Place and spend a few days away from her sewing.

When her supper came she ate every bite, then spent the rest of the evening washing her hair and polishing her nails, determined that Edward should see her looking her best.

Chapter 22

Two days passed. Susan found herself watching the audience more than the models at each style show, trying to pick out her husband. She could not imagine his missing more than one show, nor sitting anywhere else but the front row. Once she thought she glimpsed Mark, his assistant buyer, but when she looked again, he was gone.

A vague fear began growing. For some reason Edward might not have come to Paris —he might be ill, might have been in an accident. How would she know? Christmas was the last time she'd heard from him. But if anything were wrong, she would have heard about it at the fashion houses where she'd been received with such excitement. "Oui, Madam Columbus," one little French girl had said, "An aisle seat with our compliments."

The third day, as Susan sat waiting for the Balmain show, she was close to losing hope. If she didn't see Edward soon, all would have been for naught. She'd have to go back home, for it would be unfair to Mary and the girls to stay any longer.

Balmain was dead but the house was continued under Erik Mortensen. Assaulted by the sounds of wild pulsating music, she kept scanning the audience. At first the expensive fashion displays had thrilled her, but now her eyes were over-saturated with colors and her ears with loud music. She had slept little on her lumpy bed the last two nights and wondered if she had wasted her savings by coming. Perhaps a glimpse of Edward would hurt more than help her. And if she saw him, what could be accomplished? So far she had accomplished nothing of note to tell him.

For some reason, the show was late in starting. Men in black suits and bow ties scurried back and forth, adjusting lights and passing out programs. Sitting on her left was a woman in beige silk holding a French poodle in her arms. There was a vacant seat on her right, but as the show was starting one of the men who had been adjusting the lights slipped into it. The music swelled and the first model glided out.

While the first six models sashayed up and down the runway, the man beside her stood up and sat down at least four times. As usual,

Susan scanned the front rows for Edward's blond head, and when she saw two vacant seats, her breath caught. Often Edward attended only parts of shows, explaining his reasons logically. "What I want is an overall look. If I see what a designer does with one skirt in one season, I can bet it will be repeated. My assistants can choose which numbers to buy."

Feeling something on her arm, Susan turned and looked down at the poodle who was pawing her. She bent to unhook one of its claws entangled in her loosely woven skirt. The owner rose and took the dog out, blocking Susan's view momentarily with her wide hips. When Susan was able to see the runway again, a man was sitting in one of the front row seats that had been empty. One glance at his shining blond hair and bleached white collar told her it was Edward.

He leaned forward and scribbled something on a pad that he held on his lap. He was the same as she had imagined—as well groomed, as handsome, with that serious thoughtful set to his head that she loved. He was leaning back now and crossing his long legs as the next model came onto the runway.

Susan couldn't sit still. Some of the spectators were leaving their seats and walking down to the front with cameras, which flashed on and off like strobe lights. As if propelled by some strange force, she moved down with them and stood beside the row where Edward was sitting. The tempo of the music increased. The hour was almost over and all eyes were fixed on the runway for the final, most dramatic styles of the collection. On impulse, she walked down the front aisle and slipped into the vacant seat on Edward's right.

The next model came out wearing a black velvet skirt and silver-threaded blouse with bat sleeves. Leaning forward, Edward marked an X opposite number 84.

"Yes, that one's exceptional," Susan said.

At the sound of her voice, he turned. "Sue!" Then one eyebrow went up. "New hair. I like it."

The last model glided away and the designer rushed onto the runway. Spectators were cheering, many standing and clapping. One by one the models came back and kissed the designer's cheek as they passed in the finale. In the midst of the excitement, Edward grabbed her arm and steered her to the exit.

Outside, he gazed at her. "Now that you've changed the color of your hair, you should wear more make-up," he said.

She touched her cheeks. "I should?"

He grinned. "Yes, you're pale. Or are you wasting away without me? How about lunch?"

She felt as though she were in the center of a miraculous dream. Lunch didn't seem necessary. In fact, seeing Edward again was so satisfying that she felt she could go through life without ever eating again. "Yes, lunch would be nice," she said.

"Let's get ahead of the rush." She followed him into the most elaborate of the nearby cafes. As usual he was two steps ahead of her. They sat at a table covered with a white cloth and ordered salads, quiche and wine. Edward seemed genuinely pleased to see her. After the waiter had left, he began telling her about the orders he'd placed during the last few days.

"I've been working—really working," he said. "I know I can get a lot of response from Henri's line. Understatement, that's his specialty. I was wrong about the nautical look of last season. When I saw it wasn't going to go over, our stores dumped it. Country—everything's country. If you watch the streets, the white T-shirt is also big." He paused only long enough to nod at two men, well-known buyers, seated at the opposite table.

When Edward began talking again, she listened carefully. There was no doubt that he was a fashion oracle and had many successful years ahead of him. She wondered if he would ever lose that unique enthusiasm that kept his face so young and bouyant. She also wondered if he would always turn, as he was doing now, to see who was watching him.

After more talk about the fashion business, he paused. "How's London, by the way?"

She smiled and lowered her eyes. "Good. My designing is going well, but I wanted to check the current styles so I came here. I've been taking courses at St. Martins School of Design, and there's a professor there who thinks I have talent."

"You're here for the show, then?" He seemed to have missed her last remark.

She nodded. "I got an experienced seamstress to manage my workroom while I'm away."

She told him about her projects but he paid little attention. It seemed fixed in his mind that she was wasting her time in London.

He put down his fork. "My life is as hectic as it's ever been. I'm always racing for appointments. Maybe I just should get an office in New York and wait for the designers to come to me."

She laughed. "That would be totally out of character. You wouldn't be able to sit still that long. You're too energetic."

"You're right. It takes that little something extra to do what I'm doing. Even you couldn't stand the pace."

Her fingers tightened around the stem of her wine glass. "Edward, that's not why I left."

"I know. It was because you had to try out your independence, get your feet wet. I hope you got it out of your system."

She finished her salad in silence. The

waiter, a napkin over his arm, came over and asked if they would like dessert.

Rubbing his flat stomach, Edward shook his head. "Two expressos, please."

The Frenchman removed their empty salad plates and brought their coffees. "You didn't want anything, did you?" Edward asked, as if the thought had just occurred to him.

Lifting her cup of espresso to her lips, she shook her head. The coffee was hot and satisfying.

"If only I'd known you were coming—if only I didn't have to leave," he said.

Her cup rattled down on her saucer. "Leave?"

"I'm taking the plane to Milan at 5:00 for an appointment this evening."

"I see." Surprises—her life with Edward had always held upsetting surprises. A coldness began creeping over her. He had acted as though he were glad to see her—now he was leaving. "Well, I can't stay long either. I was able to get away for only a few shows," she managed to say. Better had she viewed him only from a distance—better anything than this!

He motioned to the waiter for the bill, and when it came, paid it with his credit card.

Outside, he placed his hand lightly in the small of her back and bent down his head so that his mouth was close to her ear. "We still have this afternoon," he said softly. She turned and their eyes met. There was no mistaking the suggestion.

Her heartbeat quickened. "Yes," she whispered, "we still have this afternoon."

Hand in hand, they began strolling up the avenue. The sun was shining through the bare branches of the trees, and a wind blew, casting moving shadows over their path. They had not gone far when running footsteps sounded behind them, then Mark, Edward's assistant, came up beside them.

"Nice to see you again, Mrs. Thorwald," he said, and turning to Edward thrust a sheet of paper in his hand. "Lucky I found you. Here's that designer's name and address and a list of the styles she has on hand. Call her at that number. She'll let you see all twenty. I've got to get back to turn in the orders." He waved his hand and raced down the pavement, his thin coat ballooning in the wind.

Edward walked more slowly now, studying the information on the paper. "A new gal with lots of promise," he said. "Her showroom is on the Rue Bonaparte. We'll take a cab over."

"Now?"

"I leave at five. It has to be now," he replied sharply.

He seemed to assume that she would follow along as usual. She could visualize the rest of the afternoon—Edward smiling at the designer and she waiting in some corner while he made his deals and counter-deals.

"Edward, I can't go with you," she said. "I've got someone working on my orders while I'm away, and if I'm not back by tomorrow to check them, they won't be delivered on time."

His face clouded. "Orders? What orders?"

He's already forgotten what I told him during lunch, she thought. "As a designer, I have my own studio. I run a business," she said, with an edge to her voice.

"So do I, my dear, so do I," said Edward coolly.

"That doesn't mean we can't get together. You'll be coming to London one of these days. I'm still at our house . . ." she began.

"After Italy I go to New York for a buyers' meeting of all the members of the Association," he said, looking down at the list again.

He doesn't really care about me at all, she thought. Meeting me is no more important to him than if I'd been a casual acquaintance—certainly nothing to delay his work for. She plunged her hands in the pockets of her jacket. When she was rich and famous, he'd *have* to care!

He took his eyes from the list only long enough to flag a cab. After they'd climbed into the back seat, she told him the name of her hotel and asked to be let off there.

"By the Arc de Triomphe? The cabbie should drop me off first. You can pay him later," he said, laying the list on the seat and reaching for his wallet.

"Never mind, I have it," she said.

"No, use this." He pressed some bills in her palm as if to compensate for his absence. "Sorry this had to come up, but it's a perfect chance to buy a collection before the prices soar."

Her lips quivering, Susan turned to the window. This was what she deserved—showing up unexpectedly, acting impulsively.

When the driver drew up along the Rue Bonaparte, Edward hopped out, then turned and quickly kissed her through the open window. "You're welcome to come," he said, flashing the professional smile he used on all designers.

"I wish I could," she replied, careful not to meet his eyes.

Giving a little wave, he turned and strode to a tall stone apartment building and began mounting the steps. As the cab moved away, she watched his tall slim figure out the back window until it vanished into the dark entryway.

That evening, she sat on the Paris-Calais train, tears of frustration filling her eyes. Far ahead the engine gave out a hoarse whistle, a plaintive cry that always made her melancholy whenever she heard it. She had wept ever since her meeting with Edward. Why couldn't he have asked her to go to Milan with him? Why couldn't he have seen the new designer another day? How insignificant she was in his life—causing barely a ripple in his calm, successful sea.

She leaned back and closed her eyes, swaying with the speeding car, feeling too warm, opening the window, then feeling too cool.

Until she was important, she would get neither help nor interest from Edward. She stared at the vacant seat across from her and the mouse-colored upholstery swam in her vision. By coming to Paris she had only made her misery greater.

The train sped on for miles before she got all the weeping out of her system. Finally she took out a fresh tissue, dried her cheeks and eyes and settled back in her seat. In the lives of those closest to her there seemed to be no place for her. Her fingers tightened around the arm of her seat. *She'd make a place.* She'd be that woman in the diamond tiara that she'd seen in the magazine on the plane.

She saw it all before her. Her mailbox would be full, her phone busy. Nothing or nobody would stop her. She didn't need Edward. She didn't need Michael. *She didn't need anybody!*

Chapter 23

The resolutions that Susan made on the train were not forgotten. The psychological devastation she had undergone produced a zealousness within her, and as soon as she returned home, she threw herself into her work. Mary had done an excellent job in seeing that the orders were finished, and it seemed a good idea to hire her as workroom manager on a permanent basis. The arrangement would give Susan the needed time for designing.

When she was offered the job, Mary's face flushed and her eyes sparkled. "The independence—the control," she kept repeating. "At Dior I was insignificant. Now I shall be chief."

Over the next few weeks, Susan began to wonder if she'd made a mistake in hiring her.

Immediately Mary set about reorganizing the workroom. The parlor was the warmest and lightest room in the house, and she suggested selling the buffet, sofa and easy chairs so that the entire space could be utilized. Next she began complaining about storage space, so Susan gathered her clothes from the wardrobe and emptied her dresser drawers, moving her possessions to the first floor bedroom so that the room upstairs could be used for bolts of fabric. Although Mary silently glowered, Susan kept the sofa as a place for their clients to sit. The dining room downstairs was the only room left where she could entertain friends.

Over the next few weeks, Mary's demands increased until there was a staff of six girls whom she ruled like a drill sergeant. The skirts were still selling well, and there were enough clients to enable Susan to meet the payroll each month. She would have liked having a wider safety margin, however.

Susan often wondered what Michael would think if he came and found a workroom instead of a parlor. After their quarrel he had not called. For business purposes, she arranged that someone be on hand to answer the phone at all times, as well as having another telephone installed in her bedroom downstairs. It was important to have the phones covered since she often was off on shopping expeditions for unusual fabrics and accessories.

One cool windy day she was waiting for a bus when Michael turned the corner. It was a shock to see him so unexpectedly, and her first reaction was to run away. He had already seen her, however, so she waited uneasily while he approached.

The sudden encounter had unnerved her. Her fingers moved anxiously up and down the strap of her purse, and there was a lump in her throat so large she had difficulty swallowing. Except for her heart, which was thumping wildly, nothing seemed to be functioning—not her mind, her legs, her arms. She neither moved, smiled nor waved.

He walked up to her. The tan from Italy had faded and there was pink scar tissue above his eye from the cut he had received. Seeing those familiar dark eyes brought happy memories flooding back.

"I hear you've been away," he said without looking at her.

"Yes, how did you know?"

"Mary told me you had taken a trip. Paris, wasn't it?"

She nodded, anger at Mary mingling with joy. So he had called after all, and Mary had forgotten to tell her. But perhaps he had called for business reasons. "Do you need more information for your story?" she asked.

A look of pain filled the dark eyes that were gazing at her. "You have very little faith in me," he said. "The story was published the day after we talked."

She glanced around. Without either of them noticing, the bus had come and gone, swallowing up the people who had been waiting beside them at the bus stop. Knowing that it would be at least ten minutes before another one came, she motioned to the empty bench behind them. They sat down with a large space separating them.

"Did you keep a copy of what you wrote?" she asked.

He did not look at her but stared across the street. "Yes, I have the clipping with me. I'll be glad to show it to you, but first I want to get something straight. Whether or not you believe me, I didn't visit you only for information. I did write about Marie La Joy, but I had most of the facts even before you mentioned her."

Could she believe him? This man who had come so often then deserted her? She remembered the vow she had made on the train. No, she wouldn't be fooled again!

Far down the street there was a glimmer of red, and settling her purse strap on her shoulder, she rose to her feet. "I have to leave. My bus is coming."

He got up from the bench. "The Times is sending me to Scotland. I'll be out of town for a few weeks."

The bus rumbled up to the curb and without a backward glance, she nodded her head and climbed aboard. She found a seat near the middle, sat down and peered through the smudged window. Michael was already walking down the street, his head lowered and his shoulders bent. The wind was flapping the corners of his raincoat. *He had been coming to apologize*, she thought. *He might have shown me the story had I given him a chance*.

The bus moved out into traffic. Frantically, she jerked at the stop cord. The driver drew up to the pavement at the end of the block, and she rushed down the aisle and off the bus, her purse swinging wildly from her shoulder. It kept swinging as she raced towards Michael. "Wait, Michael, wait!"

He turned around, a puzzled look on his face.

"I want to see the story," she cried when she reached him.

Drawing a large folded newspaper clipping from his pocket, he held it before them and began opening it. The wind lashed at it and almost tore it out of his hands. "How about reading it over a cup of coffee?" he suggested.

Around the corner was a sidewalk cafe where they'd been several times before. It was so windy that only a few people were seated at the round tables there, huddled in coats and drinking coffee with their gloves on.

They found a side table, and when the coffee arrived, Michael spread the newspaper clipping between them. The wind whipped the corners and they had to press it against the flat surface to keep it down. The two pages of newsprint described Marie La Joy's undercover activities in great detail. By the time Susan had read to the end, she was certain that the designer would never dare show her face in fashion circles again. If Edward had been seeing her, as Susan often suspected, he no longer would, disappearing as usual whenever there was a hint of trouble.

She smiled and gave the clipping back to Michael. "You did a good job."

"Thanks."

"There's a lot of information there that didn't come from me. I can see that."

He folded the clipping carefully and shoved it into his pocket. There was another blast of wind, and he hunched his shoulders and cradled his cup in his red hands. Most of the other patrons had left; it was no day to be sitting outside.

"Michael," she said, "you were coming to my house when we met, weren't you?"

He nodded.

"Then why don't we get out of this wind? The parlor has been turned into a sewing room, but we could use the dining room downstairs."

They got up and headed in the direction of her house. As if oblivious to the wind,

Michael walked tall and straight, and there
was such a spring in his step she had to hurry
to keep up with him.

Chapter 24

Now that she'd made up with Michael, Susan's only conflict was with Mary. If only the seamstress were less fussy! If only she'd relax! But little by little as Susan talked with Mary and learned more about her background, she grew more understanding.

Mary was born in the Netherlands in a fisherman's family, and when she was seventeen, her father died at sea. To help support her younger brothers and sisters, she went to England to work as a seamstress. Success was crucial, and she ripped and re-sewed the seams on garments until they were perfect. Even after her mother had died and her brothers and sisters were earning their own incomes, Mary's early habit of perfection persisted. Her compulsive behavior was a source of much displeasure in the workroom, and there was little Susan could do about it.

Physically, Mary was attractive. Her prematurely white hair was always clean and professionally set, and her make-up looked as if it had been applied by an artist. Although she'd spent most of her life bending over a sewing machine, her back was as straight as a young woman's and she walked gracefully with her head held high.

She not only sewed fast, but expertly. The linings of skirts made of even the thinnest material never produced a wrinkle, and her plackets were works of art. Her extreme competency frustrated the younger seamstresses for they never could meet her critical standards. Even Susan was not exempt. Mary sometimes made changes on her designs, producing a different effect than the one intended. On one dress for Tamar, she lowered the hem to a point where it was unbecoming. Susan was firm when she talked with her. "Ask, consult, but never change without permission!" she said.

Angry, Mary countered by making nitpicking demands. The tea served during the break must be a certain brand and fresh lemons must always be on hand. She complained about the condition of the kitchenette following the employees' breaks, and to appease her, Susan stretched her budget and hired a second cleaning woman. She also had a carpenter come and partition a section of the workroom into an office. Behind its closed door she and Mary could argue without being heard by the other workers.

Along with Mary's stern insistence on perfection, there was a softer side to her nature. The ongoing romance between her and Professor Barnes became a source of interest for the entire staff. Whenever Barnes came for a visit, Mary's dimple would flash and her eyes would glow. If he stayed long enough, she'd serve him tea, made as meticulously as the garments on which she worked.

The fact that Barnes saw Mary at work, rather than during her off-hours, puzzled Susan. He never left the workroom without coming into her own office and giving advice. His comments were prosaic: "Expanding a business is always a bit shaky but unless we grow, we stagnate," or "One must spend money to make money." He never stayed long. He would rush in and out of the workroom, often forgetting his raincoat which Mary would shake out and fold carefully until his next visit, as if touching it gave her pleasure.

Sometimes Susan's conflicts with Mary turned into outright battles. According to Mary, the best place for a skirt zipper was the left side, and most of the gathers should be near the seam if there were a choice. Susan had to go into long explanations if she wanted them differently. With a smug air, Mary would bring back sleeves cut so narrow that they would rip when a model tried them on, and suggest linings for bias pieces which would never hold their shapes alone. Mary's knowlege was awesome, and Susan suspected that the seamstress would prefer working for a designer more experienced than herself. But she fought for what she felt was right in her designs, regardless of Mary's objections.

One month Susan fell behind and had to take money from her savings account to meet the payroll. When Mary found out, she asked advice from Professor Barnes and relayed it to Susan. "Frederick says there's a ratio of accounts receivable to work currently in progress. He suggests that you get an accountant to help you."

"I am an accountant," Susan replied. "I used to do all the bookkeeping for a buyer." Determined to make it in the fashion world by herself, Susan had told no one of her relationship with Edward.

"You are not an accountant," Mary said before Susan could go on. "You are a designer. To how many did God give talent? Are you going to waste your time adding columns of figures? Ridiculous!"

As she walked back to her desk, Susan smiled. It was the first sign of approval Mary had given her, and it touched her heart. As long as Mary has faith in me, she decided, I can tolerate whatever else she does.

Although they were almost too busy with

general orders, each week brought less
business from Tamar. Over each gown that
Susan designed for her the Iraqi exclaimed
delightedly, but she gave her fewer and fewer
new orders. Susan was sure Tamar was
buying new fashions, but buying them from
Joel Adams.

Her worries ceased when Teena's ordered
two hundred skirts like the ones that had
been selling so well at Veronica's Boutique.
The dark-haired manager who had refused
the spaghetti-strapped dress had seen a
display of the skirts at Veronica's and,
realizing they could be a sell-out on Oxford
Street as well, had called in the order. The
only drawback was that she wanted them as
soon as possible. With her customary
efficiency, Mary marshalled the seamstresses into teams, each responsible for one
section of each skirt, then put herself in
charge of sewing the parts together.

Susan planned to use the profits from the
large order to pay for the fabrics necessary
for her style show. While Mary and the staff
worked on the skirts, Susan hunted for
unusual silks, cottons and wools. Not surprisingly, Mary did not always agree with
Susan's purchases.

When Michael returned from Scotland,
Susan complained to him about the seamstress.

"I had to have a section of the workroom

enclosed to give Mary and me more privacy. Sometimes our discussions turn out to be real battles."

Surprisingly, Michael defended Mary. "You've told me more than once what an excellent seamstress Mary is."

"She's an absolute perfectionist. The girls complain because they never can meet her demands. Sometimes I think we might be better off without her."

"Would you want her to be sloppy?"

It was the sort of question Michael often used to make a point. He had a way of putting her world into perspective by his objectivity, yet often her stubborness kept her from agreeing with him.

"I wouldn't want her to drive away my staff," she replied with a smile.

Chapter 25

Michael stopped in at the workroom at least once a week, but Professor Barnes came almost daily. He strode down the aisles between the sewing machines like a conductor on a train, smiling and patting the seamstresses' heads as he passed. Susan had ten girls working for her now, and many of them had attended classes taught by the professor.

Two sample outfits for Susan's collection had been completed—a cocktail dress of a spangled jet fabric and a maize wool suit. As proud as a new mother, Susan showed them to Barnes, who, although he said a hearty "first-rate" in front of Mary, was less positive in the privacy of her office. "Rather different," was all he would say.

Around noon, several days later, on one of those bright warm days that surprisingly occur during a British January, Susan tried on her third design, an organza ball gown with a peacock design on the bodice embroidered in tiny sparkling beads. She was standing in the workroom by the bay window when Professor Barnes came in unannounced. He paused in the open doorway and stood gazing at her silently.

She lowered her eyes, feeling something electric in the room. The sun was lighting up everything—making the metal on the sewing machines glisten, the pin trays sparkle, the beads on her dress shimmer. Wearing the gown made her feel like a television star bathed in spotlights. Raising the hem of the dress to keep it from getting dirty, she hurried to the professor's side. "Mary's gone out to lunch. Would you care to come into my office and see the sketches we'll be working on next?"

He nodded and followed her.

Once in the office, he continued to gaze at her, his eyes grave and luminous.

"What do you think of this one?" she asked, pirouetting before him.

As if struggling within himself, he turned away. "I remember coming into the classroom that first day of school," he said. "Remember looking over the heads of the students and seeing a woman in a finely tailored suit, draped exactly the right way— gorgeous—then catching sight of smooth blonde hair and shining eyes. I remember telling myself, 'Slow down, chappie, you're a middle-aged man . . .' " He moved over and, with his back to the door, took her hands in his. "When I look at you, I feel no older than I felt at thirty. I am like a spring day in winter." His grip tightened on her hands and he bent his face so close to hers that she could smell the scent of after-shave. "Why do I come here? Not to see Mary, nor to see the charming clothes you make, though I *am* proud of you. I come for the chance smile, the sight of those violet eyes, the sound of your warm voice . . ."

She could not let him go on. He would be sorry he had said these things—sorry he had succumbed to the mood of the brilliant sun-filled day.

Letting go of her hands, he raised his arms and drew his slim fingers over her bare shoulders. "Ah—that smooth white skin that makes a man want to bury his face in it. When have I seen skin like this?" Suddenly he bent his head and kissed her right shoulder. His affectionate words and the impulsive act surprised her so much that she froze, unable to move. Before she could stop him, he bent his head still further and let his lips travel over her bare throat above the low-cut bodice. As she tried to back away, his head bent lower and lower until she was able to see past him through the glass of the office door. She gave a little cry. On the other side of the door, Mary was standing in her hat and coat. Her face was a pearly white and her blue eyes were filled with a look of horror.

Susan went through the next moments in a daze. She was scarcely conscious of Professor Barnes' hurried departure from the office after her cry of alarm and wondered how her trembling legs got her to the dressing room. The elaborate gown now seemed tainted, and she lost no time in taking it off and putting on her dress and smock.

When she came out, Mary's machine had a cover on it. Her lips pursed, the older woman was scooping measuring tapes, packets of pins and various sizes of scissors into a small satchel. She would not look at Susan, but kept searching the corner where she worked until she had gathered up all her belongings.

The other girls had stopped sewing, aware of, but not understanding, the drama that was unfolding before them. The angry growl of a zipper ripped through the silence, then Mary raised her chin and picked up the bag. No one moved. With puzzled, shocked expressions, all watched as Mary marched out.

Susan's first reaction was to burst into tears, but she knew ten pairs of eyes were watching her. Opening her own sewing machine, she sat down and tried three times to insert the thread into the needle. The other machines in the room began to hum. The sun shone over the bent heads of the seamstresses as it had done during the morning and early afternoon. Nothing had changed except Mary's corner, which echoed with emptiness.

That night, for the second time, Susan phoned Michael at his flat. "I wonder if you could come over," she said. "Something's happened. It's really quite awful."

"Edward wants a divorce?"

The question startled her. In the rush of meeting orders for skirts and designing for her style show, she had rarely thought of Edward.

"No, that's not it," she said. "Mary has left. Under unusual circumstances."

"You caught me at a bad time but I'll be over as soon as I can," he said and hung up.

He came a half hour later. He told her he had been in the midst of writing a news article which was due at midnight and could stay only a few minutes. He was wearing jeans and an old tan sweater thinning at the elbows, and his fingers were smudged with typewriter ink.

The once warm day had turned cool. She brought him upstairs to the sewing room and they sat down near the fire. Minus the hum of the sewing machines, the room seemed strangely quiet. Sleet started pelting against the window panes, making a rattling sound, and periodically the fire would sizzle from drops of moisture coming down the flue.

When Michael heard her description of Barnes' behavior, he did nothing but raise his brows. "So the guy—bedazzled by the evening gown—nibbled at your neck. No big deal. He might have flung you down to the floor and done all the things a man dreams of."

The remark made her cheeks burn. "Mary will never forgive me," she said.

He leaned back in his chair, matching the tips of his fingers. "Actually, you had no part in it other than to wear a seductive, low-cut gown."

"And ask Barnes to come into my office," she added.

"You couldn't anticipate his losing control."

She got up, took the coal scuttle by the handle, and dumped some briquettes on the fire. She stood watching the corners of the tiny coal nuggets turn white. "Mary used to put out the fire when she left—just one of the tiny things she did. I don't know what I'll do without her."

"That's easy," Michael said. "Don't let her go."

"She thinks I'm a scarlet woman, ready to vamp the only boy friend she's ever had."

Michael suddenly got up. His lips were stretched into a taut line and his eyes flashed with anger. "Barnes got you into this. Let him get you out." Turning to the door, he drew a long breath. "That, my dear, is my advice. Now it's back to my typewriter, or I'll miss my deadline."

* * *

After Michael left, Susan continued to think about Mary. She wondered if she might have depended too much on her to supervise the girls, run the workroom, oversee the sewing. But before the sewing could be done, fabrics had to be purchased, sketches made, patterns cut. How could she do it all alone?

The next day, she waited until almost noon before she called Professor Barnes. Much as she dreaded talking with him, she was willing to do anything to get Mary back.

"Mary's left," she said as soon as he answered.

"I know," he replied. "I phoned her, hoping we could have a little chat, but she wouldn't speak to me. Just sniffed and mumbled something about going back to Dior."

"She wouldn't. She's one of a number there. Couldn't you explain to her what happened?"

"Explain an indiscretion? A bit difficult for the chap involved."

"She thinks it's my fault. In her eyes, you're the one who's perfect," she said.

He paused, "Well, I must say, it's never happened before. Perhaps I'm a little in love with you. Might that be it? Or was it the gown or . . ."

"Professor Barnes," she interrupted. "I don't want to cause any more friction than I have already. Mary is my friend. She's waited for you for a number of years . . ."

"And it's time I made a decision. Is that

what you're saying?''

"Exactly."

He paused. "She probably won't have me now. We do get on. Similar interests and all . . .''

"She's a jewel. I'm just beginning to appreciate that."

Chapter 26

Over the next week Susan realized even more how much work Mary had saved her as manager of the workroom. When Susan inspected the garments that the girls produced, they were always faulty. They needed to be shown how to insert zippers more neatly and make bindings. "Mary, Mary, Mary," she said under her breath, as if by invoking the name she could get the seamstress back.

Susan had managed to sandwich in one or two classes at St. Martins during this period, but now so much work fell on her that she had to give up school entirely. She was glad, in a way, for it prevented any further encounters with Professor Barnes.

Without Mary's help and organizational abilities, the other seamstresses had little

time to work on Susan's collection. Of the ten
designs she had sketched, only five had been
produced, and as back orders began piling
up, she wondered if she would have to post-
pone the style show. It was almost March and
eighty more garments had to be made before
spring. She gazed at the five creations
hanging in her office. Not a single idea for a
design had inspired her since Mary left. As if
in response to her low spirits, the weather
turned even colder, and on Tuesday evening
there was a freak snowstorm.

Michael appeared the next afternoon and
suggested that they go for a walk together.
She gazed out at the strange white world. A
break from work might be exactly the thing
she needed! She instructed the girls to lock
up when they left at 5:00 as Mary had done on
the days when Susan was out shopping.
Fifteen minutes later, she and Michael were
on their way.

Outside, the wind blew against her, biting
into her cheeks and numbing her thinly
gloved hands. The cold seemed even fiercer
than she remembered as a child along Lake
Michigan. But the scene before her was en-
chanting. A flock of gulls, as if bewildered by
the whiteness beneath, hovered over the bare
trees.

Scooping up snow in his hand, Michael ran
on ahead. He was wearing a wool shirt over a
turtleneck sweater.

"That's a nice shirt you're wearing," she cried. "I like the plaid."

"I bought it from a woolen mill in Scotland."

Another blast of wind hit and she sheltered her face with her collar. Slipping his hands into his pockets, Michael stopped and stood gazing at the magical scene before him. Snow clung to the rooftops from which hundreds of chimneys were sending up hundreds of ribbons of smoke. Even the lamp posts had a layer of snow. Shreds of sunlight peeked out from the gray clouds, making whatever they touched glisten.

She hurried to reach Michael so she could walk by his side. When she did, he was walking at such a brisk pace she had difficulty keeping up with him. "How are you managing without Mary?" he asked.

"Not well. I miss her dreadfully."

"Heard from her?"

She shook her head. She knew it would take time for Mary to accept overtures from anyone, even Professor Barnes. It would be futile if she, herself, should try to make up with her.

"She'll come around," said Michael, lacing his bare fingers in her gloved ones.

"You seem very happy today," she said. "Does snow always affect you like this?"

He smiled. "It isn't the snow. The chief at the paper is giving me a raise. We'll celebrate by having dinner at a fancy restaurant."

She stopped. "Michael, I can't. I need the evening for sketching."

"Afternoon tea, then?" He gazed down at her, squinting in the bright snowy light.

She agreed. Later, they hailed a cab and went to a tea shop on Bayswater Road where the waiter brought cucumber sandwiches along with apple tarts floating in thick rich cream.

"I feel sinful, eating all this," Susan said as she finished the last morsel of pastry.

He laughed. "Ah, if you only were!"

She had never seen him in such high spirits. He had not mentioned Edward once, nor did he tease her or look at her in his watchful way. Catching some of his enthusiasm, she bantered with him, relaxing for the first time in weeks.

It was dusk when they left the restaurant. He hailed another cab and they rode home, laughing and talking all the way. They had just rounded the corner of her block when Susan looked past the driver through the windshield. A crowd of people were standing on the pavement in front of her house. She peered out the side window. Clouds of smoke were billowing from her second story windows, and as she watched, horrified, a tongue of flame shot out. She grabbed Michael's arm. "The house is on fire!"

The cab driver drew up beside the small knot of pedestrians who stood with their chins up, oblivious of anything else but the sparks and flames shooting out from the story above. A siren sounded and a fire truck lumbered past, its red lights flashing in the semi-darkness. As it pulled up in front of the cab, Michael hopped to the curb, stuffed some bills in the cabbie's hand and helped Susan out. By now the crowd was so thick they had to elbow their way to the front door. Trembling, she pulled the key from her purse and inserted it in the lock.

A fireman ran up. "Anyone in there?"

"I don't think so," she said. There couldn't be. Everyone usually left at 5:00 and it was almost 7:00.

She pushed open the door and went into the foyer, expecting to be met by a gray haze. The air was clear except for wisps of smoke trailing down the stairwell. "The downstairs is untouched," she said, glancing back at Michael.

Two firemen stomped past. "Everyone outside until we get the bloody thing under control!"

Dazedly, Susan watched heavy black boots race up the stairs, then felt Michael's hand on her elbow. "Let's go outside," he said gently.

The cause of the fire was easy to guess. The seamstresses, more careless than Mary, had left a fire burning in the grate and had probably forgotten to sweep the scraps of fabric from the floor. One spark—that's all it would take to start a blaze.

She was on the porch when suddenly she remembered that the gowns for the style show were hanging in her office. Impulsively she turned, bolted through the open door and raced up the stairs. A wave of hot air met her at the landing. She struggled on as smoke stung her nostrils, making her eyes smart. She could hear the axes of the firemen in the room beyond. She had to get the gowns before they were ruined! When she was almost at the top she felt an arm around her waist, felt herself being lifted up and held in a tight grip.

"Don't be a fool," Michael cried. "The firemen said to stay out."

She struggled against him. "Let me go. The designs—I've got to save them. Oh, Michael— please!"

Silently he carried her downstairs. Once outside, she clung to his shoulder sobbing and gasping in an effort to clear her lungs of the stinging smoke. There were shouts, and a hose hissed as a huge stream of water shot into the air. She buried her face in the rough wool of Michael's shirt, afraid to look.

Not until the fire was completely under control were she and Michael allowed in the parlor. Fortunately, the stairs were still intact. When they reached the top, they stood silently, peering through the open parlor door at the settling smoke. There was nothing left. The new office had been burned beyond recognition. In addition to consuming the drapes, the fire had charred the woodwork around the windows as well as that on the sewing machines. The stench of burned fabric permeated everything. On the gutted floorboards water gathered in puddles, liquifying the ashes.

Susan turned to Michael. "I'll have to call Edward. I'll have to tell him. Oh God!"

They went back downstairs.

More smoke had crept down the stairwell and the odor of burned fabric was as strong as upstairs.

"You can't sleep in this," Michael said.

Together they opened the windows in her bedroom. Cold air rushed in, scattering the fashion clippings on her bureau. She went about the room collecting them, then used her hand mirror as a paperweight. Michael was adjusting a flapping shade. Suddenly the window he was working on banged down.

"You're not going to stay here. You're coming home with me!" he said.

She stared at him in disbelief. Never before had he suggested that she even visit his flat.

"It's not what you think," he explained. "You can sleep in the bed, and I'll use the sofa. You shouldn't be alone. It would be all right if you could leave the windows open, but here on the first floor that would be unsafe. Pack whatever you need and we'll leave." He picked up the phone. "I'll call a cab while you're getting everything together."

"I have to call my staff. I have to find Edward and let him know about the fire," she said.

"Tack a note on the door saying 'Closed due to fire.' You can call Edward tomorrow."

The whole situation seemed unreal. Too numb to resist, she found a satchel and threw her nightgown, comb, underwear and make-up into it. She had fought so long and so hard. And for what?

Michael lived on the other side of town and the cab ride was a long one.

"This is costing you a fortune," she said as she sat beside him in the back seat.

"I usually take the tube, but we don't need that hassle just now." He smiled. "I would have spent the money on a fancy dinner anyway."

Michael's flat was on the third floor of an ancient building without lifts. After they'd climbed the stairs, he got out his key and un-locked the door. He put his arm around her when they went inside.

The first thing she noticed was the thick charcoal carpeting. Michael hurried over and quickly picked up a newspaper lying on the floor beside a chair. For a bachelor flat, it was neater than she had expected. A large sparkling aquarium stood at one end of the room. There was a typewriter on a stand beside a table loaded with file folders and yellow paper. Strewn over the carpet were tiny tubes of scrap paper like the ones she used to find in her parlor. Prints from the National Gallery, similar to her own, hung on the wall opposite the typewriter.

"I like your carpet," she said.

He smiled. "It's new. I installed it myself."

He hurried into the bedroom and she could hear his footsteps on the hard floor as he straightened up. He came into the doorway with two neatly folded sheets in his arms.

"I'll only be a minute. Why don't you help yourself to something from the fridge."

"I'll just sit here, thank you," she said.

She had begun to shiver. The room was moderately warm, but the shock of the fire finally was producing a nervous reaction. Her hands trembled, her knees, her chin, her whole body.

Michael caught sight of her from the hall as he was bringing fresh towels into the bathroom. "God, you're pale!" He crossed the room to the sofa and took her hands. "Your hands are like ice and you're shaking." He took off his wool shirt and threw it around her then went into the bedroom and came out with a heavy sweater which he put over it.

"Something hot—I'll make something hot to drink!"

He fixed some tea which she drank in eager gulps. Leaving his own cup untouched, he sat beside her, his dark eyes filled with concern.

"It's more than the fire, isn't it?" he asked.

She nodded. "It's Edward," she said in a low voice. "The insurance will take care of the damage to the house, but he'll blame me. He thinks I'm a poor manager." She gave a frightened little laugh. "Maybe I am." Tears streamed down her cheeks, silent tears brimming up in her eyes and overflowing before she could stop them.

He drew her to him, his warm arms cradling her and holding her close. He stroked her hair and kissed the top of her head, as if she were a child who needed comforting. His nearness calmed her. When her tears had stopped, he kissed her lightly on the lips, then jumped up and, shoving his hands in his pockets, began pacing over the carpet, his jaw set as if he were fighting some inner battle.

He finally went into the bedroom and came back with an armload of books. "All these are about London—you know, interesting background stuff. Maybe you'd like to skim through one."

They were huge, glossy books with colorful photos on the covers showing the changing of the guard, Beefeaters in scarlet costumes, castles and parks. She took one and leafed through the large pages.

She felt better. "Aren't you going to introduce me to your fish?"

"They're not mine. I'm keeping them for a

fellow reporter who's on assignment. The gold one is Bozzo and the black one swimming around and looking at you is Nugget."

Laying down the book, she got up and peered into the tank. "They're lucky to have such a nice place as this to live."

Her last remark was wasted. Michael had gone in a back room somewhere, and a few minutes later came back with a half glass of brandy.

"This will help you relax," he said. "After you drink it I'd suggest you get some sleep."

She sipped it slowly while he finished his tea. She felt comfortable here with Michael—protected—not alone—and perhaps for the first time since she'd come to London—*safe!*

Chapter 27

Michael was gone by the time Susan got up the following morning. There was a note taped to the aquarium which said, "Help yourself to juice and coffee. I'll call you tonight."

She took a cab home without eating. The morning papers would carry a news item about the fire, and she wanted to phone Edward before he learned about it from Joel.

No sooner had she arrived and hung up her coat, then she began calling her husband's favorite hotels in Milan. He had not checked in at any of them, nor was he at the auditorium. Finally, getting through to one of his assistants, she found out Edward was in New York. She hung up, annoyed at herself. Edward had told her in Paris that he'd be going to New York, but the nightmarish events of yesterday made her forget.

She battled her conscience. Although she and Edward were co-owners of the house, he had put the deed in her name to save money on taxes in case they ever rented it. She could sign all the necessary papers, and Edward would never need to know. Informing him would only point out her inadequacies. Yet the more she thought about it, the less comfortable she felt about deceiving him.

She ended her dilemma by scribbling a short note:

> Dear Edward,
> A fire broke out on the second floor of our house while no one was home. I shall report the claim to our insurance agent and take care of all repairs. Good luck with your meeting.
>
> > Love,
> > Susan

She sent it to his business address on Seventh Avenue, then made a list of things she needed to do: Phone the staff and tell them when work would be resumed, call the claims adjuster, send the sewing machines out to be cleaned and repaired, buy more fabric, inform the manager at Teena's that her orders would be delayed, and find a good contractor.

Within a month the second floor was

restored and the machines back in place, but the new rooms had lost their Victorian atmosphere. Instead of the pocked oak boards, new birch planks, gleaming with varnish, covered the floor, and the fireplace had been replaced with an efficient modern stove, giving off more heat. The office was now in a more convenient location at the top of the stairs, and in its place, a coffee area with shiny steel cupboards and stainless steel sink, clean enough to satisfy even the fastidious tastes of Mary, had been installed.

Everyone was happy to return to work, especially Susan.

One cloudy afternoon about a week after the new workroom opened, Michael burst into her new office. "I can only stay a minute," he said. "There's someone waiting downstairs to see you."

"Show him up," she said, suspecting it was one of the insurance adjusters who had been plaguing her with inspections.

Beneath Michael's thick brows, his brown eyes glowed. "I can't. It's a she. Come down."

Susan rose, came out from behind her desk and followed him. Halfway down the stairwell she wondered if it were some sort of trick. Beyond his broad shoulders, she could see nothing except the shadowy walls of the foyer. It was not until she was almost to the bottom that she caught sight of a white head.

"Mary!"

The older woman, her hair coiffed and shining, stood by the door in a pale yellow coat, looking as shy as a primrose. Rushing up, Susan took Mary's gloved hands in hers. "How we've missed you!"

"I didn't have the courage to go upstairs," the seamstress said. "In fact, unless someone had nudged me, I shouldn't have come at all." She smiled at Michael who was standing by the door. "Frederick told me about that dreadful fire, and I thought I should offer my sympathy and help. He said that all the clothes for the show had been burned."

"Come now, Mary," Michael broke in, "that's not the only reason for your visit." His dark eyes were dancing.

Withdrawing her hands from Susan's, Mary slipped off her glove and held out her left hand. A large diamond set in gold sparkled in the light of the overhead bulb. "I wanted to invite you both to our wedding. The ring belonged to Frederick's first wife who died of influenza shortly after their marriage. I told him not to buy another, and I was right, for a little cleaning and polishing did wonders. We've found a semi-detached house where we'll live after the honeymoon, and if we both work, we can manage the payments." She lowered her eyes. "I didn't mean . . ." she stammered.

"Mary told me that she has a job teaching at the School of Design," Michael said quickly.

Susan's heart sank. She was grateful to Michael for easing Mary's embarrassment, but she had hoped the visit meant that she was coming back. There was a long silence, then Michael reached for the doorknob. "I can't stay. I'm due back at the Times."

"Where shall I send your invitation to the wedding?" Mary asked him.

"Just address it to me at the paper. It'll get to me," he replied as he went out.

Susan tried to catch his eye, but he didn't look back. After the door closed behind him, she turned to Mary. "I'm glad things worked out for you . . . and for the professor."

Mary glanced down. "He told me it was his fault . . . that you had nothing to do with it. At the time I thought you had."

"I know. I need you, Mary. If there's any way you could manage to come back . . ." Then an idea struck her. "You haven't seen our new workroom. It's much improved. There's a new stove and a bright wooden floor that makes sweeping up easy. Would you like to see it?"

Mary hesitated. "I'll come another day. I couldn't face the girls just now. They must have thought it very odd when I walked out."

"Whatever you wish. Will you come soon?"

Mary smiled. "As soon as I can." Slipping on her glove, she turned to the door. "It's only a part time job at the college, and I could come back here if Frederick wouldn't mind. The extra money certainly would be helpful."

The following Monday Mary visited the workroom but did not give Susan her final answer about returning until several days before the wedding.

"There's been so much to do," she explained over the phone. "Arranging for the flowers, the reception, the food. I made my gown myself. At first we planned on having a few guests, but Frederick has so many friends our list grew larger and larger. We wanted to go to the River Wye on our honeymoon but are using the money for the reception instead. We'll take a week to settle in, and after that I could begin work."

"Wonderful," Susan cried, sure that her troubles finally were over.

Chapter 28

Mary's wedding was to be on Saturday, and Susan looked forward to it with trepidation. Nothing unforetold must happen to change Mary's mind about returning to work—a few too many dances between Susan and the Professor, or too much champagne and a misinterpreted glance exchanged. It was a delicate situation and she decided to stay close to Michael's side.

Susan spent the week before the wedding awaiting some bolts of fabric which were holding up production. When the bolts didn't come Friday, she asked one of the seamstresses to sit in the office on Saturday and wait for them, promising to pay her overtime. She gave her the address of the hotel where the reception was to be held and told her to call if there were problems about the delivery.

Saturday was a cool bright day. As Susan was dressing for the wedding, she had a vague premonition of something unexpected and naturally connected it to Professor Barnes. He had not visited the workroom since the day Mary left, and having convinced Mary of his love, Susan hoped he would do nothing to spoil the relationship.

The feeling persisted as she slipped into the rust silk gown she'd designed especially for the wedding. It was fastened by an expensive gold belt around her waist with the bodice held on her shoulders by two braided straps. A stylist had done her hair, and she had bought new shoes to match the outfit.

When she stepped out of the cab before the church, her heart sank. With its stone walls and statues near the roof, it reminded her of the cathedral in the little Austrian village where she and Edward had been married. Theirs had been a short ceremony with only two witnesses, friends in the fashion world. Sadly, she climbed the sunny stone steps and went into the cool confines of the narthex, assaulted by memories of a young Edward in a morning coat and she, herself, in a white lace dress—making promises they had not kept.

Michael was waiting for her by the entrance to the sanctuary. He looked darkly handsome in his black suit and ruffled shirt.

"Friends of the bride?" an usher asked.

"Yes," Susan replied. She took his arm, and Michael followed.

The only remaining seats were on the side, and after they were seated, Susan felt as if she were in a vault with not enough air to breathe. She gazed up at the high pulpit with its elaborate wooden carvings and the candles shining out into the dimness.

"This church is really old," Michael whispered.

She nodded, absently. The organ was playing softly, flooding the towering space in the same manner as the purple, rose and golden rays which streamed from the high stained glass windows. The stir of the audience and rattle of programs quieted as relatives were escorted to their seats by the ushers.

Some of them were older than the groom and one walked with a limp.

When the relatives were settled in their seats, Frederick and the best man stepped through the side entrance and stood at one side of the pulpit. The portentous chords of "Mendelssohn's Wedding March" were struck, and Mary, dressed in a blue satin gown, came sedately down the aisle. Frederick, his cheeks flushed and chin thrust forward, met her at the altar. Then the minister began speaking in a sonorous voice.

Hoping to block out the significance of the familiar words, Susan tried to think of other things—the delivery of the bolts of fabric, a design for a wedding gown—anything to keep her mind occupied.

"Do you take this man to have and to hold, in sickness and in health . . ."

"I do," Mary said.

Susan wanted to put her hands over her ears. The same vows she had made seven years ago! She glanced at Michael who was gazing at the couple with a rapt expression.

After the lighting of one candle by the bride and groom, the pronouncement of the marriage and the jubilant trip up the aisle by the happy couple, everyone relaxed, commenting to their neighbor—everyone except Susan who sat motionless beside Michael, waiting for the usher to signal that their row could leave.

"Nice, wasn't it?" Michael said.

She nodded. What was she doing here with this dark stranger? Where was the husband to whom she rightfully belonged? She had wanted to rejoice with Mary on this day, but memories kept her from it.

The usher came and stood before their row and everyone got up. "I must smile when we go through the receiving line," Susan told herself as she stepped into the aisle. The queue did not move, and they stood amid strangers, waiting. Susan leaned her head against a sandstone pillar and stared at the Norman arch over the exit, remembering how happy she'd been seven years ago as a bride.

An eldery lady standing nearby smiled. "A bit of a crush, isn't it?"

Susan nodded. She would feel better once she was at the reception where she could get a glass of champagne.

As she and Michael entered the ballroom of the hotel, her spirits rose. An orchestra comprised of a cello, a few strings and a saxophone was playing music of the fifties. The highly waxed dance floor seemed to dare anyone to step onto its shiny surface. Smiling waiters, holding trays filled with fluted glasses of champagne, moved through the crowd which, like captured insects, emitted a loud collective drone. She and Michael moved to a corner and stood watching the guests.

He laughed. "I always wanted to go to one of these affairs. This is the real England."

"Wait until you hear the speeches," she said, grabbing a glass of champagne from one of the waiter's trays as he passed. Michael also took one and stood drinking it. His dark good looks were attracting glances from some of the women nearby.

"I'm going to have fun. That's why we're here," Susan said, smiling. But her gaity was forced. If only she could stop thinking of Edward!

The dinner, during which at least a hundred guests were served, went faster than she expected. Since Mary's father was dead and couldn't give the traditional speech accorded the bride's father, and the best man forgot part of his speech, that part of the evening was blessedly short. A few telegrams were read, then the dancing began.

The bride and groom danced the first number, clumsily as if it might have been the first time they'd danced together, then other couples joined them. Michael led Susan onto the floor and they began to waltz. The lapel of his coat was smooth against her cheek and she relaxed for the first time, gliding to the strains of the music.

She drew back so she could look at him. "You dance very well," she said.

He smiled. "Thanks. When this is over, let's go to a disco. This isn't quite my style."

"Excellent idea!" she said. Going to a disco seemed the perfect way to end the evening.

When the music stopped, one of the professors from St. Martins came up to them. "Susan, you look stunning. What a smashing dress!" he remarked.

He asked her for the next dance, and the following one she danced with another professor. When Michael found her again, the room was quite crowded and the air warm and heavy with the scent of roses. For the first time Susan noticed the tall flower stands filled with cut blossoms at each corner of the dance floor. With the heat from the crowd and faster tempo of the music, the dancers' faces grew flushed. Then the orchestra began a number almost too slow for dancing.

"Have you tasted the passion fruit ice?" Michael asked.

"No."

"I had some while you were twirling with your professors. Shall we go over?"

They circled the dance floor, stopping for a moment to speak to the bride and groom, who were standing at one side. Mary's eyes were sparkling, and her blue gown looked as fresh as if the party were just beginning. Frederick's eyes did not meet Susan's—nor did he ask for a dance.

"Have a capital time," he called out after them as they headed toward the refreshment table.

The music stopped the moment they arrived. Michael got her a plate of ice, then began talking with the girl pouring tea, whom he had met at Susan's party. Susan was standing with her plate in her hands facing the door when a blond-haired man stepped under the broad archway and stood with his chin held high, scanning the crowd.

The mound of ice on Susan's plate began to tremble as if shaken by an earthquake, and at that moment, the band struck up a familiar tune that she could not have named had her life depended on it. All she could hear was the thump of the cello beating in time to her own heart.

"Edward!" she gasped.

Chapter 29

Forgetting all else, Susan quickly set down her plate and rushed to Edward's side. They hurried through the hall and once outside, climbed into one of the waiting cabs.

"Sumner Place," Edward said to the driver. "It's a short block in Kensington. I'll tell you which house it is when we get there."

Edward was sitting in one corner of the back seat and she in the other. The darkness hid him so that except for the orange glow of his lighted cigarette, she would not have known anyone was there at all. She remembered how he had looked when she'd first seen him—his stylish gray suit and the gold pendant that glittered on his neck in the V of his open collar.

When she asked him how he'd found her, he explained that he had booked an inter-city

flight from New York to Paris with a short
layover in London. The girl who was waiting
for the fabric delivery at her workshop had
told him where she was.

"I wanted to check the repairs of the house
before I went on," he said.

Susan almost gasped. The sight of him
standing there at the hotel had meant only
one thing to her. He was here for a reunion.
She might have known his visit would have a
purpose. Her fingers tightened into fists.
Why did she always trap herself this way?

She sat silently in the shadows, glad
Edward couldn't see the disappointment on
her face. She hadn't a clue as to his expression. Occasionally stop lights would shine on
his face, turning it pink, green or yellow but
only momentarily. Couldn't he trust her to
oversee the remodeling of a house? Had he so
little confidence in her that he had to check
everything himself? She regretted leaving
Michael, shocked and wide-eyed, and was
sorry she hadn't said goodbye to Mary and
the professor. She had simply set down her
plate containing the sherbet and followed Edward like a teenager trailing a rock idol.

"How much did the repairs cost?" Edward
asked.

"We were only out the deductible amount.
The insurance paid for the rest."

"Did the contractor use good materials?"

"The best."

The cab swung around corners and raced over tram tracks. She braced herself to keep from leaning towards a man whose priorities were business and real estate, never her.

The trip took only ten minutes. Once they had arrived and she was leading him upstairs to the parlor, she grew anxious. She had been satisfied with the renovation, but suppose Edward didn't approve? Suppose there was something about the Victorian atmosphere that he wanted to keep?

She was relieved to see that the ten bolts of fabric had arrived and were stacked neatly in the hall at the top of the stairs. Passing them, they went down the hall to the workroom where she switched on one of the lamps. The girl who had been there that afternoon had swept up the fabric scraps, seen that the machines were lined up neatly, and draped a red satin gown over a mannequin in preparation for what the staff called "Susan's magic touch with pins." The room was more inviting than other designers' workrooms she had visited with Edward, and she couldn't help but be proud.

As soon as Edward stepped into the room, he pulled out his comb and ran it through his blond hair. It was a habit of his she remembered well. "Looks like quite a busy place," he said, glancing about him. He strode over to the new stove and stood looking down at it.

Hurrying over, she stooped and turned up

the gas. "It's cold in here. I'll switch on more lamps so you can see what we've done," she said.

He put out his hand to stop her, his fingers warm against her bare shoulders. "Don't. The lamps, I mean. Leave it dark."

She looked up and their eyes met. His meaning was clear. For a moment a tingling sensation passed through her, then she remembered his visit was fleeting. She stood up, but before she could move away, he grabbed her, taking her in his arms. His lips closed down on hers. They held the same urgency, the same bruising pressure, but the response she used to feel was missing. His hands began moving over her hips but she wrenched herself free. "No, there isn't time!"

He ignored her. His hands slipped up to her breasts and under her arms, then he pulled her close, drawing her body to his until all she could feel was warmth and desire. There was time? There wasn't time? Suddenly she knew there *had* to be time.

Edward threw off his coat and began unbuttoning his shirt, his fair skin glowing in the semi-darkness of the room and the gold pendant glinting in the light from the hall. Unclasping her belt, Susan tossed it on one of the machines, then unzipped the bodice of her dress and slid the straps from her shoulders, letting the soft silk fall in a circle around her feet. Edward took her in his arms and she felt her slip being pushed up, her hose pulled down, felt herself being dragged to the sofa in the corner, the new dress, which was caught around her ankles, trailing on the floor. The cushions sank beneath their weight. A brief moment of throbbing ecstasy —then it was over.

When she opened her eyes, Edward's face was turned toward the clock. Jumping up, he grabbed his shirt. "Can I get a cab on the street or do I have to call one?"

She raised up on one elbow. "Couldn't you take the plane tomorrow?"

With a shake of his head, he continued to dress. When he'd finished, he took out his comb and drew it through his blond hair a second time. It occurred to her that every-thing happened so swiftly she hadn't once touched his hair.

She shivered. The stove had not yet warmed the room, and only her slip covered her. Her new dress was lying in a dusty heap at the foot of the couch.

Edward picked up his coat and began shoving his arms into its sleeves. Once it was on, he buttoned the one button required to make it fashionable. "You did okay," he said as he strode out.

What did he mean? Then slowly she began to comprehend. *The workroom*, she said to herself. *He was talking about what I'd done to the room!*

Chapter 30

When Susan awoke the next morning, disillusionment was her only feeling. Over the past months, everything she'd done had been in the hope that Edward would grow to respect her. Now she knew that even if that were so, she wouldn't want him. Up until now, he'd succeeded in masquerading behind a cloak of glamour, but last night revealed him as he truly was—selfish and demanding with only his own needs in mind. She felt as if her body had been violated.

The more she thought about it, the clearer it became that what had happened last night was only one in a series of insults that she'd endured throughout her marriage. In some way she now wanted to pay Edward back for all his slights, for his lack of respect. Just how she didn't know.

Her change of attitude affected her thinking in other ways, too. Despite wanting independence, she'd secretly relied on Edward in case of financial trouble. Now the idea of his helping her seemed repugnant, and she began shifting her thoughts to the trust her mother had mentioned. If her fashion business failed, she could still rely on that.

Then again, she might not need the trust. Skirt sales were increasing and other orders for new designs were coming in. She looked forward to Mary's return, hoping it would bring an increase in production.

Mary arrived one week after the wedding and it was not long before Susan noticed how much she'd changed. She was more relaxed in dealing with others, efficient without her previous nit-picking and exuded a general well-being that brought peace instead of dissension to the workroom.

One morning before the rest of the staff arrived, Susan watched Mary dusting off her sewing table and laying out her equipment for the day's work: tailor's chalk, pins, scissors, spools of colored thread and matching bobbins. She was wearing a blue dress with an immaculate white collar fastened with a brooch. A fine layer of powder covered her face, as smooth and radiant as a young girl's.

Susan strode down the aisle between the machines until she reached her. "Good morning, Mary. You look lovely. It's easy to see that marriage agrees with you."

Mary's face dimpled. "Having a place of our own is delightful. I've been planning the garden this weekend while Frederick's been painting walls. You must pop in once we're settled."

"I shall. I never did tell you how nice I thought your wedding was, and what a handsome couple you made."

"Why, thank you." Pulling open a drawer, Mary lifted out a packet of new needles. "I like to sew with a sharp needle. A dull one can snag the fabric."

Susan decided to return to the former topic. "Tell me, what happened after I left the reception?" She had not heard from Michael since that night and was sure he was angry.

Mary looked up. "Everything about the wedding is rather hazy in my memory. I don't know who left when but I do recall how strange it was to see Michael leaving with another girl. Did you two have a row?"

"Not exactly. Who was with him?"

"That girl who came to your party last November. I can't recall her name. The two of them had a chat with Frederick and me right before they left."

The seamstresses were starting to come in, chattering and rattling their lunch boxes as they hung up their coats. Lacking the privacy to continue, Susan turned away, only to feel a hand on her arm.

"I've always been fond of Michael," Mary

said. "Tell me, he's not an alcoholic, is he? He seemed to be having trouble that night."

"Michael—drunk?"

Mary nodded. "His face was flushed and he seemed to weave on his way out."

"Michael is a thoughtful, wonderful person, and I've never seen him drink to excess. You must have been mistaken."

She left Mary's corner, surprised that she had rushed to his defense. As she walked slowly back to her office past the girls and their whirring machines, her heart thumped wildly. She had not heard from him. Was he dating this girl now? What a fool she'd been to leave so abruptly, especially after she'd promised to go to a disco with him.

Going into her office, she closed the door, picked up her sketch pad and sank down in a chair. She was accustomed to having the charcoal move swiftly over the page, but somehow today it did not. She drew a side view design but could go no further. She left the room and went out to help the girls with their orders.

Two weeks went by, during which she heard nothing from Michael. She tried to brush thoughts of him from her mind, and when she was devoid of design ideas—an ever more frequent occurrence—she helped sew orders. Her skills now ran the gamut: making patterns, cutting, sewing and fitting.

One day Mary approached her. "Susan,

you're looking pale. You must get out more."

The weather had been cold and rainy. A rash of orders had come in with scarcely enough time to fill them, and she had been working overtime, hardly stopping to eat. "We'll never have a style show unless I put in long hours," she replied.

Mary paused. "When I was young I was ambitious too. Now I realize there are other things as important as work."

Susan envied Mary's happiness. But Mary had waited all her life. She wondered if anything similar were in store for her.

That night, after everyone had left, Susan studied herself in the mirror. Mary was right. She was pale and tired-looking. It's not the work that's bothering me, she thought, but the fact that for weeks I haven't seen anyone but the girls in the workroom.

She had better sense than to call Michael, who undoubtedly was either angry or involved with someone else or both. But memories of him drifted back to her—the way he had studied her with those soft brown eyes, how he had turned away at times so that she couldn't see his face.

She turned from the mirror. The house was cold and so dreary she could hardly stand it. Despite the grim drizzle outside and predictions of snow, she decided to go out for dinner at Frye's Restaurant, five blocks away. She changed into a comfortable plaid wool dress, which she'd brought from the

Continent, and put on a heavy coat.

As she stepped out, driving sleet and wind rushed to meet her. Drawing her collar around her chin, she walked rapidly, her delicate shoes slipping at times on the slush beneath. Two young men with lighted cigarettes passed her, then swirling blackness returned. On the corner ahead, the lights of a chemist's shop shone out over the sidewalk. Beyond it was a number of darkened shops, closed for the day.

She hurried her steps, wondering what it would be like eating at a restaurant alone. She might have called Tamar, but she hadn't decided in time. When she arrived, windblown and chilled, the maitre d' led her to a corner table downstairs where she had to wait forever to be served. She sat listening to the swish and thud of the swinging doors as waiters, their dark trousers splotched with food stains, went in and out of the kitchen.

The wick of the candle on her table melted into the wax and was snuffed out. By the time her order of chicken arrived, she was no longer hungry. She poked at her rice, ate a few bites of her salad, then called for the bill.

The walk home was frightening. The sleet had turned to snow and was coming down rapidly over the deserted streets. To keep dry, she tied her scarf over her head, but the clinging snow made her face as wet as if it were flooded with tears. She trudged on, searching for familiar landmarks until she finally reached her lighted steps. Brushing the snowflakes from her shoulders, she unlocked her door and stepped inside.

The house seemed even more dreary and silent than when she'd left. Leaving her wet coat on the newel post, she put on a heavy sweater and climbed the stairs. A few minutes later, she sat down at her desk and reached for her sketch pad.

Her mind was blank. She could not imagine one dress, sports outfit or evening gown. For some time she sat gazing down at the blank white page, which glared back at her defiantly from under the bright desk lamp. The wind rattled the panes and blew chilly drafts around the window casings. Finally she got up, went into the kitchen and made herself a cup of hot tea. Bringing it to the desk, she sat down and began again. Not one line, fabric or color came to her. She had heard of designers "going dry," as they called it, but never dreamed it could happen to her.

She opened the drawer and put away the pad. "I'm tired and chilled," she told herself. "In the morning, when I'm fresh, all kinds of images will come."

Chapter 31

Over the next weeks, Susan's inspiration lay dormant and her sketch pad remained blank. She dared not tell the staff of her predicament. They expected her to come up with at least sixty more sketches, and like her, were looking forward to the show as an opportunity to display their work.

Susan went to see Tamar, hoping that her usual chatter about fashions would prove stimulating. When she came home, she sketched the dresses Tamar had described, but could think of nothing original. She tried to invoke the feelings that had made her so prolific, when she'd been unable to stop sketching. Was it summer and the fragrance of flowers, the sunshine, the soft sweet air surrounding her? Was it Michael's visits, unexpected and exciting?

One afternoon, after struggling for ideas, she suddenly left the workroom, went downstairs to her private telephone and hesitantly dialed Michael's extension at the Times.

"Michael Everett. Can I help you?" His voice, as usual, was calming.

"Michael . . . it's me."

There was a pause. In the background typewriters were clicking and a chair squeaking.

"How's life with Edward?" The soothing voice suddenly had turned brusque.

"Edward isn't with me. He left the night of the reception."

"That was three weeks ago." He did not go on, and the silence was agonizing.

"I need some help," she said. "Is this a bad time? I mean, I don't want to bother you if you're busy . . ."

"How about if I call you back?"

"Fine." She hung up, not at all surprised by his coolness. She could expect no more after she'd left him standing alone at the reception. She climbed the stairs and went into the workroom, doubting that she would hear from him.

In her absence, someone had dressed the cloth dress form in one of her designs for the style show. The dress, made of lilac crepe, had pleats starting at the bust line falling into a swirling floor-length skirt. She stopped before it. The workmanship was excellent, the fabric fit the pattern well, but something was missing. She had not been standing there long when Mary came up beside her. "It worked out well," Mary said, "though the lining was a bit difficult."

"It needs a train," Susan said suddenly. Hurrying to one of the tables at the side of the room, she brought back a bolt of the same lilac crepe and, shaking out several lengths, gathered the open end and held it at the back. "See—like so!"

Mary stepped back to get the effect. "You're right!"

Susan began draping the train on the cloth model, adding widths of material until she was sure it had the proper fullness. After she had made a pattern, she asked Mary to check it. When she approved, Susan told her to cut out the train and add it to the dress. "We'll have a model try it on. I want to see how it looks in motion," she said.

Nodding, Mary removed the dress from the dress form while Susan went back to her desk. She sat staring at the clutter on top— the pile of bills, the stacks of fabric samples and the blank sketch pad lying open before her. She had solved a problem, and solving problems was close to designing. Could it be that her dry spell was over?

That night, after everyone had left, Susan went into the kitchen and began heating up some soup. It was obvious Michael wasn't going to return her call.

She had scarcely finished eating when the door knocker rattled, and on peering out, she saw the figure of a man on the steps. His face was indistinguishable in the fading light but she knew it could be no one but Michael.

"I thought I'd come instead of calling," he said when she opened the door. His hair was windblown, his cheeks flushed. The dark eyes she remembered so well were fixed on the newel post behind her.

"I didn't think I'd hear from you," she said.

"My conscience finally prodded me. Do you really need help?"

"I needed help when I called. Things are better now," she said.

A corner of his mouth went up. "At night all is solved, is that it? Or did I come at the wrong time? Expecting someone else?" There was a biting tone to his voice.

It had been a mistake to call him—he was still too angry for forgiveness. The fact that he would not look directly at her told her even more than the icy tone of his voice. He had come only because he felt he must.

"Would you like a drink? I have some sherry in the dining room," she said.

He took off his raincoat and hung it on a hook in the hall. Once they were seated on opposite sides of the mahogany table with glasses of sherry before them, she began. "I need advice . . ."

One of his eyebrows went up but he said nothing.

"I seem to have lost my ability to design. Over the past two weeks I haven't been able to create one outfit. If I can't function, that means work comes to a standstill." Was she foolish telling him? Would he laugh?

But he neither laughed nor smiled. He sat with his head down, hunched over his tiny glass, his thick fingers twisting the stem. "A bit like the newspaper business—groping around for a lead or the proper treatment of material."

"Yes, I suppose it is similar. So what do you do when you can't think of anything?"

He paused as if weighing one answer against another. "Sometimes I play solitaire, work a crossword, go to a pub, try to keep my mind receptive and open . . ."

She studied his large hands, his huge shoulders, the dark shadows where a beard might have grown. His masculinity had always created a sexual tension within her. His touch, even the lift of an eyebrow, affected her. Suddenly she wanted to cover his hand with hers and blurt out that she'd missed his visits, his laughter, even his teasing—but she didn't dare. He was not the old carefree Michael, but someone deliberately trying to hide his emotions. It was up to her to flush them out.

"Mary told me that you left the reception with Audrey," she began.

His fingers stopped twisting the stem of the glass and he shot her a quick glance. "Mary says too much." Abruptly he pushed back his chair and rose to his feet. Giving a little bow, he said icily, "It's been nice visiting with you, Mrs. Thorwald. I'm sorry I can't furnish you with more concrete answers to your dilemma. I can only extend my wishes for your success."

She jumped up, almost tipping over her glass of sherry. "Michael, don't be like that!"

"How should I be?"

"Be my friend again. I need you."

He turned away, strode to the window and stood gazing out. "If you thought at all, which sometimes I doubt, you'd realize it's rather strenuous being your friend. Edward bounced back like a lost tennis ball and you're out the door before I can turn around."

"I don't blame you for being upset. I was rude to leave so suddenly."

"But well worth it for the delights involved, I dare say?"

Her cheeks burned. He could be vicious when he wanted to.

Suddenly he turned to face her. "If I remember correctly, I thought I heard you promising to go to a disco with me," he said.

"I imagine you still went. Or were you too drunk to remember?" she shot back.

The flush in his cheeks told her she'd scored a direct hit. "So you and Mary *have* been talking?" he said. "Yes, I did go to the disco and got even drunker. But I wasn't alone so it turned out to be a rather pleasant evening." He strode over to the table, picked up his sherry, and gulped it down. The crystal clicked down briskly on the table, and just as briskly he strode from the room, leaving her standing there watching. His footsteps echoed on the slate floor, then the front door slammed behind him.

She sank down in her chair. This was their first real quarrel. He was proud—much too proud—and she knew that her sudden departure from the reception had hurt him beyond measure. It would be a long time before he'd forgive her.

Chapter 32

It was an envious cousin who gleefully wrote the news to Susan: Alan Hennessy had broken the trust set up by Susan's father, invested the money in small computer stocks and lost her and her mother's fortunes. The only asset remaining was the condominium in Florida that the couple jointly owned.

The news explained the quiet desperation that Susan had sensed in her mother's letters during the last few months. Too proud to reveal that her life was less than glamorous, the older woman had told about days in the sun, games of shuffleboard or backgammon, deep sea fishing excursions. She often mentioned that Alan was away in New York, and because her letters usually were written during his absences, they were more and more frequent.

Loss of the trust was the last thing Susan wanted to hear. She had depended on borrowing from it to finance her style show, and now that was out of the question. Would the show even be possible? The costs of renting a hall, hiring models and paying an orchestra were stupendous.

But perhaps she'd never reach that point. Unless she got over her dry period, there would be nothing to show, and her sketch pad remained as glaringly white as ever.

She began working on orders along with the seamstresses, hoping she could get past whatever was blocking her. She was discovering that to create at will was virtually impossible.

The next time Susan saw Michael she and Tamar were having lunch at a sidewalk cafe. She glimpsed his dark head first, then the bulge of his hand as he reached in his pocket for his wallet to pay the bill. For a second, she thought he wouldn't see her, but he was too observant not to notice. He glanced in her direction, then looked away.

She would pretend not to care, and she turned toward Tamar.

"There's a man standing there, looking at us. I think he's an American," Tamar said.

"I know him. He's a friend of mine."

"You must call him over." Before Susan could stop her, Tamar had waved to Michael.

Hesitantly, he made his way over, circling

around tables until he came to theirs. When he reached them, Susan introduced him to Tamar and asked him to sit down. He drew up a chair and sat beside Tamar.

"Do you eat lunch here often?" Susan asked.

"Only on sunny days."

"Would you care to have coffee with us?"

He hesitated, then nodded. Shedding his suit jacket, he lounged back in his chair, a bright strip of sunlight across his face. He was wearing a short-sleeve shirt, and the curly black hairs on his forearms and in the V of his open collar accentuated his masculinity.

He turned to Tamar. "How do you like London?"

She smiled and simpered, letting her painted blue eyelids fall over her dark eyes as if she were basking in the sun. "I like it today when it does not rain."

He laughed. "And the other days?"

"It is not so good."

The waiter set down two coffees and Susan ordered another for Michael, who continued focusing his attention on Tamar and directing his conversation to her.

"I like London because of its history. Did you know that the ancient city had a wall around it in Roman times? During the Middle Ages there were seven gates entering into it. That's why many streets are named Ludgate, Newgate, Aldersgate . . ."

"I didn't know that, Michael," Susan said.

He glanced at her quickly. "It's true. A part of the old wall still remains in some sections of the city. The White Tower was built in 1066 by William of Normandy in a break in the wall."

"The Norman Invasion—1066. How I used to drill my students on that," Susan said.

"Did you learn about it, too?" he asked Tamar.

"As a child, very little. Later in college— then is when I have the history."

The waiter brought Michael's coffee and he drank it in nervous sips, keeping his eyes away from Susan's. Tamar mistook his attention to her, assuming that he was attracted.

Fingering the red and blue bracelets on her arm, she looked down and said, "I should like it if you would visit me at the De Vere Hotel sometime. I think you would like the history of Iraq, my country. I have many books . . ." She glanced up. "You'll come, yes?"

Susan smiled to herself. There was nothing shy about Tamar when men were concerned. She wondered if Tamar would keep Michael waiting as she herself was kept waiting for fittings. Would Michael have to compete with the parrot for attention? With Joel?

But she needn't have worried. Michael retreated as fast as a soldier under machinegun fire and said little to Tamar during the next few minutes. Quickly finishing his coffee, he set down his cup and got up. "It's been a pleasure meeting you, Tamar," he said. "Have a pleasant afternoon."

When he had gone a few steps, he turned and looked at Susan over his shoulder. "I'll call you," he said, then disappeared into the crowd.

Chapter 33

And so their dates began again. Michael never mentioned the reception, and although he asked about Edward once or twice, he did not press her to tell him more than the minimum. Leasing a Ford Leyland from a neighborhood garage, he concentrated on taking her sightseeing whenever she was free.

Susan felt guilty about spending time away from her work. Along with the news of the loss of the trust came the realization that she was truly on her own. Pride had kept her independent before, but now she knew it was a matter of survival. Yet in order to survive, she must create. The car trips with Michael seemed to free her from the dullness that had descended upon her in the workroom. Gradually she began sketching again—flowing, exiting clothes with imaginative color combinations.

Soon Michael's passion for history got the better of him, and he dragged her to some of London's famous landmarks. In two weeks, they visited the Tower, the Inns of Court, Hampton Court, the Cutty Sark in dry dock at Greenwich and the Old Curiosity Shop.

One evening they attended a concert by the London Philharmonic Orchestra at the Royal Festival Hall. Up until now, aside from a few goodnight kisses, Michael had avoided any intimacy with her. But during the concert she caught him gazing at her frequently, his face dark and moody.

When he brought her back to her house, he strode into the dining room with a determined step, switched on a corner lamp and put his hand under it to check his watch. He gave a start, but said nothing. Unhooking the cape she had worn over her black silk evening dress, she slipped it off and laid it over one of the chairs.

"A drink? Wine . . . coffee?" she asked.

"Nothing, thank you," Michael said.

She felt uncomfortable. Like the other men at the concert, he was wearing a tuxedo which, contrasting with his usual wardrobe of T-shirts and sweaters, made him look like a stranger.

He crossed the room to the window and stood with his hands clasped behind him, staring out at the pale moonlit night. Outside all sounds were stilled, and only the ticking of the clock on the buffet and his heavy breathing broke the silence. Besides the corner lamp, the only other illumination in the room came from the hallway light that she had switched on when they first came in. Turning from the window, Michael walked over to her, his white shirt front incadescent in the shadowy room.

Lifting his hands, he put them on her shoulders. His face, silhouetted against the window, was blank and dark, and she couldn't see his eyes. He stood there a moment as if he wanted to say something to her, but instead took her in his arms. Tonight his kiss was different. She did not relax in his arms, but tensed, fighting off the passion evoked by his demanding mouth and tongue. Drawing away to look at him, she tried again to find his eyes but saw only the dark shape of his head moving near as he pressed her body tightly to his.

She did not like the disturbing sensations his lips were sending through her—or the fact that her former yearning was tripled in intensity this time. It made her want to grab him by the neck and draw him down—nearer and nearer until he would melt into her. The need to be loved was so strong that when his kisses became more intense, she could scarcely bear it. She drew back.

"When?" she whispered.

"Whenever you say," he replied, his breath

warm against her face. Then his lips were closing down on hers again. Amid the roaring in her ears, she could hear the clock strike two.

Later she wondered how he could leave—how, if he felt as she did, he simply could drop his hands at that moment and walk away.

She wondered again when she heard the crunch of the tires of his Ford Leyland on the pavement outside, and the sound of the engine shifting from low to second.

In the days that followed, Michael began permeating Susan's thoughts as Edward previously had. But was this attraction on her part due to physical need? Was it a sexual pull which always tugged at her whenever she was near him, or was it more? There was so much about him that she had yet to discover.

"A man needs—a woman loves," her mother had once told her. But, like herself, her mother had been wrong about so much. She wished Michael would be sent away on assignment, for it was difficult to concentrate with such yearning inside her, made sharper whenever she saw him.

Refusing some of his invitations, she spent long hours in the workroom, eating sandwich lunches with Mary while listening to her tales about life with Frederick Barnes—of their cozy semi-attached house, of Sundays spent entertaining friends with dinners of leg of lamb and roast browned potatoes and fizzy apple cider. She even could picture Mary's immaculate table settings. But these carefree conversations were rare. The majority of her time she spent sketching.

Money was coming in—more than she'd once thought possible—yet it was not enough to cover the costs of a style show. Susan never refused an order, but each day, after all were filled, she put the girls to work on garments for the show. She did not hesitate to pay them overtime, and sometimes kept them well after 6:00 o'clock.

She envied the girls when they left. Like Mary, they went home to cozy houses or flats, where they could forget their work for eight or ten hours. She was trapped here with hers.

Ever since she'd moved downstairs, she'd been even more dissatisfied with the house. Except for the huge dining room, the downstairs rooms were drafty and dull, and there seemed no place where she could spend a comfortable evening relaxing. She entertained visitors like Michael either upstairs in the workroom or downstairs in the dining room, but on nights when she was alone, she turned off the upstairs stove to save money and stayed in the kitchen where the tiny gas stove and waist-high refrigerator were dwarfed by the high ceiling. She used the kitchen table for sketching and reading, often turning on the gas oven to take away the chill.

But her living quarters were the least of her problems. Foremost was her increasing concern over the upcoming style show. She knew that her collection was far from ordinary. She'd shed her timidity and created with flair and emotion—she'd been daring and innovative. But would the public like her designs?

She could scarcely believe that the show would soon be a reality. Sixty-five garments had been completed, twenty more sketched with only four more left to design. Mary and the others were plunging ahead with the work as if engaged in a frantic dance which, as it nears the end, gains momentum until everyone is dizzy and overheated.

Night after night she sat in her bleak kitchen wondering how she would pay the fees for the auditorium, wages for models, and the costs of flowers and an orchestra. The profit she'd made from orders had gone for fabrics and trim. If demands for her designs kept on at their present rate, eventually she could finance the show. But she might have to wait another six months, and that would make the fall fashions in her collection outdated.

As the days went on, she finished the four remaining sketches, but still had not solved her financial problems. She turned the matter over in her mind until she hit upon the only solution possible—one that she had pushed from her thoughts dozens of times—*borrowing.*

Chapter 34

Once Susan had accepted the fact that outside help was needed, it didn't take her long to decide on a course of action. There was one person who could loan her money easily—Tamar! Hadn't she offered financial help after the fire? Hadn't she hinted at being a business partner when work was progressing again? Tamar had faith in her, had an abundance of money and would be happy to put it to good use. Of course it would be foolish to approach a matter that delicate over the phone, so she arranged to come to Tamar's hotel for a meeting on Thursday.

When the time came, Susan set out for the hotel on foot, in much the same mood as on her first visit—determination mixed with apprehension.

It was a warm spring day. There had been

rain early that morning, but now a bright sun was out and drops were falling from the awnings, making dark patches on the pavement under her feet. As she walked through Kensington Gardens, a warm breeze played over her face, and she imagined herself sitting in Tamar's hotel now, the sunshine slanting in through the wide windows as they discussed plans for the show. Tamar's olive-colored face would have that special glow that always came when they talked about clothes, and her dark eyes would be large and shining.

It seemed to take longer than usual to reach the hotel. Perhaps her anticipation had stretched out the moments. As she climbed the steps of the large brick building, a door-man in a navy uniform with gold buttons stepped before her and swung open the door. Thanking him, she went inside and hurried across the lush carpeting of the lobby to the lifts, entering one standing ready.

The lift stopped at floors two and three and each stop seemed to drain away some of Susan's courage. As it neared the fourth floor where Tamar lived, her strength suddenly deserted her. Tamar was her one hope. If she were aloof and distant, as sometimes occurred, all would be lost. The lift shuddered to a stop. She stepped out and was walking down the corridor when Joel swiftly passed her in the hall.

At her cry of recognition, he stopped and waited while she approached.

"Been seeing Tamar?" she asked.

He looked down at the carpet. "Just came from her room." A flush reddened his fair cheeks, and his fingers clasped and unclasped the edges of his coat. If he had been showing Tamar photos of the gowns he was trying to sell her from Thadius, where was his briefcase? And why was his shirt so rumpled?

"Listen, Joel," she said. "Don't be embarrassed. I don't mind if you're selling to Tamar. I don't need her business now. In fact, we've been so busy on the collection for the style show that any orders from her would be a delay."

"Then what are you doing here? You're on your way to see her, aren't you?" he asked.

"Yes."

"So?"

Because of their mutual dependence on Edward, she felt a lingering kinship with Joel. Why not tell him her plan? They both had enough experience in salesmanship to know that Tamar, with all her riches, was fair game. "I'm going to try to arrange a loan with her to help finance my show," she said.

"Tamar . . ." he said, his eyes shining with a special glow, " . . . a generous lady indeed."

"I mustn't keep you," she said, anxious to get on with her business.

His eyes met hers for the first time. "Good luck with your show, Sue. I think what you're doing is great—the way you're making a go of it by yourself and all . . ."

"Thanks, Joel."

He strode to the lifts, and she continued on to Tamar's room. When she knocked on the door, muffled sounds of footsteps came from the other side, then a bolt clicked. The door opened several inches and Tamar peered out from a room that was unusually dark.

"I'm putting the polish on my nails," she said.

Opening the door only wide enough for Susan to enter, she slammed it shut and hurried back to a chair by a small table where she sat down and continued to apply the polish.

Rather than the sunshine Susan had anticipated, the shades in the room were drawn and only one lamp was on. Tamar, her strawberry hair glowing in the circle of light, was stroking one nail after the other with a tiny brush. Susan found a chair and waited for her to finish. The pungent odors of nail polish and polish remover caused a wave of nausea to sweep over her. Fighting it, she studied the top of Tamar's bent head. This woman, who had given her her start, might be the culminating means to her success.

Holding out the red-tipped fingers of one hand, Tamar raised her head and inspected them. "They call it sizzling ruby. What do you think?"

"Nice. It looks good with black."

"You have it?"

"I've heard of it. Actually, I have a hard time keeping my nails long enough to polish. Handling fabrics and pins makes them break."

Tamar seemed to take forever polishing the nails on her right hand. Finally, placing the tips of her fingers on the table so that the polish could dry, she leaned back. "So. You wanted to see me?"

Susan cleared her throat, not knowing quite how to begin. "Yes."

"The style show? When will it be?" Tamar asked.

"That depends, Tamar. I need a loan." Immediately she wished she could take back her words and start again. She had blurted out the reason for her visit without a proper build-up.

The Iraqi leaned forward, her brows drawn down towards the bridge of her nose. "A loan?"

"For musicians, flowers, renting a hall. About 5000 pounds. Could you possibly lend it to me? I'll pay you back as soon as I can."

Tamar held out her hand again, turning it admiringly so that the bright crimson polish caught the rays of the lamp. She did not look at Susan, but kept her eyes on her nails. After

a long silence, she said, "If I had the money
. . . if I had any money, I would not be doing
my own nails."

Susan gasped. What sort of game was
Tamar playing? "You live in this hotel. You
buy from Thadius. You go to Paris . . . and
your closet is overflowing with clothes. How
can you not have money?"

Tamar studied her nails again. "One must
keep something on one's back, yes. My money
is not here, but in Iraq. I am—how do you say
it?—hard up for cash."

"I can't believe it . . ." Susan cried. She did
not mention the lavish way that Tamar spent
in restaurants, nor her many offers to help in
the past. Susan stared at her for a few
seconds, then glanced about the room. There
was a well-stocked liquor cabinet in one
corner, an expensive tapestry on the wall,
valuable figurines from every country in
Europe and the Middle East.

Over the months, Susan had bent over
backwards for Tamar, hurrying with gowns
she needed. Now she marveled at how Tamar
could remain so calm and self-possessed. She
might have been denying Susan a minor
whim, some small favor, so little did the
refusal affect her. Abruptly her friend rose
and crossed the room to a phone by the
windows.

Picking up the receiver, she turned to
Susan. "Over our tea we shall talk. But
nothing of money. Money should never enter

a friendship." She put her mouth to the speaker, "Please. Room 418. Tea—enough for two, today."

Susan sprang to her feet, a multitude of emotions rising up within her. There was no way she could sit facing Tamar, smiling and eating sandwiches with the crusts cut off. Her hand would shake if she tried to lift a cup to her lips!

"Tamar, I'm sorry but I can't stay. Have them send tea for one."

She hurried to the door, said goodbye and left without a backward glance.

Once outside, she walked for a time, puzzled and hurt. Tamar's praise and their many luncheons had led her to believe that the Iraqi was her friend. How could she be so aloof now?

She was crossing the street when she noticed the bank. It stood there on the corner in granite-like splendor with the sign "Barclay's Bank" in gilt lettering across the front window.

Borrowing. It had taken Susan a long time to decide on such a course. Should she still go through with it?

She passed the bank, then slowly came back and pushed open the glass door bordered in shiny brass. A woman was sitting at a desk in the entryway.

"May I help you?"

"Could I see a bank officer, please?"

The woman motioned to a plush chair and

Susan sat on its edge. Was this absurd? How could she—a stranger and an American—borrow? True, she had a savings account in one of Barclay's branches, but the balance was minimal. The only collateral she had to offer was the Sumner Place house, remembering again that the deed was in her name. But that was only on paper. It was understood that she owned it jointly with Edward, and she questioned her right to borrow on it.

Before she could reach a decision, a dark-haired man appeared, introduced himself as Erik Van Horst and ushered her to his desk. From the name, she guessed the man was Dutch. London was filled with people of many nationalities—Indians, Pakistanis, Europeans, Africans. She tried to concentrate on this and other dry objective facts to keep her mind off Tamar.

She requested £5000, and when she asked what rate of interest she would have to pay, Mr. Van Horst quoted the current rate, double-checking in one of his folders.

"The matter of collateral?" he asked.

"My husband Edward and I own a house here in London. The deed is in my name," Susan replied.

"Not Edward Thorwald! He's borrowed from us before. Where is the property located?"

She gave the address and he smiled. "That will do nicely. Bring in a copy of the deed.

Meanwhile we'll fill out these forms," he said opening another folder and drawing out two sheets of paper covered with small print.

Within a week, a bank check for £5000 was in Susan's hands. Without Edward's approval or knowledge, she had used their house as collateral, leaving herself quite vulnerable if the show failed. Tamar could have saved her from this. Now the stakes had doubled—not only was she about to display daring fashions, but she had put her place of business in jeopardy.

Late on the afternoon the check came, she was sitting alone in the dining room, staring at the varnished table when three taps sounded on the front door. There was only one person who rapped that way—Michael.

"Come in," she called without moving.

There were footsteps in the hall, then Michael's dark head appeared around the door frame. As he came into the room, he switched on the overhead light. She had been sitting in the dusk, and the sudden bright glow hurt her eyes.

He pulled out a 'chair and sat down opposite. "How did you know it was me?" he asked.

"I know the way you rap."

"You left the door unlocked. Not a very wise thing to do."

She shrugged. "I would have locked it in a

few minutes. I barely got home myself, and some of the staff were still upstairs. That's why it was open."

"Everyone gone now?"

She nodded.

"You're pale and your eyes look frightened. What's wrong?"

Looking down, she rubbed her fingers slowly on the shiny surface of the table. "I borrowed 5000 pounds from the bank for the style show and used this house as collateral."

She looked up just in time to see his smile fade and his eyes turn grave. There was a long silence. "Was borrowing from the bank your only choice?" he asked.

In a monotone, she told him everything, beginning with her visit at Tamar's. When she'd finished, he frowned. "Did it ever occur to you that I might have been able to help?" he asked.

"I'd never use you," she said. "I don't like using people who have to struggle the same as I do."

He laughed. "You're a strange one. You'd visit Tamar, risk Edward's wrath, squeeze the bonds tight enough to choke you—all before you'd come to me."

She averted her eyes. "It's better this way. I'm obligated to no one."

"If that's the way you want it," he said. His voice had been sympathetic before, but now there was an edge to it. Slapping the table with his hand, he rose. "Owing the bank is something like owing your soul to the company store." He strode to the door. "I wish you luck," he said, then turned and went out.

Someone else had wished her luck—but it seemed so long ago. It was Joel. She sat there, dully staring out the window. The twilight was thickening into blackness like a huge dark wave covering the house. It was time to close the blinds, but she felt too weak to move.

There were dark ghoulish-shaped weeds in her garden, making the entire scene like something in a nightmare. Finally she dragged herself up, went down the hall and locked the front door. If she could only push away this weight descending upon her—lock out all her doubts! What she had done could easily bring her to her knees.

Chapter 35

The gravity of the bank loan, especially using the house as collateral, made Susan reconsider having a style show. Her collection was almost ready, but were the clothes worth displaying? She hired two models to try on the finished outfits, a final test as to whether she should go ahead with the further expenditures a show required. She then lined up her staff for a viewing. As the models sashayed before them, Mary kept smiling and nodding her head.

There were tailored jackets with off-center closings, calf-length skirts that fit smoothly over the hips, feathers flying at necklines, sarong draped skirts, high-waisted empire gowns.

"Each woman must choose depending on her age, waistline, shoulders and legs," said

Mary, viewing a white satin windbreaker covering a slinky long black dress. "That one surely isn't for me."

"By seeing the designs on live models, I can tell where the clothes hit the body and how they should be accessorized," Susan told her. "How do you think that Donegal tweed came out?"

"Fine, but I like the next one, trimmed in plum velvet," Mary said.

Susan switched her gaze to the staff of seamstresses who, eyes round and faces flushed, were studying each model intently.

"The proper shoes will help," Susan said, loud enough for everyone to hear.

When the informal showing came to an end, Susan was pleased. A few garments needed more work but most had turned out as planned.

"Your eyes never have had such sparkle," Mary said after the models had left.

"It's going to work, Mary. I wasn't sure, but now I see the clothes moving—see that their fullness flatters rather than looking bulky—I'm satisfied. You and the girls have done a wonderful job."

Mary averted her eyes. "The clothes are unusual, I'll say that. Experimental . . ."

"Tomorrow's clothes, today."

"They'd never make it without those lovely colors and fabrics."

Susan laughed. "You're telling me that you

think they *will* make it, aren't you?" She waited breathlessly for Mary's reply.

The white-haired woman nodded her head slowly. "I think so. I think they might even prove to be a bit sensational."

Knowing that her designs had both the staff's and Mary's approval eased Susan's concern, but there was still much to be done. Previously, she had felt that once her collection was designed and made, the rest would be easy. Now she was learning that "creating" was only the first step.

Michael was the only one who knew to what extent she'd gone to finance the show. The rest of her friends were oblivious. Professor Barnes joked in his usual manner, the seamstresses giggled with excitement, and Mary, who had been through many shows at Dior, took it all calmly. It was only Michael's earnest eyes when they met hers that reflected her own painful concern. But with everyone's anticipation at such a high peak, she knew she could not back down now. She engaged an auditorium in the center of London, hired models, arranged for music and photographers, and bought shoes for each costume.

The show was to be held on a Friday. Thanks to Michael, a small news story was scheduled to appear in the fashion section of the Sunday Times prior to the date. Susan began collecting names and addresses of the people who should receive invitations and put Mary in charge of hand addressing them and sending them out. Michael furnished her with the names of members of the press to contact, and she used the files Edward had left in the house for the names of important buyers.

But there was one buyer whose attendance was vital—*Edward*. Although she had lost all respect for him as a husband, she still needed his opinion as a fashion authority. She wanted her designs evaluated in his eyes— wanted him to watch *her* runway for a change, hear applause for her. If the show were successful, Edward's presence would give her great satisfaction. In addition to Edward, she planned to invite Michael, Veronica and her husband, Professor Barnes and Joel, among other friends. She left Tamar's name off the list.

She addressed Joel's invitation herself, then took the bus to the London branch of Thadius, hoping to give it to him personally while finding out where to send Edward's.

When she arrived, a strange woman, in a dress identical to that worn by her predecessor, was at the front desk. Susan went up to her and asked to see Joel.

"Mr. Adams has gone on an important business errand this morning," she said. "Could someone else help you?"

"I'm Susan Thorwald. I want to see him personally."

At the name Thorwald, the woman drew to attention. "I know where he is. I'll let him know right away," she said in a fluttery voice. She picked up the phone immediately and began dialing.

Susan took off her gloves and opened her coat. Ten minutes later, Joel rushed in the front door of the shop, his forehead glistening as if he'd been running.

"Sue, what a pleasant surprise. Nothing wrong, I hope?"

"I'm excited and nervous, that's all. My show is scheduled for the first of the month," she said. She drew his invitation from her purse and handed it to him.

Removing it from its envelope, he studied it, then smiled. "Did Edward get one of these?" he asked, waving it in the air.

"That's just it. I don't know where to send it."

Joel shook his head, gazing again at the invitation. "Your timing is off—terribly off."

Before he could finish, the door opened and a woman in a white ermine jacket strode in. "Good morning, Joel," she said rather sharply.

Joel nodded, and leaving Susan's side, hurried to the girl at the front desk. After a few seconds of conversation he returned.

"Am I keeping you?" Susan asked.

"I had an appointment, but Nancy promised to take care of her," Joel said.

While Nancy went back to get some gowns,

the customer stared at Joel and Susan, her eyes hazy with disappointment. She stayed only long enough to view two, then swished out the door, her head held high.

"Thadius is losing business," Susan whispered.

"Thadius is doing mighty fine—at least this store is. Edward gives us very little attention, however. Of course you know he's in Japan."

"Japan!" Her heart sank. There would be little chance of his getting back for her show.

"It's against the rules, but I could give you his address. He left last week and will be there for a couple months."

"No, never mind." It would be pointless to send Edward's invitation to Japan and get Joel into trouble. She would send it to his Seventh Avenue office in New York and let his staff forward it.

Joel's eyes gleamed. "Edward's a busy boy, I hear."

Sensing he was about to furnish her with some unwanted gossip, she drew her coat together and began buttoning it. "That's all I wanted—to give you the invitation. I hope you can come."

"I wouldn't miss it. I'm really excited for you."

She wished she could be more sure of Joel's friendship. When he was with her, he lavished her with attention, but like Edward, he was accustomed to treating all women with a frail allegiance. That was evident from the woman in the ermine jacket who had come in and whom he had avoided. Women were a segment of the population who fed Edward and Joel, angered them, delighted them, wore their fashions—but they were merely women.

Pulling on her gloves, she turned toward the door.

"Going home?" Joel asked. "I'll drive you."

"I'd appreciate that, Joel. Sure you have time?"

"I have lots of time. Just give me a few minutes to get my car."

They left the shop together, and she waited under the awning while he disappeared down an alley. A short time later a sleek white Jaguar pulled up to the pavement. Joel reached over from the driver's seat and opened the door for her.

She climbed in, noticing the plush red leather interior. "I must say, Thadius *is* doing well," she said. "This is a beautiful car."

"It's a Jaguar XJS. I've never seen such beauty and styling and speed all in one sports car." Reving the engine, he merged with the traffic.

"Want to cruise down the M-1 with me sometime?" he asked ten minutes later as they neared her house.

"I'd like to Joel, but I have hardly any time before the show."

"You should get out some, you know."

She was silent. If she went out at all, it

would be with Michael. Joel reminded her
too much of Edward.

When they arrived, she thanked him for the
ride and asked if he would like to come in to
see her workroom.

"Where can I leave the car?" he asked.

"Here—where it's parked."

"Can't take that chance. This baby needs
supervision in protected parking lots. But
thanks anyway."

He waited until she was at her front door,
then drove off, the car a white streak under
the brilliant sun.

There were so many details to attend to
that the weeks sped by. When the final week
came, it was hard for Susan to wait for the
moment when the first model would appear
on the runway. "The clothes represent the
best I can do at this time," Susan reminded
herself, trying to steel herself for the public's
final decision.

She was so exhausted that she slept well
the night before the show. The following
morning, dozens of unexpected problems
popped up. Belts were missing, collars
soiled. One model called in sick and had to be
replaced. Susan handled each of these emergencies without losing her composure,
staying within reach until the clothes had
been transported to the auditorium,
numbered and put on racks. Over each
hanger was a bag containing accessories that

were to be worn with that outfit. Reluctantly she returned home to ready herself. It had begun to rain and she gazed at the sea of bobbing black umbrellas from the top floor of the bus, fearing that the foul weather might be an unlucky omen of some sort.

Once she arrived home, she drew herself a hot bath, stepped in and sank down in the warm soapsuds. Usually a bath calmed her, but tonight the hot water made her jittery. She had planned to grab a bite to eat before she left for the auditorium, but now the act of swallowing even a morsel seemed impossible. She was glad she'd refused Michael's offer to drive her, for in her present numb state she wouldn't be able to respond to anything he said.

She covered her face with a hot washcloth and let the steam pour into her skin, wishing it could warm the inner recesses where her brain was frozen by fear. She sat up suddenly, the water swishing around her. What time was it? Silly to lie in a hot tub— she must arrange for a taxi and dress.

As she stepped out onto the bathmat, the cool air rushed against her bare body and made her shiver. She dried her skin with swift frantic strokes of the towel, slipped into her chenille robe and hurried to the phone to call a taxi.

While dressing and applying makeup, she tried not to think of the possibility of failure. But no matter how much she forced herself to block out such fears, they crept into her thoughts, making her hand tremble as she tried to brush on her lipstick and paint her lids with blue. I'll have to let the make-up man at the auditorium do a touch-up job, she thought as she laid down the brush. She had decided to wear a simple black wool dress— calf-length with a white linen collar and cuffs and a black poet's bow at the neck. She slipped it over her head, and after zipping up the back, hurried out in the hall to wait for the taxi.

There was a lump in her throat so large that she could scarcely swallow. She paced up and down in the foyer for what seemed like a half-hour, ready too early, yet obsessed with the feeling she wasn't ready at all. A layer of wetness covered her palms and the collar of her dress seemed to be choking her. When the headlights of the cab finally shone through the window beside the front door, she quickly slipped on her raincoat, dashed out and climbed in, mumbling the address to the driver in such a low voice that he twice had to ask her to repeat it.

Chapter 36

Only after she entered the dressing room at the auditorium and a half dozen emergencies claimed her attention did Susan calm down. When she finally had time to peek out at the audience, she sighed with relief. The auditorium was packed. Pale eager faces shone out in the gloom, and she even recognized some in the seats closest to the stage. Michael and Professor Barnes were sitting together in the second row. Having not invited Tamar she was surprised to see her sitting next to Joel. Veronica and her husband were coming down the aisle, the blond woman sporting one of the suits Susan had designed for her boutique.

Letting go of the curtain, Susan turned backstage just as Mary came hurrying from the coat rack. Her white hair was freshly styled and her makeup, as usual, was flaw-less. In her hand was a satchel containing emergency sewing equipment. The sight of the older woman was reassuring to Susan. With Mary here, the floor would not open up and swallow her nor would her knees give way as they were threatening to do. Mary came up and pressed her hand.

"It's going to be O.K.," Susan whispered.

Mary nodded, and they moved to an area where they could keep an eye on most of the backstage activity.

The air was heavy with perfume, hair spray, cigarette smoke and tension. The dressers, noted for their talents of putting on one gown while taking off another, were unbuttoning, unzipping and unbuckling garments hanging on the rack so that no time would be lost when it came time to put them on. The make-up man was standing at the mirrors, adding blusher and eye shadow to several models at once. "A fashion pit crew" Michael had jokingly called it.

The sixteen models who were to participate were dressed in their first outfits and now were adjusting hats, hiking up hem-lines and making sure garments hung properly on their shoulders. Susan came over and re-tied a belt and yanked at a loose thread. The director signaled for them to form a queue and the lights dimmed.

The pulsating music, now swelling to a loud pitch, seemed to penetrate Susan's

entire body. It grew even louder as the
models waited. The director studied her
watch, and a moment later signaled the first
girl to go out.

Tossing back her head, the model strode
onto the runway and glided to its end while
Susan and Mary, out of view, stood watching.
It was all happening the way Susan had
dreamed.

The pace of the show was professional. The
models pranced across the stage and back,
the music changing according to the mood of
the clothes. With the expert help of the
dressers, they changed into other costumes
and went out again perfectly orchestrated, on
cue. Occasionally they strutted across the
stage in pairs. There were no interruptions.

Mary leaned toward Susan and whispered,
"The audience is quiet, isn't it?"

Susan listened and nodded. There were no
cheers, no loud blasts of applause. Everyone
seemed as numb as she. Cameras flashed
periodically, heads remained facing the
stage, but the customary stirrings in the
crowd were missing. A dreadful thought took
possession of her. "I'm failing—oh, I'm failing." Whirling, turning, prancing, the models
became a blur before her eyes. As in a nightmare, she watched them swish across the
stage and come back towards her, throwing
down purses, furs or jewelry as soon as they
were out of view of the audience. Then came
the traditional finale—a daring wedding

gown. Surely that would bring a response.

No one cheered. The model who was wearing it glided off the stage, and Susan hurried onto the runway to make her bow. A still greater hush came over the audience. To fill the gap, the musicians began to play a medley of songs they had used as background music for the show. Spectators stood up, put on coats, and gathering up purses and umbrellas, merged into the aisles.

Susan came backstage and joined Mary. They had not been standing there long when Michael and Professor Barnes pushed back the curtain. Although Michael said nothing, she could tell by the glow in his eyes that he was impressed.

"First rate," Barnes cried in his heartiest manner. A queue formed behind them and somehow Susan got through the next moments of greetings. Veronica and her husband each shook her hand, and following them, a buyer from one of Harrod's fashion departments. She could see Tamar and Joel standing together near the end of the queue. Tamar's right arm encircled Joel's slim waist.

"Why is Tamar here?" Susan whispered to Mary.

"I sent her an invitation. I thought you'd forgotten her," Mary replied.

Her agony was great enough without having to face her former friend again. When the couple finally reached her, Tamar acted as if nothing had changed.

"Susan, this is Joel Adams," Tamar said, looking up at him fondly.

"Yes, I've met Mr. Adams before," Susan said.

Tamar's brows rose in surprise, and Joel flushed and kept his eyes averted as he shook her hand. "Nice show," he said.

"We go now in his little car," Tamar said. "He wanted the black leather on the seats. I chose the red. I tell the salesman when I buy it, 'My friend is too young for black.' "

Joel flushed again and moved on. It seemed ironic. Joel had been bought—bought with the money that had been denied her, bought with a shiny car worth much more than the amount she had asked to borrow from Tamar. And Joel had made her believe it was the profits from Thadius that had allowed him such a luxury!

She continued shaking hands. The overhead lights made everything a glare. She had witnessed many designers after shows in much the same setting. They had been jubilant—laughing, receiving congratulations and chattering—but tonight all seemed hollow. The adjectives "fabulous" and "outstanding" were meaningless tributes—polite amends to make up for the hushed, glum audience that had rejected her designs. Her face ached from the forced smile frozen on her lips.

Finally Michael came up to her and whispered, "You're getting pale."

"Let's leave," she said. "This is about all I can take."

He drove her home in the Ford Leyland. She leaned towards him. Michael was the only one in her shaky world who made sense. Joel was a womanizer, Tamar a liar, Edward miles away. She wished there was someway she could tell this man beside her how much he meant to her. She sat very still with her eyes glued to the middle white line of the roadway, thinking of the right words.

"Would you like to go to a restaurant— some quiet place?" he asked, watching the road.

Tears sprang to her eyes. "I couldn't," she said. "It would be impossible to face people just now. Let's go home."

Once they were back at her house and had come into the dining room, she burst into tears. "I failed—failed horribly. How can I face the seamstresses who worked so hard, or Mary? I let them all down," she sobbed.

Without a word, Michael drew her to him and let her weep. All the while his hand caressed her hair and neck, pulling her nearer. The shoulder of his jacket felt so smooth, his body so strong. Suddenly she was tired of fighting—of forcing herself to be cheerful and bright when she was human, subject to despair like anyone else, wanting support and warmth. She knew that the next step was inevitable—a force stronger than herself was pulling her to the one place where she wanted to be.

"Now. Please, now," she said, and taking his hand, led him into her bedroom.

Tenderness was new to her. Unlike Edward, Michael's style of love making was what she'd read in books—slow, sensitive, allowing time for her own enjoyment. He was sweet and unselfish, raising her to heights of new feeling.

"I've lived more in this one night than I could ever imagine," she whispered.

He did not answer, but drew his arms around her and, stroking her hair, pressed his lips to hers. She drifted off to sleep in his arms, wondering if intimacy rather than success might not be the dream she had hungered after so long.

At dawn when she woke, Michael was gone. She stretched, feeling a new vibrancy in her body. Last night came back as though it were only a moment away. She had staked everything on the style show, had lost and to her surprise had made it through. There had been no remorse, only the joy of her night with Michael. Reaching down over the bed, she adjusted the covers around her and, shutting her eyes, slept some more.

She woke again at nine o'clock, pulled on a robe and stood gazing out at her weedy patch of garden. Next to the dry tan stalks that had been there all winter, bright yellow daffodils were blowing in the wind. Spring had come without her noticing.

Going into the bathroom, she splashed her face with cold water, thankful it was Saturday and she didn't have to face the girls in the workroom. It was difficult to concentrate on other people when Michael dominated her every thought. Was he in love with her? He had whispered endearments and to stop her tears had covered her wet cheeks with kisses. She had never felt such comfort. Failure was supposed to make one feel abandoned, but she felt wonderful.

She went into the kitchen where she plugged in the electric kettle to boil water for instant coffee. Having missed supper last night, she was ravenous. For breakfast she would have eggs, meaty English bacon and a tall glass of fresh orange juice. She was squeezing the oranges when the phone rang.

It was Michael. "Have you seen the morning paper?"

She groaned. "Not yet."

"How about these headlines: 'Designer Stuns Fashion World. Audience Mute.' I'll bring them over."

"When?"

"In about half an hour."

Forgetting about breakfast, she hurried through her bath taking more care than usual with her make-up. She didn't care what the world thought. The man who was coming to see her was the one who mattered. She put on everything but the white linen blouse she intended to wear, unlocked the front door, then rushed upstairs to get the sample matching the one that had been in the show. As she was slipping it on, the door creaked open and she heard footsteps in the foyer. She rushed to the landing. "Is that you, Michael?" she called.

"The news stories are good, Sue," he said. "It looks promising. Come down. I can only stay a minute."

Buttoning her blouse as she went, she rushed down the stairs. Michael was wearing a business suit, white shirt and tie, and on coming nearer, she saw that his face was closely shaved.

"Why are you wearing a suit? Why can't you stay?"

He was silent. Something about meeting his eyes after last night embarrassed her and she quickly glanced at the newspapers he was holding. Taking them from his hands, she laid them on the stairs.

"What do you mean you can stay only a minute, Michael? Where are you going?"

"I have to cover a story in Beirut."

"Beirut? So far away!"

"If I'm lucky, I'll only be gone a week." His eyes did not meet hers. "Pity we didn't know last night."

"Know what?" What was he driving at?

The phone began to ring. Picking up the clippings from the stairs, he thrust them in her hands. "That you've made it," he said with a smile.

Ignoring the phone, she sorted through the headlines: "Colossal Collection Unveiled." "Designs Become Sensation." There were photos of some of the dresses in the show and interviews with fashion authorities. She swallowed. She should be overjoyed, but all she could think of was that Michael was leaving. She gazed at him, a hard lump in her throat.

Averting his eyes, he reached for the doorknob.

"Goodbye, Michael," she said. Inside a voice was screaming, *Stay, live with me!*

"Goodbye and good luck."

Was he going to leave without even kissing her? How could she bear it?

He grinned. "Don't lose those papers. They should prove something to Edward."

He was scarcely out the door when the phone began ringing again. She made no move to answer it but stood holding the clippings—and just waiting, as if a miracle might bring him back.

Chapter 37

On the day Michael left, Susan became so busy that she scarcely had time to think. There were interviews with the media, while buyers and other designers began courting her, absorbing all the time she formerly spent in the workroom. Besides demands for her collection designs, the publicity connected with the show increased the popularity of her "Whitaker" skirt, and soon there was a backlog of orders. After several conferences with Mary, Susan decided to buy two dozen more sewing machines, hire more staff and convert the unfinished third floor into a second workroom.

While carpenters hammered overhead, Susan added as many machines as possible to the present workroom. The girls sewed there. When the pounding became too distracting and working conditions over crowded, she reluctantly gave away the mahogany dining table and established a small workroom downstairs where it was more peaceful.

Three floors turned into work areas! There was no place left for personal living, but she felt so fortunate to have the orders—to be able to pay back the bank—that she couldn't care less. "I don't mind as long as I have a place to sleep," she told Mary. Even that was in danger of being taken over. Bolts of fabric were stacked from floor to ceiling in one corner of her bedroom, along with boxes of thread, lace and ribbons. But rather than resent this intrusion, she gratefully accepted it. To her ears, the hum of machines on the floor above and in the dining room sounded like a symphony.

What was most exciting was the constant flow of designs that emanated from her. Following long evenings during which she was entertained in lavish restaurants, she would come home and sketch original designs inspired by gowns she'd seen that evening. The same enthusiasm she'd had at the start of her career possessed her, only now she valued it, knowing its fleeting nature.

The present dinners reminded her of those she used to attend with Edward, only this time she was the one in the spotlight. With her sucess came an inner glow—a pride of having accomplished something on her own, a feeling of worth. "No one can take that away," she whispered to herself when she grew lonesome for Michael.

Success brought problems as well as joy. The phone rang incessantly with a number of "would you?" requests: "Would you come to such and such an art school to speak?" "Would you look at my line of fabrics?" "Would you allow us an appointment?" Then there were the usual crackpots, who only wanted to hear her voice.

She hired a secretary, a Miss Nesta Jones, to screen her calls.

"If a Mr. Michael Everett asks for me, keep him on the wire until you find me," she instructed her. "Or an Edward Thorwald," she added.

She would be amused to see the look on Edward's face when a secretary answered, but chances were against that happening. His secretary would talk to her secretary before he picked up the phone.

Like a backdrop to the brilliant events in her life, spring was spreading itself over London. The lilacs were out, rose buds appeared on tall thorny stems in Kensington Gardens, and daffodils shed their golden warmth over the flower beds. During her years with Edward, Susan had used this season as a crutch, glorying in the warm days and the green grass and budding flowers to make her days more endurable. This year the season melded with her own life, accentuating its high color.

The third floor workroom was finished, orders still kept pouring in, and Susan toyed with the idea of knocking out walls and filling the entire first floor with machines as well. Mary began devoting all her time to supervision of the staff, while Susan interviewed and hired two business managers: Paul Stott as credit supervisor and Richard Tice for personnel and payroll. If her business continued to boom, even more staff would be necessary. Meeting the payments on her bank loan was easy, and she might have paid it all up if another idea hadn't come to her.

She wanted to buy a home. There was no space left in the three-story house at Sumner Place to entertain or relax. The sewing machines produced a constant hum during the day, and at night her bedroom was so crowded she could scarcely move. "I shall buy a house in the suburbs with raspberry and current bushes and pear trees in the backyard," she decided. But when she went over the books with Paul, shuffling sheets in exasperation, she could see that the costs of expanding the business, her loan payments and the payroll, plus a necessary reserve, would not allow for a down payment on a home. She was also sending monthly checks to her mother, who had left Alan and was now living in Chicago with her two poodles.

Susan's financial status did not stop her from looking however, and nearly every weekend she visited at least three houses for sale. One Saturday she found her dream home, a three-story Tudor-style house in Croydon with a small shopping area two blocks away. Its downstairs' rooms were arranged with a view of the garden overflowing with glorious flowers and shrubbery. Upstairs on the third floor was a studio with skylights that could easily be converted into a room for sketching and sewing. An easily accessible commuter train made several daily trips to and from London.

She loved everything about it and returned to see it several times.

On the third visit she said to the owner, an artist, "I want to buy your house, but I need time. How long can you wait?"

He was a short little man with a mustache who wobbled when he walked. "Until June," he said.

"Only one month?"

"I'm moving to France then and need the money for a down payment on a house there," the artist said.

"How many people have been through it?"

"Three parties are interested, including you."

He crossed the room to a cabinet, and pulling a pipe from his pocket, stuffed tobacco in the bowl and lighted it. He peered at her through the spiral of smoke. "Haven't I seen your picture somewhere?"

"I'm a fashion designer. I had a show a short time ago."

"Ah yes, I remember. The local newspaper made a big splash about it. I wish they'd give a bit more print to us painters."

She laughed. It was refreshing to meet someone who didn't fawn over her. "Let me know if you have another offer for the house. I know I want it, but I can't buy it at the moment." Fishing in her handbag, she drew out one of her business cards and handed it to him. How far those cards had taken her, she thought.

As she rode back to London on the train, Susan recalled the artist's comment about her show. If he had seen the "splash" of publicity as he called it, others had too, especially Edward who paid several staff members to collect fashion news. With the publicity and her announcement, Edward *had* to know about her debut. She wondered how long it would be before he called.

One afternoon several days later, Susan was returning from a luncheon date when she passed Nesta on the phone. Motioning to Susan, she covered the mouthpiece and whispered, "A man is ringing up from France. He refuses to give his name."

This was it—the call from Edward that she'd been expecting. Pausing a moment to gain her breath, she took the phone from Nesta.

"Mademoiselle Whitaker," said a voice with a French accent. "My name is Pierre De Moray. I'm calling from Grasse, France."

"Yes?" Obviously he thought she was single by his form of address.

"I plan to be in London at the end of the week and should like to see you. I work for a perfume manufacturer called Gallieni."

Susan gasped. "Yes, I've heard of the firm." It was a well-known company with some of its perfume endorsed by film and stage stars.

"May I make an appointment with you for dinner?"

"My secretary keeps my appointment book. Perhaps you can arrange it with her."

She quickly handed the phone to Nesta and sank down on a chair. Endorsing a perfume meant royalties. With the extra income, she could buy the artist's house!

"Next Tuesday night all right? Your calendar is open then." Nesta said, flipping the pages of Susan's appointment book.

Susan took the book from her and shuffled through it. Tuesday was a week away, and unless they met sooner someone might buy the house. "Cancel my appointment with the textile manufacturer on Friday. I'll have dinner with Monsieur De Moray then."

Leaving Nesta to handle the details, she went into the workroom where twenty girls were bending their heads over twenty humming machines, and the sun lit up the bright colorful fabrics flowing under the twenty needles. Life had become so wonderful that she was not quite sure whether she was awake or dreaming.

Chapter 38

Susan was to meet Monsieur De Moray at Taylor's, the same restaurant where she had eaten with Michael and which now had a growing reputation. The Frenchman was not there when she arrived, and she stood in the lobby surveying the changes that had been made since her last visit. There was a new rose-patterned carpet, and at one end of the dining room, a man in a tuxedo was playing a baby grand. Her thoughts were on Michael when Monsieur De Moray hurried in, complaining with a French accent about traffic and a slow cab driver.

The table reserved by the Frenchman was under one of the ceiling globes which shed a tiny watery light over the white cloth. They sat down, and when the waiter came, Monsieur De Moray ordered their dinners carefully with great attention to her likes and dislikes.

The service had improved. In minutes they were served two colorful glasses of Compari and orange juice, transformed into a rosy tangerine by the candlelight on their table.

Susan picked up her glass and raised it. "Cheers, as they say here."

He laughed. "We say Bon Appetit!"

He had straggly black hair and a rather long thin face with gray half-moons under his eyes. What saved his image from tackiness was a finely tailored black suit and an immaculate white shirt and collar. "The people of Europe know how to enjoy beautiful things," he said. "France excels in couture, perfumes and cuisine—luxuries, but always in demand."

Susan was impressed by his good English, but she knew it would take the entire dinner for him to come to the point. Europeans rarely approached subjects with the directness of Americans.

Over the next course of oysters, he described how perfume essences were distilled. When their entrees of venison with rose pepper sauce appeared, his eyes grew dark and intense, and she sensed he was about to bring up the reason for his visit. However, not until the last dish was cleared away did he begin.

"Congratulations," he said. "Your designs have been received well in our country. Your collection is so outstanding that the fashion world is—what is the word?—reeling!"

Susan's cheeks reddened. The light shining down on her from the ceiling and the wine she'd drunk were making her extremely warm. Opening her handbag and pulling out a tissue, she blotted her forehead.

"Our company would like you to endorse our new floral scent—a secret scent that inspires amour." He smiled so broadly that all his teeth showed.

She jumped up. "Would you please excuse me for a moment?" she said. One of the most momentous events in her career was about to take place, and she didn't want to sit opposite this important Frenchman and arrange a future of royalties with half-eaten lipstick and a shiny face.

He rose. "Shall I order a dessert while you're gone? Or perhaps a cognac?"

She smiled as he came to her side of the table to pull back her chair. "No dessert, but a cognac would be nice."

She stayed in the loo only long enough to repair her make-up and make a quick check in the full length mirror. She was wearing a black woolen jacket, matching pants and a violet satiny blouse, the top button of which she opened to make it cooler. When she came out, several people were getting up from a large table, making it necessary for her to circle a number of tables to get back to her own. At last she found an empty aisle where she could walk freely. She raised her head just in time to see the maitre d' standing at the entrance with a man and a black-haired woman who had just come in. Susan stopped and stood still. She tried to redirect her gaze but it was too late. Michael's eyes met hers in a hideous moment of recognition.

The shock of seeing him with a date stunned her so that she almost forgot where her own table was. Had it not been for the two glasses of amber liquid beckoning her like beacons, she might not have found it. As she approached, Monsieur De Moray jumped up and pulled out her chair. She sank into it, her mind in a tumult. *Michael was back in town and had not called her!* She glanced around to where she had seen him, but he and the girl had vanished.

The cognac—half of which she drank in one gulp—revived her enough so that she could think of a plan.

"Monsieur," she said, "I would like to show you my workroom in South Kensington. Perhaps we could continue our discussion there."

He nodded and motioned to the waiter for the bill which seemed to take an endless time in coming. Susan was so uncomfortable that she could scarcely sit still while Monsieur De Moray slowly finished his drink, elaborating on future plans of the Galieni firm.

They finished their discussion at her workshop, then she signed a contract with fingers almost too shaky to hold the pen. By now she didn't care if the perfume smelled like gasoline; she just wanted to be alone. When the Frenchman finally left, smiling so broadly that he was all teeth and gums, she rushed down the hall to her room and flung herself on the bed.

Up until now, her success had brought her nothing but joy. Now all that was cancelled by the sight of Michael and the girl standing together in the restaurant. Nothing was turning out as she'd planned. Edward wasn't calling. Michael had come back and ignored her. What good was money and fame if she lost the one person who mattered?

Chapter 39

The next morning Susan was more hurt and puzzled than angry. Her thoughts made little excursions here and there, trying to fathom what she saw the previous evening. Perhaps Michael was interviewing the girl for the Times, or perhaps she was a relative on a visit. Then again perhaps she *was* a date —a crushing thought. Was Michael the sort of man her mother often warned her about— one who left after he got what he wanted? Had she spoiled the chase by succumbing? But it was different now than in her mother's day. There were no more chases—people often went to bed together on the first date.

A ringing phone and questions by her staff kept her so busy that she was forced to brush away all personal problems. It wasn't until afternoon that she told Mary about the perfume contract. Surprisingly, the older woman was horrified.

"You don't endorse a perfume carte blanche," Mary cried. "You see that a combination of flowers are combined to make exactly the right scent. *Then* you put your name on it. You are so careful about other things—fabric, colors, accessories—it isn't like you to be so careless. And why the rush? Why didn't you stall Monsieur De Moray?"

"I was not myself," Susan replied in a scarcely audible voice. She couldn't tell Mary what she had seen at the restaurant or else the tears that she held back all day would rush out.

"With all the orders we put out each day, you could have waited before signing the contract. Never have I seen a more lucrative business. Twice as much as we used to do at Dior, and more customers than we can possibly take care of."

Susan shrugged. "What's done is done. I can't cross my name off the contract."

Mary smiled grimly. "Let's hope the scent Galieni selects will sell."

Leaving Mary's corner, Susan went into her office and picked up the phone. The perfume contract had been all she needed to reach a decision. She dialed the number of the artist who owned the house in Croydon and, finding it still available, arranged to come later that afternoon and give him a down payment.

She caught the 4:00 o'clock train. It was the first break in her work-filled day. As she sat in the sunny car, gazing out the window at the backs of apartment buildings and walled garden plots, her thoughts returned to Michael.

Michael had deceived her, but then again wasn't she used to Edward deceiving her? Hadn't her mother been deceived? Were all men alike?

Warm sun shone through the window. Outside, green playing fields swept past, round-abouts, a patch of sooty daffodils growing near the tracks. As she watched the whirling landscape, she planned the future. The new house would set her free. She would begin again. She would hire a housekeeper and a cook and spend more time outdoors. She would give dinner parties. "The house will keep me from being lonely—will keep my spirits up," she decided.

The train reached her stop, and she stepped out onto the platform and began walking towards the artist's house, wondering what it would be like to be one of London's many commuters.

Once the house was hers and the artist had moved out, Susan threw herself into redecorating. She bought dark pine furniture and

gingham shades and bright copper vessels—
all the homey touches she'd missed in her
stiff Victorian house. She hung lithographs
from local art dealers, and filled every corner
with green plants from a nearby flower
stand.

Her life style radically changed. As soon as
everyone had finished work, she locked up
her workshop then rushed to the train. Sometimes the streets were shiny and wet when
she arrived in Croydon, but whatever the
weather, her new house and its surroundings
delighted her.

On weekends she gloried in the open
quality of her new neighborhood, contrasted
to the crowded sidewalks near her old house.
She grew to know the butchers and bakers
and fruit vendors who often stood in the rain
with their produce covered by heavy plastic
sheets. A Chinese woman who padded along
from shop to shop with her window-washing
pail became another familiar sight.

The house was so pleasant that she often
lingered over breakfast. One day she was
sitting at the table drinking coffee and gazing
out when a seagull flapped its wings, and
using the blustery air to advantage, caught
an air current and soared. Like the gull, she
felt as if she had caught luck and was riding
it. The past months had been the most
exciting in her life. Then an awful realization
came over her. "I'm better off without Edward. I don't even love him anymore," she

whispered as she watched the gull fly over her neighbor's roof and off into the morning sky.

Chapter 40

Susan was close to losing hope of ever hearing from Michael when he phoned her one day at work. His voice was low and serious. She mentioned her date with the French perfumer, expecting him to tell her about his date at Taylor's, but he said nothing.

"I have a favor to ask you," he said. "One of my editors, Alan Morgan, is giving a dinner party a week from tonight at his home in Chistlehurst. He's invited me and whomever I choose to bring. Could you come with me?"

She answered almost too quickly. "Yes, I can come. Is it formal?"

"No, a cocktail dress is fine," he said. "Morgan's great. You'll enjoy meeting him and his wife. I'll pick you up around 7:00

o'clock." He seemed relieved that she'd accepted.

"I live in Croydon now," she said and outlined the roads he should take to get to her house.

On the night of the party, Michael came for her in a red Ford Leyland.

"I had to turn the blue one in. I'm not sure how well the heater works in this one. Better put on something warm," he said.

She went back upstairs and came down with a black gabardine coat covering her beige and scarlet jersey dress, a design of hers that had been praised by the workroom staff for the flowing lines of its gored skirt and long, hip-length bodice. Sitting beside Michael in the front seat reminded her of the times when Edward used to rent cars in various European cities, but she quickly brushed the thought from her mind.

"How are you going to introduce me?" she asked, wondering if Mr. Morgan knew she was married.

"Susan Thorwald. I've told them nothing of your fame."

She laughed, but Michael did not respond. There seemed to be an icy wall of formality between them. He concentrated on his driving, keeping his eyes on the road. Chistlehurst was on the outskirts of London, and by the time he pulled the car up in front of the Morgan's house, it was 8:00 o'clock.

"We're not late?" she asked.

"These affairs always start at 8:00."

"You've been to others?"

He nodded.

As they walked to the entrance, she wondered if she'd be judged against other girls who had dated him—perhaps the girl he had been with at Taylor's. Hurrying up the porch steps, Michael pressed the doorbell, which clanged musically. A moment later the carved oak door flew open.

"Ah, Michael," the man cried out. He was about fifty, with a slightly balding head and eyebrows that seemed to shoot off into space.

"Come in, please," he said cordially.

They stepped onto the dark slate of the entryway, and Michael introduced her to his host. As they were shaking hands, a golden retriever with glistening reddish fur bounded up and nuzzled his nose in the folds of Susan's coat.

"Tawny, no!" the host said, grabbing the dog's collar and leading him to one side. "I'll take your coats, then come along to the living room for a drink," he said. "Mrs. Morgan is in the kitchen, attending to some thing or other about dinner."

He hung their coats in a huge closet in the foyer, and they and the golden retriever followed him through the high-ceilinged hallway into a softly lighted room with French windows and a red Persian carpet. Two slender woman were sitting on a long sofa opposite one man with tinted glasses and another one with a red spot on each cheek. A fire was burning in the grate and the room was very warm.

For some reason everyone was silent when she and Michael entered. Tawny's claws clicked on the shiny wooden floor as he trotted around the carpet to his basket in the corner. Then, as if a camera had snapped, everyone moved. Mr. Morgan introduced them to the others, but Susan was so nervous that she caught only first names: Tony and Lynn, Thomas and Allison.

A large mahogany liquor cabinet stood beside an amber Victorian desk topped with leather. Amid repetitions of "Thank you so much," the host proceeded to take orders and serve the cocktails. Almost immediately Susan sensed Michael's popularity. When important topics came up, everyone asked for his views and listened carefully to his answers.

"The American is clever," Allison whispered to Lynn, who was wearing a simple taupe silk dress adorned with a long string of pearls. She sat with her slim legs crossed. Allison had a rather large nose, but her shining, neatly arranged blond hair made up for it. As the conversation progressed, Lynn mentioned to Susan that Allison painted in oils. Finally their hostess, Elizabeth, took the glass of sherry her husband held out to her and joined them on the sofa.

At dinner Susan was placed next to Alan, who talked about current affairs in Britain. "Too many people deciding how it should be done and not enough people doing it. Our leaders are a pretty dreary lot," he said, but a pleasant laugh tempered his words.

In this atmopshere, Susan thought, her host would have difficulty convincing her that anything about this country was wrong. The damask tablecloth, the shining, exquisitely designed silverware and muted colors of the dining room enchanted her. As she dug her spoon into the honeydew melon, the faint odor of roses reached out from the centerpiece and seemed to touch her like a hand from the past—gentle and loving.

As the melon plates were being cleared, Mr. Morgan leaned closer to her. "That chap of yours—a sensation in the newsroom. Born reporter if you believe in that sort of rot. Not that we don't have able British writers, but Michael gets to the bottom of things, as you Americans put it." He laughed. "It's his slant, actually. We English can't be objective enough. More wine?"

He poured her a bit more then began replenishing glasses all around, the clear liquid sparkling in the glow of the tall candles. Susan was pleased over his praise of Michael.

She caught the women at the other end of the table talking about their trips to Spain. They seemed to be making a pet of Michael who sat between them showing more

confidence and animation than he ever did
with her.

They proceeded through courses of
consomme, ham in peach sauce with carrots
and broccoli, choice of raspberry or plum
cake, Brie with port and crackers. It was
after 11:00 when they returned to the living
room to drink black or white coffee out of
small demitasse cups. The women congre-
gated together by one of the French windows
and began talking about the merits of various
make-up bases. When the conversation
switched to gardening, Susan thought of the
blossoming plants behind her home and
promised herself that tomorrow she would
hire a gardener.

She joined in the conversation whenever
she could. Michael was sitting by the fire at
the other end of the room, talking softly to
the men around him.

Susan watched them. Michael was looking
at ease and amazingly handsome in his finely
cut suit, his eyes glowing with interest. She
had never taken the time to really study him,
never from across the room like this. He had
always been at her side, so much a part of her
life that she had taken him for granted. A
rush of warmth swept through her—and she
suddenly knew she loved him!

She sat very still, marveling at her dis-
covery. She had spent years worshipping the
wrong kind of success—the glittering world
of Edward, a runway of tinsel brightness.

Here was a man who was valued not for what he controlled but for what he was.

The warmth of the room, the cheerful fire, the voices rising and falling put her in a kind of trance. The golden retriever padded over from his corner and lay at her feet, his silky fur glowing in the lamp-light. She wished she could stay forever in this room filled with lively chatter and domestic serenity that made her own life seem empty. But mintues later, as if in response to an invisible baton, everyone got up to leave.

Mr. and Mrs. Morgan stood side by side in the foyer while their guests put on their wraps. As they went out, Lynn and Allison kissed the hostess, mentioning plans for shopping excursions. Susan shook hands with the host and hostess and thanked them warmly.

Outside it was cool and she and Michael hurried to his car. Once they had started out, Michael drove in silence, his face expressionless.

"Enjoy yourself?" he finally asked.

"The evening was fantastic."

As if surprised, he turned his head swiftly to look at her, then turned back to the road. "I wondered if you were having a good time. You made quite an impression when we first came in."

"Really? Maybe it was you they were looking at. Everyone seems to admire you, Michael."

"And I, them. They're fine, intelligent people."

He did not speak again until they were on the motorway. "I invited you to come with me for two reasons," he said. "First, I wanted to show you off to my friends, and second, I knew the long drive would give us a chance to talk. You're too busy to see at work."

She smiled, wanting to draw near him, but the serious look on his face stopped her. "Talk away," she said.

"What I'm about to say stems from my self-protective instinct, and because I know that in the next few weeks you'll be making some important decisions. You're rich and famous now and can have almost anything you want. I guess I'm lucky to have watched you on your way to the top, but the fact is . . ." He paused. "You don't need me anymore. You can go on alone now."

She gasped and was silent. His words were far different from those she expected.

The soft voice went on. "Maybe for once I'm thinking of myself. I have this terrible fear of rejection that began in childhood. I avoided telling you this before, but my family had a bad reputation in the town where we lived."

"You were poor?"

"More than that. My dad couldn't work. Silly in the head—the brunt of the town jokes. They called him 'Crazy Luke'."

"Oh no, Michael!"

"It made it tough when we kids went to grade school. In a small town something like that is hard to live down. Peers can be merciless." He paused. "You know I haven't told this to anyone over here? That's why I came to London. I tried working for a newspaper in Denver but stories about my dad even followed me there. Here I can be free. Here, no one knows."

She said nothing. So this was his shame—the secret he'd kept hidden all these months.

"You've often asked me why I wasn't married," he continued. "The gossip about my father put a lot of girls off. I'm telling you this because it has stopped mattering . . ."

She wanted to touch his hand but he was holding the wheel in a tight grip, his face pale under the highway lights and his jaw tight.

"No, it doesn't matter," she said. The emotion she felt was relief—and regret that he had not told her before. Whatever his father was had nothing to do with him. And what she had seen tonight was an intelligent, almost brilliant man, admired by those with whom he worked.

"It doesn't matter," he said, "because I think we should stop seeing each other. Edward is yours now, if you want him. We've been on a yo-yo course for a long time and we shouldn't punish ourselves any longer."

He had said it so calmly—as calmly and intelligently as he had talked this evening before the group by the fire. *It doesn't matter now,* he had said. He felt no emotion for her —that's what he was trying to say. Tears sprang to her eyes.

"I don't want to wait for Edward to make up his mind," he said. "I don't want you telling me—Look, Joe, this is the way it is."

"Edward has nothing to do with us," she began. He was being absurd and didn't know it. She would never take Edward back now!

She glanced at him. His face was flushed. Then what he was trying to say hit her. He was telling her he didn't want *her!* All the preliminary talk about his dad was merely a dodge—a way of letting her down easy. He had another girl—the black-haired girl from Taylor's!

"You really want to break it off, then?" she asked in a whisper.

His eyes remained on the road, but in the light shining up from the dashboard she could see his chin was firm and his mouth pressed in a line. "Yes, I do."

They drove on in silence. I have finally seen him as he is, she thought, have realized that I love him—only it's too late. She wanted to bury her head in her hands and weep, but instead she stared at the twin circles the head-lights were making on the road ahead until they began to swim in her vision. Michael was going faster now, probably anxious to be rid of her. All the former glow of the evening had diffused into the black night surrounding the white ribbon of road. Drawing her coat around her, she turned her face to the window.

Darkened buildings swept past, then familiar landmarks rose up in the gloom as they neared her house. Perhaps seeing her in a group had the opposite effect on him. Perhaps he had realized she didn't fit.

"I want to be with you. I love you," she wanted to cry, but her pride would not let her. He could explain until he was blue about his fear of rejection, but the truth was he had found someone else.

Michael pulled the car up to the curb in front of her house, slid the gearshift into neutral and switched off the lights. Darkness and stillness enveloped them. He turned to her but before he could speak she groped for the door handle. In a second she was outside, her high heels clicking on the pavement as she ran to her house. Unlocking her door, she stepped inside and slammed it behind her, heedless of the sleeping neighbors.

Chapter 41

Edward's phone call came on a busy afternoon two days later. When Susan took the phone from her secretary, the only slight pleasure she could feel was in being right that he'd call.

"How are you, Sue?" Edward asked in his professional voice.

"Fine. I've never been better."

"Good. I'm a month late, but congratulations on the show."

"Thank you, Edward." Holding the phone with a steady hand, she kept her voice confident and cool. She wasn't going to volunteer anything.

"No doubt you know why I'm calling," he said.

She was silent. He wanted to buy her collection—that was the reason. Why didn't he come right out and say so? But then, Edward had never been direct in business matters.

"Your designs are going over amazingly well here in Paris."

"Good."

"I'd like to see you."

"That might be possible."

"I'm sorry I missed your show, but I was stuck in Japan. When shall I come?"

It was all happening as she'd dreamed. Edward would buy her collection and bring her name to the States. She stared at the desk, thinking of her months of tedious work, the times she'd pounded her fist on the desk, frustrated, waiting for this moment. But the joy she expected was missing.

Her thoughts returned to his question: When and where? Wanting to make it without Edward's help, she'd told no one except Tamar and Michael that the famous Columbus was her husband. If he came to Sumner Place, Mary and the staff would be shocked.

"I'll meet you at the Kensington Hilton at 2:00 o'clock next Monday. I'll have my secretary make arrangements to use one of their conference rooms."

"Monday it is," he said and hung up.

She had dreamed of this meeting so many times that there was no problem deciding what to wear on Monday. She chose a fuchsia suit with bold white piping. The jacket, lined in striped silk, was boxy and short with the neckline scooped in a flattering way. The wrapped skirt was of the same color. She bought expensive white pumps and a bag and gloves of kid to go with it. She knew it was a look sophisticated enough for Edward. It was even possible that he might want to feature it in Thadius' resort line for the coming season.

The hotel was not far from where she lived, but to save time she took a cab. Gone were the days of long walks to calm her churning emotions. True, she was slightly nervous, but never had she felt more in control. For once she could sit back and react to Edward's proposals—it was she who had the upper hand.

The cab went up tree-lined Holland Avenue and pulled up in front of the hotel. A doorman rushed up to open the cab door, and as she stepped out, several tourists turned to watch her.

Under the canopy, through the open glass doors, then into the spacious Crescent Lounge with its geometric scatter rugs and lush green plants.

She saw Edward almost immediately. He was sitting in an easy chair, reading a news-paper under a lamp, his blond hair gleaming in the light. It had been over six months since they'd been together, and he looked as if he had gained at least ten pounds. His face had grown jowly. He glanced up from the paper, starting in recognition, and as she crossed the orange carpet, studied her every movement. Shoulders back, head held high, she strode up to him. When she was almost at his side, he folded his newspaper and stood up.

Other people seeing him for the first time would be impressed by his good looks, but Susan noticed that his waist was larger, his shoulders more rounded. Nor were his eyes the brilliant blue she remembered. His smile was the same, however.

"You look great, Sue," he said.

"The conference room is number ten," she said, avoiding his eyes, wanting to get the meeting over with as soon as possible. She didn't mind selling her collection to his firm, for the exposure in New York would do her a great deal of good, but she wished she could do so without meeting him. The encounter was already churning up too many emotions that should lie fallow.

Edward slipped his hand into his pocket and pulled out a key. "I booked a room on the sixth floor," he said. "I thought it would give us more privacy."

She had kept her emotions in check until now, but the idea of the private room angered her. Suppose he tried what he had the last time they were together? Suppose he insisted? "The conference room will do nicely," she said.

"I canceled the conference room," he replied, not looking at her.

Her secretary had engaged it in her name. How could he cancel it? But both their names were Thorwald and who would question instructions from the famous Columbus? "It's like you to do something like that," she snapped.

"I didn't mean to upset you," he said. "We could meet somewhere else if you'd like."

His next move would be to suggest taking a cab to their home. If she were to keep him away from her workshop, she had better accept the arrangement. "We shan't be meeting long. The room will do," she said.

They walked down the hall in the direction of the lifts. She was surprised to see him slow his pace so that he remained at her side. One of the lifts was standing open and they stepped in. The doors silently slid shut, but the quiet thud as they met seemed to Susan like the clang of a jail cell. The car moved up and she stared ahead, her stomach flip-flopping as the lift wavered and stopped at the sixth floor. Her fists were clenched so tightly that the leather of her white gloves squeaked.

The large hotel room reminded her of anonymous others where she and Edward had stayed. The tile roof of the Beacon House next door could be seen from a window bordered by sheer cream draperies hung in pleated folds. On the table in front of the window were cut blue hyacinths in a shiny black bowl.

She had scarcely finished laying her purse

on the blue bedspread and peeling off her long gloves when Edward grabbed her by the shoulders and bent his head to kiss her. She slipped out from under his grasp.

"Edward, I'd rather you wouldn't."

It took no more than those words to stop him. It was astonishing how much respect he had for her now. He crossed the room and picked up the phone. "While I was waiting, I ordered champagne."

"Champagne? For what?" Again she was annoyed.

Ignoring her question, he told room service they were ready.

She surveyed all the chairs in the large room and finally picked one by the window.

Edward had scarcely put down the phone when a waiter tapped on the door and came in carrying an ice bucket with a large green bottle of Mumm's. In his other hand were two goblets with white ribbons tied around their stems. Once the waiter had left, Edward took the frosty bottle, skillfully opened it and filled the glasses in the careful way he always did, matching the level of each without spilling a drop.

"I thought the ribbons would make it more festive," he said, handing her a goblet.

She set it down on the table beside her. "The House of Thadius wants to buy my second collection, is that what we're celebrating?"

He took a large sip of champagne, gazing at her over the rim of his glass. "I don't know what Thadius wants. I'm celebrating because I'm here with you."

"What do you mean?"

"That I've left Thadius. Alfredo took over as head, and I couldn't stand the way he was running things. He's an asshole. I'm doing men's clothing now. I got a good line on what was selling when I went to Japan, then I stopped off in Hong Kong. Men care more about clothes than a decade ago. They're willing to pay fancy prices for the tailor-made stuff . . ."

She stared at him in anger and amazement. "You don't quit something you've spent almost ten years building up—something as successful as Thadius!"

"I do. Change—that's the name of the game. You change—I change. Flexibility. It got to me after a while—all those fashion shows, the constant traveling. I can make as much now with less sweat. From the beginning I could always sell."

"So why are we meeting?"

He gazed at her. "I think you can guess." There was no mistaking that look in his eyes.

She could hear the hum of the elevators far away, but nothing else. The modern hotel had a cooling system and the windows were closed, blanketing all outside sound. The morning cleaning women had finished, so even the corridors were quiet.

A wave of courage shot through her. "Edward, before we go on, I think I should tell you something. Mother married again—an attorney named Alan Hennessy. He broke the trust my dad had set up for me, invested the money in small computer stocks and lost it. Mother is so poor I have to support her."

"Your mother wrote me the news. She's always been on my side." He smiled. Glass still in his hand, he sat down on a chair opposite. "I was thinking that we never really talked during our marriage, that I barely knew you, that we were caught up in some sort of unending marathon. I was thinking about how unfair I was to you. Now I want to make it up to you, Susie."

Susie? How long had it been since he'd used that name? She leaned forward and began twisting the ring on her finger.

He set down his goblet on the table beside him. "I want to go back to the way things were before," he said without meeting her eyes.

She gazed at him, her mouth open. "I don't. I don't think you ever realized how awful it was for me."

"No, I don't think I did. But it would be different now—less travel, more time together, more fun." He pulled his chair nearer to hers. There was a haziness about his eyes that she'd never seen before. He had changed all right—but his eyes still held the glint of a salesman.

"What made you realize there was more to life than working?" she asked.

He shifted in his chair. "I don't know. The passage of time—lessons learned." He laughed shakily.

"There have been rumors about other women."

"Not other women—one woman, and that was only for a short time."

"Who?"

"Her name was Tina. She was a model who left me after four months. She showed me sunny days on the beach, white sands on the Riviera and birds that warbled by the water. But that's all over now."

"She showed you what I couldn't?"

He reached for his champagne and took a sip. "Maybe it's all a matter of timing. I wasn't ready when you tried to show me."

The room was very still. Edward seemed far more relaxed than when she was living with him. He had lost a great deal—of youth, vibrancy, drive. But talking quietly here, away from the activity that had smothered their lives, he seemed much more mature.

She smiled. "I'm glad we can talk together now. We never could talk when we were married."

"We're still married!"

"I don't feel married anymore. I don't think I'm ready, Edward, for what you have in mind. I'm seven years younger than you, and I've lost a good deal of time and want to make it up. The life you describe is not for me."

He nodded.

One thing you could say for him at least—you never had to spell things out for him. His mind was as sharp as ever, and she could forget the trite excuses about being unable to pick up where they'd left off or being a changed person. He was a salesman who knew when the selling game was over—knew when the customer wasn't buying and would never buy. She got up, slipped off her two rings and laid them in his palm.

He looked up at her. Above the blue eyes that used to hold her spellbound, moisture glistened on his forehead. But like all salesmen, he covered his true emotions well. For the first time she could admire him without the frustration she'd always felt.

Picking up her gloves and purse, she crossed the room to the door. "Goodbye, Edward."

He nodded but did not reply.

She left him sitting there with the rings clutched in his left hand and the glass of champagne in his right, staring at the blue hyacinths in the black bowl before him.

Chapter 42

The next day Susan phoned a solicitor and arranged to begin divorce proceedings. She had come close to the decision three months ago after Mary's wedding reception. Why should it be so painful now?

There was a window seat in her new house where she often sat staring out into the garden with her feet on the cushions and hands clasped around her knees. She sought this refuge now, hoping the peaceful view and a chance to reflect would ease some of the hurt inflicted by the two men in her life. Early that morning she'd told Mary she would not be at work. "Handle whatever comes up any way you see fit," she had said.

Any other day, the colorful scene outside would have restored her spirits. Verdant ivy poured down a wall of rocks, dotted by clumps of bright yellow daffodils. Amid the green leaves of the hydrangia bushes, puffy white blossoms appeared, new since last week. But instead of its rainbow glow, the garden might have been layered with volcanic ash, so much had gone out of her life. Along with her dreams, had beauty died as well? Unclasping her hands, she brushed at her eyes, wondering if anything would seem lovely to her again.

She shifted her position so that she could see another part of the yard, arranged her hands around her knees, and listened to the birds chirping in the trees. Suddenly the chime of the doorbell interrupted them. *The cleaning woman—it's her day!* Swinging her feet off the velvet cushions, she hurried to the door and opened it.

Mrs. Stuart, a heavy-set woman with silver hair and ruddy cheeks, stood on the porch. "The door was ajar so I knew someone was home. It won't bother you if I clean, mum?" she asked.

For a moment Susan considered telling her to leave. She wanted to roam through the house without being disturbed. She felt like a sleepwalker, needing to bump into things to awake—familiar, kindly things that wouldn't hurt her. But Mrs. Stuart lived a distance away, and it would be cruel to send her home.

"No, come in," Susan said, swinging open the door and forcing a smile. She chatted with her a moment then climbed the stairs to her third floor studio.

Doors banged below amid the sounds of Mrs. Stuart's heavy footsteps as she collected the cleaning equipment. The air in the studio was stifling, and a hard white light shone down from the skylight. On Susan's desk an empty sketch pad waited. Designing seemed impossible now.

She began to pace the floor. Her dream was gone—she had lost Michael and there was nothing to fill the void. Sinking down in her desk chair, she dropped her head in her hands. She was suddenly tired, more tired than she'd ever been in her life. She had made a double mistake. She had been loyal to a man who had been meaningless and lost a man whose worth she'd never recognized. How could she go on?

During the next few days, her spirits failed to improve. Always before she had been able to summon an extra bit of strength to get through an emergency. *My personal life is a wash-out*, she thought. *I've messed it up until all I have left is my work*. But work was no solution. One worked for something, and her incentives were gone. She had more than enough money and her goals were achieved—what was left?

She spent the next week strolling around her garden, answering the necessary mail, sitting for hours in her window seat. Nothing helped.

One morning, as she was reading the Times, a headline caught her attention: "Editor to take position on New York paper." Beside the news story was a photo of Michael.

Michael, the man she loved—was this really him? He would go out of her life forever now. The man in the dark suit in the photo looked like a young executive. The man she knew wore sweaters, had sensitive eyes capable of seeing other peoples' distress, smooth hands that held a special tenderness. Tears flooded her eyes and dropped onto the newspaper.

The phone rang and she hurried to answer, with all her heart wanting it to be Michael.

"How are you? Not ill, I hope?" Mary asked.

"Half-ill."

"Your voice sounds husky. Hope you haven't picked up a summer cold. Everything's going fine here at work, but Frederick and I were a bit curious about that story in the Times this morning. That nice Mr. Everett. Is he actually leaving London?"

"He hasn't stopped in, has he?" Susan asked.

"No, I wish he would. I'd like to see him again before he goes. I was fond of him and should like to wish him luck."

A sob caught in Susan's throat and she couldn't answer.

"Will you pass on the message?" Mary persisted.

"I certainly hope I can, Mary."

Susan said goodbye but remained standing by the phone, remembering the night in the car when Michael told her he wanted to break up with her. Even though he wanted nothing more to do with her, she couldn't let him go without saying goodbye. Struggling with her pride, she dialed his number at the Times. A woman answered and said he was not at his desk.

Susan drew a long breath. "Leave a message for him to call Susan Thorwald at 584-4321," she said.

The phone remained silent all morning and afternoon. Susan waited until 5:00, then dialed his number again. Michael, himself, answered this time.

"Michael, it's Susan," she said.

"Yes?" His voice was flat and disinterested.

"I've seen Edward."

"And?"

"I can't talk over the phone," she said. "I want to see you."

"When?"

"Tonight. Here at my house."

"I'm busy."

"Tomorrow night, then?"

He hesitated several minutes before he answered. "As you wish." There was a loud click as he hung up.

* * *

The next day the weather was stormy. "Gale force winds and flooding on country roads," the radio warned. Michael will use the rain as an excuse for not coming, Susan kept telling herself all day.

But that night he appeared at 6:00 o'clock. He came in without looking directly at her, but once he was in the foyer, she noticed that his dark eyes were enormous from the strain of the past hour. "Traffic. Flooded roads and detours everywhere. Lightning like you've never seen. I was afraid for my poor car," he said. He smiled, but his smile was not the same. It only reached as far as his mouth.

"I didn't think you'd come," she said.

She led him into the parlor and they both sat down. He wore a tan sweater over a white shirt and brown tie—no raincoat—and the pelting rain between her house and his car had turned the wool into fuzzy little balls. His fingers moved nervously over the arm of his chair, and he sat far forward as if he were ready to leave at any moment.

Her heart reached out to him. She must have loved him for a long time without knowing it—with Edward's image casting so dark a shadow that she couldn't see beyond it. Much as she wanted to blurt out the words "I love you," her pride would not let her. She must be satisfied with this one meeting, this final meeting.

"What would you like to drink?" she asked.

"Make it a Bloody Mary—our first drink together. Or don't you remember?"

Lightning glared at the windows, followed by a whoosh of raindrops against the panes. One of the lamps faltered, then glowed again.

"I remember." She went into the kitchen, fixed two Bloody Marys, and when she came back, handed him one. As he took it, their eyes met. "I love you," she again wanted to say—but couldn't.

The business of handing out napkins and passing cheese on toothpicks eased some of the tension in the room. She sat down again, clinging to her glass as if it were a rock in a raging surf. "So you've taken another job?" Her voice sounded brittle.

"Let's cut the formalities. You know why I'm going. I told you."

"You mentioned something about chickening out. Is that girl I saw you with at Taylor's going with you?"

He looked down. "I only dated her once. Our personalities didn't really mesh."

A tiny hope sprang up inside her, flickered like the lamp had done a moment before, then died. "Then it's our relationship that's sending you away?"

He continued to gaze at his glass. "We never had a relationship. There was always Edward. What happened when you saw him?"

"He suggested a reconciliation. I refused."

He looked up in surprise, his dark brows

raised high. "Why? I thought that was what you had been working for these many months?" He was keeping his voice controlled but had inched even farther forward in his chair. The expression in his eyes had changed to that watchfulness she remembered so well.

"He had an affair with a girl who left him. He tried to sell me on the idea that our lives could be different. Edward respects me now, but I doubt if he could really love me," she said.

Michael took a long swallow of his drink and leaned back. "From what you've told me about him, I'm inclined to agree with you. He seems incapable of any real emotions."

If she could only break his reserve! They were talking about a subject they had discussed at length, yet Michael was treating it as lightly as if Edward were some cardboard character in a play. She watched as he gulped down the rest of his Bloody Mary.

"So you're going to America," she said.

"Time for a change." As if to avoid further conversation, he stood up and waved his empty glass. "Can I get another one of these?"

"Of course."

He disappeared into the kitchen while she continued to sit in the dim room. She turned to the window. Drops were rolling down the panes like tiny tributaries tumbling toward a river, and the sky was even more overcast than before. *Everything will be dark from now on,* she thought. *If he goes, how can I live without him?*

Michael came back carrying a glass so full it almost slopped over and carefully eased himself into a chair.

She leaned forward. "Stay in London. Alan Morgan will be glad to hire you back."

"It's too late. They've already found someone to replace me. I leave next week," he said, taking a gulp from his glass. His voice was as curt and positive as that of a judge.

Her breathing grew rapid, and her ears began to buzz like they did in a descending plane. "I want you to stay."

"It seems rather pointless."

"Michael, I love you!"

He stared at her. Flashes of lightning made his face white, then dark again.

She went on, one word tumbling over another in her eagerness. "I don't blame you for being surprised. I was myself when I discovered it. Subconsciously, I couldn't help comparing you with Edward and thinking how marvelous it would be living with you. Just living, without competing with a dozen other things. But I didn't want to end a marriage that wasn't working—if it could be made to work. I thought if I tried hard enough, Edward would grow to respect me and change. It worked in a reverse way. He gained respect for me, and I lost it for him. Michael, I've even started divorce proceedings."

Michael was silent as if trying to digest the import of her words. "Tell me this," he finally said. "If I had left before you saw Edward—if you had no choice but to go back to him, would you?" His dark eyes were brilliant and intense.

"Perhaps if I'd never known you, I wouldn't have realized how perversely different he was. All I knew was the world of fashion. You showed me there was more, and I'll always be grateful to you. I also saw myself. I'm self-centered and mercenary and a dozen things I ought not to be, whereas you're thoughtful and kind and deep. You *are*, Michael."

The furrow between his brows smoothed and a faint smile formed on his lips. "I kept dreaming if would end like this. I gambled that when you became successful and independent, Edward would lose his charm. Then as the days dragged on, I stopped expecting it. A person keeps hoping and hoping . . ." His voice trailed off.

Even in the dull rainy light she could see the earnest flush in his cheeks. He *had* to love her. Would he have kept coming back merely out of curiosity? Would he have offered to loan her money, helped her plan her first show, encouraged her? Even when he had teased her, he had been trying to help.

"When did you first think . . . know . . .?" She felt awkward.

"That I loved you? You may not believe it, but I fell in love the moment I met you. I don't know why, but so many things in this world happen without explanation. But I couldn't say anything. How could I compete with anyone as important as Edward whom you were so careful to tell me you loved? I thought I could wait. Then I saw all your dreams become a reality, and I knew you could have Edward as well. I just couldn't stand it any longer."

"So you decided to give up?"

He laughed. "Yes, I suppose you might call it that."

She turned to the window. The rain had stopped, and slivers of pink sunshine were filtering through the gray clouds into the garden outside. Tiny glistening drops clung to every branch and leaf like myriads of gemstones sparkling in the rays from the setting sun.

She got up from her chair. "I could come with you," she said, staring out into the green of the garden. She turned.

His smile was much broader now and his eyes held an expression of pleased surprise. Gratitude had always been one of the qualities she'd most admired in him. He expected little, then seemed overjoyed at what he got.

He quickly got up and came over to her,

took her hands in his and gazed at her face. "You'd marry me? You'd do that—give up everything you've worked for here?"

"It wouldn't be everything. I could continue my career in New York. A change, as you say . . ." She imagined the America she had missed—New York and Chicago and the many rooms in other cities where she would wake up beside Michael.

The wool of his sweater was invitingly soft. She leaned her head on his shoulder, casually at first. Letting go of her hands, he drew his arms around her, pulling her close. Ever since the night he had told her they should stop seeing each other, she had kept herself from dreaming of ever being near him again. Now all restraint was gone. How good this closeness felt—how strong his body. His lips touched hers softly and tentatively then pressed against them with a firm sureness. She felt giddy—giddy in the knowledge that he loved her, giddy from the sensations rising up inside.

The final rays of sunshine streamed over them through the wet window panes. His lips were warm, the sunshine was warm—all the darkness and cold had vanished.